THE
HAWTHORNE
LEGACY

JENNIFER LYNN BARNES

PENGUIN BOOKS

PENGUIN BOOKS

UK | USA | Canada | Ireland | Australia
India | New Zealand | South Africa

Penguin Books is part of the Penguin Random House group of companies
whose addresses can be found at global.penguinrandomhouse.com.

www.penguin.co.uk
www.puffin.co.uk
www.ladybird.co.uk

First published 2021

001

Text copyright © Jennifer Lynn Barnes 2021

Cover design based on original concept by Lisa Horton

The moral right of the author has been asserted

Printed and bound in Great Britain by Clays Ltd, Elcograf S.p.A.

The authorized representative in the EEA is Penguin Random House Ireland,
Morrison Chambers, 32 Nassau Street, Dublin D02 YH68

A CIP catalogue record for this book is available from the British Library

ISBN: 978–0–241–48072–4

All correspondence to:
Penguin Books, Penguin Random House Children's
One Embassy Gardens, 8 Viaduct Gardens, London SW11 7BW

PENGUIN BOOKS

THE HAWTHORNE LEGACY

ALSO BY JENNIFER LYNN BARNES

The Inheritance Games

For Charlie

THE
HAWTHORNE
LEGACY

CHAPTER 1

Tell me again about the first time the two of you played chess in the park." Jameson's face was candlelit, but even in the scant light, I could see the gleam in his dark green eyes.

There was nothing—and no one—that set Jameson Hawthorne's blood pumping like a mystery.

"It was right after my mother's funeral," I said. "A few days, maybe a week."

The two of us were in the tunnels beneath Hawthorne House—alone, where no one else could hear us. It had been less than a month since I'd first stepped into the palatial Texas mansion and a week since we'd solved the mystery of why I'd been brought there.

If we'd truly solved that mystery.

"My mom and I used to go for walks in the park." I shut my eyes so that I could concentrate on the facts and not the intensity with which Jameson locked on to my every word. "She called it the Strolling Aimlessly Game." I steeled myself against the memory, letting my eyelids open. "A few days after her funeral, I went to the park without her for the first time. When I got near the pond, I saw a crowd gathered. A man was lying on the sidewalk, eyes closed, covered in tattered blankets."

1

"Homeless." Jameson had heard all of this before, but his laser focus on me never wavered.

"People thought he was dead—or passed out drunk. Then he sat up. I saw a police officer making his way through the crowd."

"But you got to the man first," Jameson finished, his eyes on mine, his lips crooking upward. "And you asked him to play chess."

I hadn't expected Harry to take me up on the offer, let alone win.

"We played every week after that," I said. "Sometimes twice a week, three times. He never told me more than his name."

His name wasn't really Harry. He lied. And that was why I was in these tunnels with Jameson Hawthorne. That was why he'd started looking at me like I was a mystery again, a puzzle that he, and only he, could solve.

It couldn't be a coincidence that billionaire Tobias Hawthorne had left his fortune to a stranger who knew his "dead" son.

"You're sure that it was Toby?" Jameson asked, the air between us charged.

These days, I was sure of little else. Three weeks earlier, I'd been a normal girl, scraping by, desperately trying to survive high school, get a scholarship, and get out. Then out of the blue, I'd received word that one of the richest men in the country had died and named me in his will. Tobias Hawthorne had left me billions, very nearly his entire fortune—and I'd had no idea why. Jameson and I had spent two weeks unraveling the puzzles and clues the old man had left behind. *Why me?* Because of my name. Because of the day I was born. Because Tobias Hawthorne had bet everything on the long shot that somehow I could bring his splintered family back together.

Or at least that was what the conclusion of the old man's last game had led us to believe.

"I'm sure," I told Jameson fiercely. "Toby's alive. And if your grandfather knew that—and I know that's a big *if*—but if he did know, then we have to assume that either he chose me because I knew Toby, or he somehow masterminded bringing us together in the first place."

If there was one thing I'd learned about deceased billionaire Tobias Hawthorne, it was that he was capable of orchestrating nearly anything, manipulating nearly anyone. He'd loved puzzles and riddles and games.

Just like Jameson.

"What if that day in the park wasn't the first time you met my uncle?" Jameson took a step toward me, an unholy energy rolling off him. "Think about it, Heiress. You said that the one time my grandfather met you, you were six years old, and he saw you in the diner where your mother was a waitress. He heard your full name."

Avery Kylie Grambs, rearranged, became A Very Risky Gamble. The kind of name a man like Tobias Hawthorne would remember.

"That's right," I said. Jameson was close to me now. Too close. Every one of the Hawthorne boys was magnetic. Larger than life. They had an effect on people—and Jameson was very good at using that to get what he wanted. *He wants something from me now.*

"Why was my grandfather, a Texas billionaire with a whole host of private chefs on call, eating at a hole-in-the-wall diner in a small Connecticut town that no one's ever heard of?"

My mind raced. "You think he was looking for something?"

Jameson smiled deviously. "Or someone. What if the old man went there looking for Toby and found *you*?"

There was something about the way he said the word *you*. Like I was someone. Like I mattered. But Jameson and I had been down that road before. "And everything else is a distraction?" I asked, looking away from him. "My name. The fact that Emily died on my birthday. The puzzle your grandfather left us—it was all just a lie?"

Jameson didn't react to the sound of Emily's name. In the throes of a mystery, nothing could distract him—not even her. "A lie," Jameson repeated. "Or misdirection."

He reached to brush a strand of hair out of my face, and every nerve in my body went on high alert. I jerked back. "Stop looking at me like that," I told him sternly.

"Like what?" he countered.

I folded my arms and stared him down. "You turn on the charm when you want something."

"Heiress, you wound me." Jameson looked better smirking than anyone had a right to look. "All I want is for you to rifle through your memory banks a little. My grandfather was a person who thought in four dimensions. He might have had more than one reason for choosing you. Why kill two birds with one stone, he always said, when you could kill twelve?"

There was something about his voice, about the way he was still looking at me, that would have made it easy to get caught up in it all. The possibilities. The mystery. *Him.*

But I wasn't the kind of person who made the same mistake twice. "Maybe you've got it wrong." I turned away from him. "What if your grandfather didn't know that Toby was alive? What if *Toby* was the one who realized that the old man was watching me? Considering leaving the entire fortune to me?"

Harry, as I'd known him, had been one hell of a chess player. Maybe that day in the park wasn't a coincidence. Maybe he'd sought me out.

"We're missing something," Jameson said, coming up to stand close behind me. "Or maybe," he murmured, directly into the back of my head, "you're holding something back."

He wasn't entirely wrong. I wasn't built to lay all my cards on the table—and Jameson Winchester Hawthorne didn't even pretend to be trustworthy.

4

"I see how it is, Heiress." I could practically *hear* his crooked little grin. "If that's how you want to play it, why don't we make this interesting?"

I turned back to face him. Eye to eye, it was hard not to remember that when Jameson kissed a girl, it wasn't tentative. It wasn't gentle. *It wasn't real*, I reminded myself. I'd been a part of the puzzle to him, a tool to be used. I was still a part of the puzzle.

"Not everything is a game," I said.

"And maybe," Jameson countered, eyes alight, "that's the problem. Maybe that's why we're spinning our wheels in these tunnels day after day, rehashing this and getting nowhere. Because this isn't a game. *Yet.* A game has rules. A game has a winner. Maybe, Heiress, what you and I need to solve the mystery of Toby Hawthorne is a little motivation."

"What kind of motivation?" I narrowed my eyes at him.

"How about a wager?" Jameson arched an eyebrow. "If I figure all of this out first, then you have to forgive and forget my little lapse of judgment after we decoded the Black Wood."

The Black Wood was where we'd figured out that his dead ex-girlfriend had died on my birthday. That was the moment when it had first become clear that Tobias Hawthorne hadn't chosen me because I was special. He'd chosen me for what it would do to them.

Immediately afterward, Jameson had dropped me cold.

"And if I win," I countered, staring into those green eyes of his, "then you have to forget that we ever kissed—and never try to charm me into kissing you again."

I didn't trust him, but I also didn't trust myself with him.

"Well then, Heiress." Jameson stepped forward. Standing directly to my side, he brought his lips down to my ear and whispered, "Game on."

CHAPTER 2

Our wager struck, Jameson took off in one direction in the tunnels, and I went in another. Hawthorne House was massive, sprawling, big enough that, even after three weeks, I still hadn't seen it all. A person could spend years exploring this place and still not know all the ins and outs, all the secret passageways and hidden compartments—and that wasn't even counting the underground tunnels.

Lucky for me, I was a quick learner. I cut from underneath the gymnasium wing to a tunnel that went below the music room. I passed beneath the solarium, then climbed a hidden staircase into the Great Room, where I found Nash Hawthorne leaning casually against a stone fireplace. Waiting.

"Hey, kid." Nash didn't bat an eye at the fact that I'd just appeared seemingly out of nowhere. In fact, the oldest Hawthorne brother gave the impression that the whole mansion could come crashing down around him and he'd just keep leaning against that fireplace. Nash Hawthorne would probably tip his cowboy hat to Death herself.

"Hey," I replied.

"I don't suppose you've seen Grayson?" Nash asked, his Texas drawl making the question sound almost lazy.

That did nothing to soften the impact of what he'd just said. "Nope." I kept my answer short and my face blank. Grayson Hawthorne and I had been keeping our distance.

"And I don't suppose you know anything about a chat Gray had with our mother, right before she moved out?"

Skye Hawthorne, Tobias Hawthorne's younger daughter and the mother of all four Hawthorne grandsons, had tried to have me killed. The person who'd actually pulled the trigger was the one in a jail cell, but Skye had been forced to leave Hawthorne House. By Grayson. *I will always protect you*, he'd told me. *But this . . . us . . . It can't happen, Avery.*

"No clue," I said flatly.

"Didn't think so." Nash gave me a little wink. "Your sister and your lawyer are looking for you. East Wing." That was a loaded statement if I'd ever heard one. My lawyer was his ex-fiancée, and my sister was . . .

I didn't know what Libby and Nash Hawthorne were.

"Thanks," I told him, but when I made my way up the winding staircase to the East Wing of Hawthorne House, I didn't go looking for Libby. Or Alisa. I'd made a bet with Jameson, and I intended to win. First stop: Tobias Hawthorne's office.

In the office, there was a mahogany desk, and behind the desk was a wall of trophies and patents and books with the name *Hawthorne* on the spine—a breathtaking visual reminder that there was nothing ordinary whatsoever about the Hawthorne brothers. They had been given every opportunity, and the old man had expected them to be extraordinary. But I hadn't come here to gawk at trophies.

Instead, I took a seat behind the desk and released the hidden compartment I'd discovered not long ago. It held a folder. Inside the folder, there were pictures of me. Countless photographs, stretching back years. After that fateful meeting in the diner, Tobias Hawthorne had kept tabs on me. *All because of my name? Or did he have another motive?*

I thumbed through the photos and pulled out two. Jameson had been right, back in the tunnels. I was holding out on him. I'd been photographed with Toby twice, but both times, all the photographer had captured of the man beside me was the back of his head.

Had Tobias Hawthorne recognized Toby from behind? Had "Harry" realized we were being photographed and turned his head away from the camera on purpose?

As far as clues went, this wasn't much to go on. All the file really proved was that Tobias Hawthorne had been keeping tabs on me for years before "Harry" had shown up. I thumbed past the photographs to a copy of my birth certificate. My mother's signature was neat, my father's an odd mix of cursive and print. Tobias Hawthorne had highlighted my father's signature, as well as my date of birth.

10/18. I knew the significance there. Both Grayson and Jameson had loved a girl named Emily Laughlin. Her death—on October 18— had torn them apart. Somehow, the old man had intended for me to bring them back together. But why would Tobias Hawthorne have highlighted my father's signature? Ricky Grambs was a deadbeat. He hadn't even cared enough to pick up the phone when my mother died. If it had been left up to him, I would have gone into foster care. Staring at Ricky's signature, I willed Tobias Hawthorne's reasoning in highlighting it to become clear.

Nothing.

In the back of my mind, I heard my mother's voice. *I have a secret,* she'd told me, long before Tobias Hawthorne had written me into his will, *about the day you were born.*

Whatever she'd been referring to, I was never going to guess it now that she was gone. The one thing I knew for certain was that I wasn't a Hawthorne. If my father's name on that birth certificate weren't proof enough, a DNA test had already confirmed that I had no Hawthorne blood.

Why did Toby seek me out? Did he seek me out? I thought about what Jameson had said about his grandfather killing twelve birds with one stone. Going back through the folder again, I tried to find some shred of meaning. What wasn't I seeing? There had to be *something—*

A rap at the door was the only warning I got before the doorknob began to twist. Moving quickly, I gathered the photographs and slipped the file back into the hidden compartment.

"There you are." Alisa Ortega, attorney-at-law, was a model of professionalism. She arched her brows into what I had mentally termed the Alisa Look. "Would I be correct in assuming you've forgotten about the game?"

"The game," I repeated, unsure *which* game she was talking about. I felt like I'd been playing since the moment I'd first stepped through the door of Hawthorne House.

"The football game," Alisa clarified, with another Alisa Look. "Part two of your debut into Texas society. With Skye's exit from Hawthorne House, appearances are more important than ever. We need to control the narrative. This is a Cinderella story, not a scandal—and that means that *you* need to play Cinderella. In public. As frequently and convincingly as possible, starting with making use of your owner's box tonight."

Owner's box. That clicked. "The game," I repeated again, comprehension dawning. "As in, an NFL game. Because I own a football team."

That was still so absolutely mind-blowing that I almost succeeded in distracting myself from the other part of what Alisa had said—the bit about Skye. Per the deal I'd struck with Grayson, I couldn't tell anyone about his mother's part in my attempted murder. In exchange, he'd handled it.

Just like he'd promised he would.

"There are forty-eight seats in the owner's suite," Alisa said, going into lecture mode. "A general seat map is created months in advance. VIPs only. This isn't just football; it's a way of buying a seat at a dozen different tables. Invites are highly sought after by just about everyone—politicians, celebrities, CEOs. I've had Oren vet everyone on the list for tonight, and we'll have a professional photographer on hand for some strategic photo opportunities. Landon has crafted a press release that will go out an hour before the game. All that's left to worry about is…"

Alisa trailed off delicately.

I snorted. "Me?"

"This is a Cinderella story," Alisa reminded me. "What do you think Cinderella would wear to her first NFL game?"

That had to be a trick question.

"Something like this?" Libby popped into the doorway. She was wearing a Lone Stars jersey with a matching scarf, matching gloves, and matching boots. Her blue hair was tied into pigtails with a thick bunch of blue and gold ribbons.

Alisa forced a smile. "Yes," she told me. "Something like that—minus the black lipstick, the black nail polish, and the choker." Libby was pretty much the world's most cheerful goth, and Alisa was not a fan of my sister's sense of fashion. "As I was saying," Alisa continued emphatically, "tonight is important. While Avery plays Cinderella for the cameras, I'll circulate among our guests and get a better sense of where they stand."

"Where they stand on what?" I asked. I'd been told again and again that Tobias Hawthorne's will was ironclad. As far as I knew, the Hawthorne family had given up on trying to challenge it.

"It never hurts to have a few extra power players in your corner," Alisa said. "And we want our allies breathing easy."

"Hope I'm not interrupting." Nash acted like he'd just happened upon the three of us—like he wasn't the one who'd warned me that Alisa and Libby were looking for me. "Go on, Lee-Lee," he told my lawyer. "You were sayin' something about breathing easy?"

"We need people to know that Avery isn't here to shake things up." Alisa avoided looking directly at Nash, like a person avoiding looking into the sun. "Your grandfather had investments, business partners, political relationships—these things require a careful balance."

"What she means when she says that," Nash told me, "is that she needs people to think that McNamara, Ortega, and Jones has the situation entirely under control."

The situation? I thought. *Or me?* I didn't relish the idea of being anyone's puppet. In theory, at least, the firm was supposed to work for me.

That gave me an idea. "Alisa? Do you remember when I asked you to get money to a friend of mine?"

"Harry, wasn't it?" Alisa replied, but I got the distinct feeling that her attention was divided three ways: between my question, her grand plans for the night, and the way Nash's lips ticked upward on the ends when he saw Libby's outfit.

The last thing I needed my lawyer focused on was the way that her ex was looking at my sister. "Yes. Were you able to get the money to him?" I asked. The simplest way to get answers would be to track down Toby—before Jameson did.

Alisa tore her eyes away from Libby and Nash. "Unfortunately," she said briskly, "my people have been unable to find a trace of your Harry."

I rolled the implication of that over in my mind. Toby Hawthorne had appeared in the park days after my mother's death, and less than a month after I left, he was gone.

"Now," Alisa said, clasping her hands in front of her body, "about your wardrobe..."

CHAPTER 3

I had never seen a game of football in my life, but as the new owner of the Texas Lone Stars, I couldn't exactly say that to the crowd of reporters who mobbed the SUV when we pulled up to the stadium, any more than I could have admitted that the off-the-shoulder jersey and metallic-blue cowboy boots I was wearing felt about as authentic as a Halloween costume.

"Lower the window," Alisa told me, "smile, and yell, 'Go, Lone Stars!'"

I didn't want to lower the window. I didn't want to smile. I didn't want to yell anything—but I did it. Because this was a Cinderella story, and I was the star.

"Avery!"

"Avery, look over here!"

"How are you feeling about your first game as the new owner?"

"Do you have any comments about reports that you assaulted Skye Hawthorne?"

I hadn't had much media training, but I'd had enough to know the cardinal rule of having reporters shout questions at you rapid-fire: Don't answer. Pretty much the only thing I was allowed to say was that I was excited, grateful, awed, and overwhelmed in the *most incredible* possible way.

So I did my best to channel excitement, gratitude, and awe. Nearly a hundred thousand people would attend the game tonight. Millions would watch it around the world, cheering for the team. *My* team.

"Go, Lone Stars!" I yelled. I went to roll up my window, but just as my finger brushed the button, a figure pulled away from the crowd. Not a reporter.

My father.

Ricky Grambs had spent a lifetime treating me like an afterthought, if that. I hadn't seen him in more than a year. But now that I'd inherited billions?

There he was.

Turning away from him—and the paparazzi—I rolled my window up.

"Ave?" Libby's voice was hesitant as our bulletproof SUV disappeared into a private parking garage beneath the stadium. My sister was an optimist. She believed the best of people—including a man who'd never done a damn thing for either one of us.

"Did you know he'd be here?" I asked her, my voice low.

"No!" Libby said. "I swear!" She caught her bottom lip between her teeth, smudging her black lipstick. "But he just wants to talk."

I bet he does.

Up in the driver's seat, Oren, my head of security, parked the SUV and spoke calmly into his earpiece. "We have a situation near the north entrance. Eyes only, but I want a full report."

The nice thing about being a billionaire with a security team brimming with retired Special Forces was that the chances of my being ambushed again were next to none. I shoved down the feelings that seeing Ricky had dredged up and stepped out of the car into the bowels of one of the biggest stadiums in the world. "Let's do this," I said.

"For the record," Alisa told me as she exited the car, "the firm is more than capable of handling your father."

And *that* was the nice thing about being the sole client of a multi-billion-dollar law firm.

"Are you okay?" Alisa pressed. She wasn't exactly the touchy-feely type. More likely she was trying to assess whether I would be a liability tonight.

"I'm fine," I said.

"Why wouldn't she be?"

That voice—low and smooth—came from an elevator behind me. For the first time in seven days, I turned to look directly at Grayson Hawthorne. He had pale hair and ice-gray eyes and cheekbones sharp enough to count as weapons. Two weeks ago, I would have said that he was the most self-assured, self-righteous, arrogant jerk I'd ever met.

I wasn't sure what to say about Grayson Hawthorne now.

"Why," he repeated crisply, stepping out of the elevator, "would Avery be anything other than fine?"

"Deadbeat dad made an appearance outside," I muttered. "It's fine."

Grayson stared at me, his eyes piercing mine, then turned to Oren. "Is he a threat?"

I'll always protect you, he'd sworn. *But this...us...It can't happen, Avery.*

"I don't need you to protect me," I told Grayson sharply. "When it comes to Ricky, I'm an expert at protecting myself." I stalked past Grayson, into the elevator he'd stepped out of a moment earlier.

The trick to being abandoned was to never let yourself long for anyone who left.

A minute later, when the elevator doors opened into the owner's suite, I stepped out, Alisa to one side and Oren to the other, and I didn't so much as look back at Grayson. Since he'd taken the elevator down to meet me, he'd obviously already been up here, probably schmoozing. Without me.

"Avery. You made it." Zara Hawthorne-Calligaris wore a string of delicate pearls around her neck. There was something about her sharp-edged smile that made me feel like she could probably kill a man with those pearls if she were so inclined. "I wasn't sure you would be putting in an appearance tonight."

And you were ready to hold court in my absence, I concluded. I thought about what Alisa had said—about allies and power players and the influence that could be bought with a ticket to this suite.

As Jameson would say, *Game on.*

CHAPTER 4

The owner's suite had a perfect view of the fifty-yard line, but an hour before kickoff, no one was looking at the field. The suite extended back and widened, and the farther you got from the seats, the more it looked like an upscale bar or club. Tonight, I was the entertainment—an oddity, a curiosity, a paper doll dressed up just so. For what felt like an eternity, I shook hands, posed for photographers, and pretended to understand football jokes. I managed not to gawk at a pop star, a former vice president, and a tech giant who probably made more money in the time it took him to urinate than most people made in a lifetime.

My brain pretty much stopped functioning when I heard the phrase "Her Highness" and realized there was actual royalty in attendance.

Alisa must have sensed that I was reaching my limit. "It's almost time for kickoff," she said, laying one hand lightly on my shoulder—probably to keep me from fleeing. "Let's get you in your seat."

I made it until halftime, then bolted for real. Grayson intercepted me. Wordlessly, he nodded to one side and then started walking, confident that I would follow.

Despite myself, I did. What I found was a second elevator.

"This one goes up," he told me. Going anywhere with Grayson Hawthorne was probably a mistake, but given that the alternative was more mingling, I decided to take my chances.

The two of us rode the elevator up in silence. The door opened to a small room with five seats, all empty. The view of the field was even better than it was below.

"My grandfather could only mingle in the suite for so long before he got fed up and came up here," Grayson told me. "My brothers and I were the only ones allowed to join him."

I sat and stared out at the stadium. There were so many people in the crowd. The energy, the chaos, the sheer volume of it was overwhelming. But in here, it was silent.

"I thought you might come to the game with Jameson." Grayson made no move to sit, like he didn't trust himself too close to me. "The two of you have been spending a lot of time together."

That irritated me, for reasons I couldn't even explain. "Your brother and I have a bet going."

"What kind of bet?"

I had no intention of answering, but when I let my eyes travel toward his, I couldn't resist saying the one thing guaranteed to get a reaction. "Toby is alive."

To someone else, Grayson's reaction might not have been noticeable, but I saw the jolt go through him. His gray eyes were glued to me now. "Pardon me?"

"Your uncle is alive and gets his jollies by pretending to be a homeless man in New Castle, Connecticut." I probably could have been a little more delicate.

Grayson came closer. He deigned to sit next to me, tension visible in his arms as he folded his hands together between his knees. "What, precisely, are you talking about, Avery?"

I wasn't used to hearing him call me by my first name. It was too late to take back what I'd said. "I saw a picture of Toby in your nan's locket." I closed my eyes, flashing back to that moment. "I recognized him. He told me that his name was Harry. We played chess in the park every week for more than a year." I opened my eyes again. "Jameson and I aren't sure what the story is there—yet. We have a bet going about who finds out first."

"Who have you told?" Grayson's voice was deadly serious.

"About the bet?"

"About Toby."

"Nan was there when I found out. I was going to tell Alisa, but—"

"Don't," Grayson cut in. "Don't breathe a word of this to anyone. You understand?"

I stared at him. "I'm starting to get the feeling that I don't."

"My mother has no grounds on which to challenge the will. My aunt has no grounds on which to challenge the will. But Toby?" Grayson had grown up as the heir apparent. Of all the Hawthorne brothers, he had taken being disinherited the hardest. "If my uncle is alive, he is the one person on this planet who might be able to break the old man's will."

"You say that like it's a bad thing," I told him. "From my perspective, sure. But from yours..."

"My mother cannot find out. Zara cannot find out." Grayson's expression was intense, everything in him focused on me. "McNamara, Ortega, and Jones cannot find out."

In the week that Jameson and I had been discussing this turn of events, we'd been completely focused on the mystery—not on what might happen if Tobias Hawthorne's lost heir suddenly turned up alive.

"Aren't you even a little bit curious?" I asked Grayson. "About what this means?"

"I know what this means," Grayson replied tersely. "I am telling you what this means, Avery."

"If your uncle were interested in inheriting, don't you think he would have come forward by now?" I asked. "Unless there's a reason he's in hiding."

"Then let him hide. Do you have any idea how risky—" Grayson didn't get to finish that question.

"What's life without a little risk, brother?"

I turned toward the elevator. I hadn't noticed it going down or coming back up, but there Jameson was. He strolled past Grayson and settled into the seat on the other side of mine. "Made any progress on our bet, Heiress?"

I snorted. "Wouldn't you like to know?"

Jameson smirked, then opened his mouth to say something else, but his words were drowned out by an explosion. More than one. *Gunfire.* Panic shot through my veins, and the next thing I knew, I was on the ground. *Where's the shooter?* This was like Black Wood. Just like the Black Wood.

"Heiress."

I couldn't move. Couldn't breathe. And then Jameson was on the floor with me. He brought his face level with mine and cupped my head in his hands. "Fireworks," he told me. "It's just fireworks, Heiress, for halftime."

My brain registered his words, but my body was still lost in memory. Jameson had been there in the Black Wood with me. He'd thrown his body over mine.

"You're okay, Avery." Grayson knelt beside Jameson, beside me. "We won't let anything hurt you." For a long, drawn-out moment, there wasn't a sound in the room except our breathing. Grayson's. Jameson's. And mine.

"Just fireworks," I repeated back to Jameson, my chest tight.

Grayson stood, but Jameson stayed exactly where he was. He stared at me, his body against mine. There was something almost tender in his expression. I swallowed—and then his lips twisted into a wicked smile.

"For the record, Heiress, *I* have been making excellent progress on our bet." He let his thumb trace the outline of my jaw.

I shuddered, then glared at him and climbed to my feet. For the sake of my own sanity, I needed to win this bet. *Fast.*

CHAPTER 5

Monday meant school. Private school. A private school with seemingly endless resources and "modular scheduling," which left me with random pockets of free time scattered throughout the day. I used that time to dig up everything I could about Toby Hawthorne.

I already knew the basics: He was the youngest of Tobias Hawthorne's three children and, by most accounts, the favorite. At the age of nineteen, he and some friends had taken a trip to a private island the Hawthorne family owned off the coast of Oregon. There was a deadly fire and a horrible storm, and his body was never recovered.

The tragedy had made the news, and sifting through articles gave me a few more details about what had happened. Four people had gone out to Hawthorne Island. None had made it back alive. Three bodies had been recovered. Toby's was presumed lost to the ocean storm.

I found out what I could about the other victims. Two of them were basically Toby clones: prep school boys. *Heirs.* The third was a girl, Kaylie Rooney. From what I gathered, she was a local, a troubled teen from a small fishing village on the mainland. Several articles mentioned that she had a criminal record—a sealed juvenile record. It took me longer to find a source—though not necessarily a reputable one—that claimed that Kaylie Rooney's criminal record included drugs, assault, and arson.

She started the fire. That was the story the press ran with, without coming right out and saying the words. *Three promising young men, one troubled young woman. A party that spun out of control. Everything, engulfed in flames.* Kaylie was the one the press blamed—sometimes between the lines, sometimes explicitly. The boys were lionized and eulogized and held up as shining beacons in their communities. *Colin Anders Wright. David Golding. Tobias Hawthorne II.* So much brilliance, so much potential, gone too soon.

But Kaylie Rooney? She was trouble.

My phone buzzed, and I glanced down at the screen. A text—from Jameson: *I have a lead.*

Jameson was a senior at Heights Country Day. He was somewhere on this magnificent campus. *What kind of lead?* I thought, but I resisted giving him the satisfaction of texting back. Eventually, my phone informed me that he was typing.

Tell me what you know, I thought.

Then the text finally came through. *Wanna raise the stakes?*

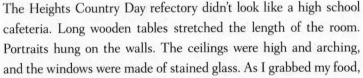

The Heights Country Day refectory didn't look like a high school cafeteria. Long wooden tables stretched the length of the room. Portraits hung on the walls. The ceilings were high and arching, and the windows were made of stained glass. As I grabbed my food, I scanned the room reflexively for Jameson—and found another Hawthorne brother instead.

Xander Hawthorne was sitting at a dining table, staring intently at a contraption he'd set on its surface. The gizmo looked a bit like a Rubik's Cube, but elongated, with tiles that could swivel and fold out in any direction. I suspected it was a Xander Hawthorne original. He'd told me once that he was the brother most apt to be distracted by complex machinery—and scones.

That got me thinking as I watched him fidget three tiles back and forth in his fingers. When his brothers had been off playing their grandfather's games, Xander had often ended up sharing his scones with the old man. *Did they ever talk about Toby?* There was only one way to find out. I crossed the room to sit next to Xander, but he was so absorbed in thought that he didn't even notice me. Back and forth, back and forth, he twisted the tiles.

"Xander?"

He turned toward me and blinked. "Avery! What a pleasant and not objectively unexpected surprise!" His right hand meandered to the far side of the contraption and a notebook that sat there. He snapped it closed.

I took that to mean Xander Hawthorne was up to something. Then again, so was I. "Can I ask you something?"

"That depends," Xander replied. "Are you planning to share those baked goods?"

I looked down at the croissant and cookie on my tray and slid the latter his way. "What do you know about your uncle Toby?"

"Why do you want to know?" Xander took a bite of the cookie and frowned. "Does this have craisins in it? What kind of monster mixes butterscotch chips and craisins?"

"I was just curious," I said.

"You know what they say about curiosity," Xander warned me happily, taking another gargantuan bite of the cookie. "Curiosity killed the—Bex!" Xander gulped down the bite he'd just taken, his face lighting up.

I followed his gaze to Rebecca Laughlin, who was standing

behind me, holding a lunch tray and looking the way she always did: like some kind of princess, plucked from a fairy tale. Hair as red as rubies. Impossibly wide-set eyes.

Guilty as sin.

As if she could hear my thoughts, Rebecca quickly averted her eyes. I could feel her trying not to look at me. "I thought you might need help," she told Xander hesitantly, "with the—"

"The thing!" Xander leaned forward and cut her off.

I narrowed my eyes and turned my head back toward the youngest Hawthorne—and the notebook he'd flipped closed the moment he'd seen me. "What thing?" I asked suspiciously.

"I should go," Rebecca said behind me.

"You should sit and listen to me complain about craisins," Xander corrected.

After a long moment, Rebecca sat, leaving a single empty chair between us. Her clear, green eyes drifted toward mine. "Avery." She looked down again. "I owe you an apology."

The last time Rebecca and I had spoken, she'd confessed to covering for Skye Hawthorne's role in my attempted murder.

"I'm not sure I want one," I said, an edge creeping into my voice. On an intellectual level, I understood that Rebecca had spent her whole life living in her sister's shadow, that Emily's death had wrecked her, that she'd felt some kind of sick responsibility to her dead sister to say nothing about Skye's plot against me. But on a more visceral level: *I could have died.*

"You're not still holding a little grudge about all of that, are you?" Thea Calligaris asked, claiming the seat that Rebecca had left open.

"Little grudge?" I repeated. The last time I'd been this close to Thea, *she* had admitted to setting me up to attend my debut in Texas society dressed like a dead girl. "You play mind games. And Rebecca almost got me killed!"

"What can I say?" Thea let her fingertips brush Rebecca's. "We're complicated girls."

There was something deliberate about those words, that brush of skin. Rebecca looked at Thea, looked at their hands—and then curled her fingers toward her palm and placed her hand in her lap.

Thea kept her eyes on Rebecca's for three long seconds, then turned back to me. "Besides," she said pertly, "I thought this was supposed to be a *private* lunch."

Private. Just Rebecca and Thea and Xander, the three of whom—last I'd checked—were barely on speaking terms with one another for complicated reasons involving, as Xander liked to say, star-crossed love, fake dating, and tragedy.

"What am I missing here?" I asked Xander. The notebook. The way he'd dodged my question about Toby. The "thing" Rebecca had come to help him with. And now *Thea*.

Xander saved himself from having to answer by jamming the rest of the cookie into his mouth.

"Well?" I prompted as he chewed.

"Emily's birthday is on Friday," Rebecca said suddenly. Her voice was quiet, but what she'd just said sucked the oxygen from the room.

"There's a memorial fundraiser," Thea added, staring me down. "Xander, Rebecca, and I scheduled this *private* lunch to iron out some plans."

I wasn't sure I believed her, but either way, that was clearly my cue to leave.

CHAPTER 6

Trying to talk to Xander had been a bust. I'd gotten as far as I could reading about the fire. *What next?* I thought, walking down a long corridor toward my locker. *Talk to someone who knew Toby?* Skye was out, for obvious reasons. I didn't trust Zara, either. Who did that leave? *Nash, maybe? He would have been about five when Toby disappeared. Nan. Maybe the Laughlins.* Rebecca's grandparents ran the Hawthorne estate and had for years. *Who is Jameson talking to? What's his lead?*

Frustrated, I pulled out my phone and shot off a text to Max. I didn't really expect a reply, because my best friend had been on technological lockdown ever since my windfall—and the accompanying attention from the press—had ruined her life. But even with the guilt I was carrying about what my instant fame had done to Max, texting her made me feel a little less alone. I tried to imagine what she would tell me if she were here, but all I came up with was a string of fake curse words—and strict orders not to get myself killed.

"Did you see the news?" I heard a girl down the hallway ask in a hushed voice as I stopped in front of my locker. "About her father?"

Gritting my teeth, I tuned out the sounds of the gossip mill. I opened my locker—and a picture of Ricky Grambs stared back at me. It must have been cut out of an article, because there was a headline above the photograph: *I Just Want to Talk to My Daughter.*

Rage simmered in the pit of my stomach—rage that my deadbeat of a father would have dared to talk to the press, rage that someone had taped this article to the back of my locker door. I looked around to see if the perpetrator would make themselves known. Heights Country Day lockers were made of wood and didn't have locks. It was a subtle way of saying, *People like us don't steal.* What need was there for security among the elite?

As Max would say, *Bullship.* Anyone could have accessed my locker, but no one in the hallway was watching my reaction now. I turned back to tear the picture down, and that was when I noticed that whoever had taped it up had also papered the bottom of my locker with scraps of bloodred paper.

Not scraps, I realized, picking one up. *Comments.* For the past three weeks, I'd done a good job at staying offline, avoiding what internet commenters were saying about me. *To some people, you'll be Cinderella*, Oren had told me when I first inherited. *To others, Marie Antoinette.*

In all caps, the comment in my hand read, *SOMEONE NEEDS TO TEACH THAT STUCK-UP BITCH A LESSON.* I should have stopped there, but I didn't. My hand shook slightly as I picked up the next comment. *When will this SLUT die?* There were dozens more, some of them graphic.

One commenter had just posted a photo: my face, with a target photoshopped over it, like I'd been caught in the sight of a gun.

>———◄

"This was almost certainly just a bored teenager pushing boundaries," Oren told me as we arrived back at Hawthorne House that afternoon.

"But the comments..." I swallowed, some of the threats still emblazoned on my brain. "They're real?"

"And nothing you need to worry about," Oren assured me. "My team keeps tabs on these things. All threats are documented and assessed. Of the hundred or so worst offenders, there are only two or three to date that merit watching."

I tried not to get hung up on the numbers. "What do you mean, *watching*?"

"Unless I'm mistaken," a cool, even voice said, "he's referring to the List."

I looked up to see Grayson standing a few feet away, wearing a dark suit, his expression impossible to read but for a line of tension in his jaw.

"What list?" I said, trying not to pay too much attention to his jawline.

"Do you want to show her?" Grayson asked Oren calmly. "Or should I?"

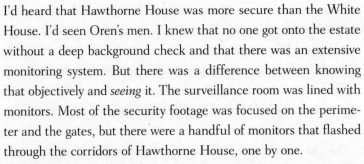

I'd heard that Hawthorne House was more secure than the White House. I'd seen Oren's men. I knew that no one got onto the estate without a deep background check and that there was an extensive monitoring system. But there was a difference between knowing that objectively and *seeing* it. The surveillance room was lined with monitors. Most of the security footage was focused on the perimeter and the gates, but there were a handful of monitors that flashed through the corridors of Hawthorne House, one by one.

"Eli." Oren spoke, and one of the guards who was monitoring the feeds stood. He looked to be in his twenties, with a military-style haircut, several scars, and vibrant blue eyes ringed with amber around the pupil. "Avery," Oren said, "meet Eli. He'll be shadowing you at school, at least until I've completed a full assessment of the locker situation. He's the youngest member of our team, so he'll blend better than the rest of us would."

Eli looked military. He looked like a bodyguard. He did not look like he would *blend* at my high school. "I thought you weren't concerned about my locker," I told Oren.

My head of security met my eyes. "I'm not." But he also wasn't taking any chances.

"What, precisely," Grayson said, coming up behind me, "happened at your locker?"

I had a brief and infuriating urge to tell him, to let him protect me, the way he'd sworn he would. But not everything was Grayson Hawthorne's business. "Where's this list?" I asked, stepping away from him and redirecting the conversation to the reason I was here.

Oren nodded to Eli, and the younger man handed me an actual, literal list. Names. The one at the top was *RICKY GRAMBS*. I scowled but managed to scan the rest of the list. There were maybe thirty names, total. "Who are these people?" I asked, my throat tightening around the words.

"Would-be stalkers," Oren answered. "People who've attempted to break onto the estate. Overly zealous fans." He narrowed his eyes. "Skye Hawthorne."

I took that to mean that my head of security knew why Skye had left Hawthorne House. I'd promised Grayson secrecy, but this was Hawthorne House. Most of the occupants were far too clever for their own good—or anyone else's.

"Could you give me a moment with Avery?" Grayson did Oren the courtesy of pretending that was a request. Unimpressed, Oren glanced toward me and arched a questioning brow. I was tempted to keep Oren there out of spite, but instead, I nodded at my head of security, and he and his men slowly filed out of the room. I half expected Grayson to cross-examine me about what I'd told

Oren about Skye, but once the two of us were alone, that cross-examination never came.

"Are you okay?" Grayson asked instead. "I can see how this would be a lot to take in."

"I'm fine," I insisted, but this time I couldn't muster the will to tell him that I didn't need his protection. I'd known, objectively, that I would need security for the rest of my life, but seeing the threats laid out on paper felt different.

"My grandfather had a List as well," Grayson said quietly. "It comes with the territory."

With being famous? With being rich?

"Regarding the situation we discussed last night," Grayson continued, his voice low, "do you understand now why you need to leave it alone?" He didn't say Toby's name. "Most of these people on the List would lose interest in you if you lost the fortune. *Most* of them."

But not all. I stared at Grayson for a moment, my eyes lingering on his face. If I were to lose the fortune, I'd lose my security team. That was what he wanted me to understand.

"I understand," I replied, ripping my eyes from Grayson's, because I also understood this: I was a survivor. I took care of myself. And I wouldn't let myself want or expect anything from him.

Turning away, I stared at the security monitors. A flash of movement on one of the feeds caught my eye. *Jameson.* I tried not to be too obvious as I watched him striding with purpose through a corridor I couldn't place. *What are you up to, Jameson Hawthorne?*

Beside me, Grayson's attention was on me, not the monitors. "Avery?" He sounded almost hesitant. I hadn't been sure that Grayson Davenport Hawthorne, former heir apparent, was capable of hesitating.

"I'm fine," I said again, keeping half an eye on the screen. A moment later, the feed flashed to another corridor, and I saw Xander, walking with just as much purpose as Jameson. He was carrying something in his hands.

A sledgehammer? Why would he have a—

The question cut off in my mind because I recognized Xander's surroundings, and suddenly I knew exactly where he was going. And I would have bet my last dollar that Jameson was on his way there, too.

CHAPTER 7

At some point after his son's disappearance and supposed death, Tobias Hawthorne had walled off Toby's wing. I'd seen it once: solid bricks laid over what I had assumed to be a door.

"Sorry," I told Grayson, "I have to go." I understood why he wanted me to leave the Toby situation alone. He probably wasn't wrong. *And yet…*

Neither Oren nor his men trailed me when I left. The threats on the List—they were external. And that meant that I could make my way to Toby's wing without a shadow. I arrived to see Xander hoisting the sledgehammer over his shoulder. He caught sight of me out of the corner of his eye. "Pay no attention to this sledgehammer!"

"I know what you're doing," I told him.

"What sledgehammers were put on God's green earth to do," Xander replied solemnly.

"*I know,*" I said again, waiting for those words to sink in.

Xander lowered the business end of the sledgehammer to the ground. Brown eyes studied me intently. "What is it you think you know?"

I took my time with my reply. "I know that you didn't want to answer my question about Toby. I know that you and Rebecca and Thea were up to something at lunch today." I was building my way up to the true gambit here. "I know your uncle's alive."

Xander blinked, his incredible brain moving at what I could only assume was warp speed. "Did the old man say something in your letter?"

"No," I said. Tobias Hawthorne had left us each a letter at the end of the last puzzle. "Did he say something in yours?"

Before Xander could answer, Jameson strolled up to join us. "Looks like a party." He reached for the sledgehammer. "Shall we?"

Xander pulled it back. "Mine."

"The sledgehammer," Jameson replied loftily, "or what's behind that wall?"

"Both," Xander gritted out, and there was a note of intensity in his voice that I'd never heard from him before. Xander was the youngest Hawthorne brother. The least competitive. The one who'd been in on their grandfather's last game.

"Is that the way it is?" Jameson eyes narrowed. "Want to wrestle for it?"

That did not strike me as a rhetorical question. "Xander, your uncle and I know each other." I cut in before any actual wrestling could take place. "I met Toby right after my mother died." It took me a minute, maybe less, to lay out the rest of it, and when I'd finished, Xander stared at me, a little bit in awe.

"I should have seen it."

"Seen what?" I asked him.

"You weren't just a part of *their* game," Xander replied. "Of course you weren't. The old man's mind didn't operate that way. He didn't just choose you for *them*."

Them being Grayson and Jameson. *Their* game being the one we'd already solved. "He left you a game, too," I said slowly. It was the only thing that made sense. Nash had warned me once that their grandfather had, in all likelihood, never intended me to be a player.

I was the glass ballerina or the knife. A part of the puzzle. A *tool.* I narrowed my eyes at Xander. "Either tell us what you know, or give me that sledgehammer."

No matter the old man's intentions—I wasn't here to be *used.*

"Not much to tell!" Xander declared jollily. "The old man left me a letter congratulating me for getting my hardheaded and much less handsome brothers to the end of their game. He signed the letter as Tobias Hawthorne, no middle initial, but when submerged in water, that signature became 'Find Tobias Hawthorne the Second.'"

Find Toby. The old man had left his youngest grandson with that charge. And there was a good chance that the only real clue he'd left him...was me. *Twelve birds with one stone.*

"I guess that answers the question of whether the old man knew Toby was alive," Jameson murmured.

Tobias Hawthorne knew. My entire body rang with that revelation.

"If we have Toby's last known location," Xander mused, "perhaps a sledgehammering is unnecessary. My plan was to search his room and see if any clues turned up, but..."

I shook my head. "I have no idea how to find Toby. I asked Alisa to get money to him, right after I inherited, before I even knew who he was. He was already in the wind."

Jameson cocked his head to the side. "Interesting."

"Is Toby's wing the lead you mentioned earlier?" I asked him.

"Maybe it is," Jameson said, grinning. "Or maybe it isn't."

"Far be it from me to interrupt banter," Xander interjected. "But this is *my* lead. And my sledgehammer!" He heaved it over his shoulder.

I stared at the wall and wondered what lay beyond it. "Are you sure about this?" I asked Xander.

He took a deep breath. "As sure as anyone holding a sledgehammer has ever been."

CHAPTER 8

The wall came down easily enough that I wondered if it had been meant to come down. How long had Tobias Hawthorne waited for someone to hammer their way through the barrier he'd erected? For someone to ask questions?

For someone to find his son.

As I stepped through what remained of the bricks, I tried to imagine what the old man had been thinking. *Why didn't he find Toby himself? Why didn't he bring him home?*

I stared down a long hallway. The floor was made of white marble tiles. The walls were completely lined with mirrors. I felt like I'd stepped into a fun house. On high alert, I made my way slowly down the hall, taking stock. There was a library, a sitting room, a study, and, at the end of the hall, a bedroom every bit as large as mine. Clothes still hung in the closet.

A towel hung on a rack next to an enormous shower.

"How long has this place been bricked up?" I asked, but the boys were in another room—and I didn't need them to tell me the answer. *Twenty years.* Those clothes had been hanging in the closet since the summer Toby had "died."

Emerging from the bathroom, I found Xander's legs poking out from underneath a king-sized bed. Jameson was running his hands over the top of an armoire. He must have found some kind of latch or lever, because a second later, the top of the armoire popped up like a lid.

"Looks like Uncle Toby was a fan of contraband," Jameson commented. I climbed up on the dresser to get a better look and saw a long, thin compartment completely lined with travel-sized liquor bottles.

"Found a loose floor panel," Xander called from under the bed. When he reappeared, he was holding a small plastic bag full of pills—and another one full of powder.

⬦━━━━━━⬦

Toby's wing was brimming with secret compartments: hollowed-out books, trick drawers, a false back to the closet. A secret passage in the study led back past the entryway, revealing that the mirrors that lined the hallway were two-way. From where I stood in the passage, I could see Jameson lying facedown on the marble floor, examining the tiles one by one.

I stared at him for longer than I should have, then retreated back to the library. Xander and I had screened hundreds of books for hidden compartments. Nineteen-year-old Toby's tastes had been eclectic—everything from comic books and Greek philosophy to pulp horror and law. The only shelf on the built-in bookshelves that wasn't full of books framed a clock that was about eight inches tall and affixed to the back of the shelf. I studied the clock for a moment. *No movement of the second hand.* I reached out to test how firmly the clock was attached to the shelf.

It didn't budge.

I almost left it there, but some instinct wouldn't let me. Instead, I twisted the clock, and it rotated, loosening. The face of the clock came away from the wall. There were no gears inside, no electronics. Instead, I found a flat, circular object made of cardboard. Closer inspection revealed two concentric cardboard circles attached with a brad in the center. Each one was lined with letters.

"A homemade cipher disk." Xander crowded me to get a better look. "See how the A on the outside disk aligns with the A on the smaller one? Twist either disk so that different letters align, and it generates a simple substitution code."

Clearly, Toby Hawthorne had been raised the same way his nephews had: playing the old man's games. *Were you playing with me, Harry?*

"Wait a second." Xander straightened suddenly. "Hear that?"

I listened. Silence. "Hear what?"

Xander pointed his index finger at me. *"Exactly."* The next second, he took off. I tucked the cipher disk into the band of my pleated skirt and followed. In the hallway, Jameson was silently lowering a marble tile back into place.

He'd found something—and apparently hadn't planned on sharing that with his brother or me.

"Aha!" Xander said triumphantly. "I knew you were being too quiet." He strode over to Jameson and squatted beside him, pressing on the floor tile Jameson had just lowered. I heard a popping sound, and the tile released, like it was on a spring.

Glaring at Jameson, who winked back at me, I knelt next to Xander. Beneath the tile was a metal compartment. It was empty, but I saw an inscription on the bottom, engraved into the metal.

A poem.

"I was angry with my friend," I read out loud. *"I told my wrath, my wrath did end."* I glanced up. Jameson was already standing and walking away, but Xander's eyes were locked on the inscription as I continued. *"I was angry with my foe: I told it not, my wrath did grow."*

The words hung in the air for a few seconds after I said them.

Xander whipped out his phone. "William Blake," he said after a moment.

"Who?" I asked. I glanced back at Jameson, who pivoted and paced back toward us. I'd thought he was off and running, but really he was thinking, concentration in motion.

"William Blake," Jameson echoed, an almost chaotic energy marking the words and his stride. "Eighteenth-century poet—and a favorite of Aunt Zara's."

"And Toby's, apparently," Xander added.

I stared down at the engraving. The word *wrath* jumped out at me. I thought about the alcohol and drugs we'd found in Toby's room. I thought about the fire on Hawthorne Island and the way the press had lauded Toby as such an outstanding young man.

"He was angry about something," I said. My mind raced. "Something he couldn't say?"

"Maybe," Jameson replied pensively. "Maybe not."

Xander handed me his phone. "Here's the entire poem."

"A Poison Tree," by William Blake, I read.

"Long story short," Xander summarized, "the author's hidden wrath grows into a tree, the tree bears fruit, the fruit is poisoned, and the enemy—who doesn't know they are enemies—eats the fruit. The whole shebang ends with a dead body. Very catchy."

A dead body. My mind went, unbidden, to the three bodies that had been recovered from the fire on Hawthorne Island. Exactly how angry was Toby that summer?

Don't leap to conclusions, I told myself. I had no idea what this poem meant—no idea why a nineteen-year-old would have had these words inscribed on a hidden compartment. No idea if this *was* Toby's handiwork, rather than the old man's. For all we knew, Tobias Hawthorne had done this after his son went missing, right before bricking up the door.

"What the hell are you kids doing in here?" That question sounded like it had been ripped forcibly from someone's throat. My head whipped toward the doorway. Mr. Laughlin stood there, on the other side of the demolished bricks. He looked tired and old and almost *hurt*.

"Just putting everything back where we found it!" Xander said brightly. "Right after we—"

The groundskeeper didn't let him finish. He stepped through the opening in the brick wall and pointed his finger at us. *"Out."*

CHAPTER 9

That night, I lay in bed, thinking about the poem and staring at the cipher disk. I turned the smaller wheel, watching as it generated code after code. What exactly had Toby used this for? Answers didn't come, but eventually sleep did. I woke the next morning with "A Poison Tree" still on my mind. *I was angry with my friend: / I told my wrath, my wrath did end. / I was angry with my foe: / I told it not, my wrath did grow.*

A knock on my door interrupted that thought. It was Libby. She was still dressed in her pajamas—skull print, with bows.

"Everything okay?" I asked.

"Just making sure you're up and getting ready for school."

I gave her a look. Libby had never, in the history of her legal guardianship of me, gotten me up for school. "Really?"

She hesitated, her right index finger picking at the dark nail polish on her left, and then the floodgates broke. "You know Dad didn't mean to give that interview, right? Ave, he had *no* idea the person he was talking to was a reporter."

Ricky had gotten back in touch with Libby around the time that news of my inheritance hit the press. If she wanted to give him another chance, that was her business, but he didn't get to use her as an intermediary with me.

"He wants money," I said flatly. "And I'm not giving him any."

"I'm not an idiot, Avery. And I'm not defending him."

She was absolutely defending him, but I didn't have the heart to say that. "I should get ready for school."

>————<

My morning routine took five times longer now than it had before I had a team of stylists, a media consultant, and a "look." By the time I finished applying eight different concoctions to my face and at least half that many to my hair, sitting down to breakfast was out of the question. Running late, I rushed into the kitchen—not to be confused with the chef's kitchen—to pick up a banana and was greeted with the sound of an oven door slamming closed.

Mrs. Laughlin straightened and wiped her hands on her apron. Soft brown eyes narrowed at me. "Can I help you with something?"

"Banana?" I said. Something about the expression on her face made it difficult for me to form a full sentence. I still wasn't used to having a staff. "I mean, could I get a banana, please?"

"Too good for breakfast?" Mrs. Laughlin replied stiffly.

"No," I said quickly. "It's just, I'm running late, and—"

"No matter." Mrs. Laughlin checked the contents of another oven. From what I'd been told, the Laughlins had run the estate for decades. They hadn't been thrilled when I inherited, but everything continued to run like clockwork. "Take what you like." Mrs. Laughlin briskly nodded to a fruit bowl. "Your type always does."

My type? I bit back the urge to throw out a retort. Clearly, I'd misstepped somehow. And just as clearly, I didn't want to be on her bad side. "If this is about what happened with Mr. Laughlin yesterday...," I said, flashing back to the way her husband had thrown us out of Toby's wing.

"You stay away from Mr. Laughlin." Mrs. Laughlin wiped her hands against her apron again, harder this time. "It's bad enough, what you've done to poor Nan."

Nan? My answer came with my next breath. The boys' great-grandmother had been the one to show me a picture of Toby. She'd been there when I realized I knew him. "Nan told you," I said slowly. "About Toby." I thought about Grayson's warning, about the importance of this secret staying a secret.

Xander knew—and now Mrs. Laughlin. Quite possibly her husband, too.

"You should be ashamed of yourself," Mrs. Laughlin said fiercely. "Playing with an old woman's feelings like that. And dragging the boys into whatever you were doing in Toby's wing? It's cruel is what it is."

"Cruel?" I repeated, and that was when I realized: She thought I was lying.

"Toby's dead," Mrs. Laughlin said, her voice tight. "He's gone, and the whole House mourned him. I loved that boy like he was my own." She closed her eyes. "And the thought of you torment-ing Nan, telling that poor woman that he's *alive*...defiling his things..." Mrs. Laughlin forced her eyes open. "Hasn't this family suffered enough without you making up something like this?"

"I'm not lying," I said, feeling sick to my stomach. "I wouldn't do that."

Mrs. Laughlin pursed her lips. I could see her biting back what-ever she wanted to say. Instead, she stiffly handed me a banana. "You should go to school."

CHAPTER 10

True to Oren's word, Eli stuck to my side at school. Despite my head of security's promise about "blending," there was nothing discreet about being a seventeen-year-old with a bodyguard.

American Studies. Philosophy of Mindfulness. Calculus. Making Meaning. As I sat through my classes, my fellow students didn't stare. They not-stared—so conspicuously, it felt worse. By the time I made it to Physics, I was ready to take my chances with the internet commenters and locker vandals of the world on my own.

"Can you just wait in the hall?" I asked Eli.

"If I want to be out of a job," he replied gamely, "sure."

Part of me had to wonder if Oren was really going to this length because of the locker incident—or if it was because Ricky was in town and making noise.

Trying to shut out that thought, I plopped down into a seat. On a normal day, the fact that my high school physics laboratory looked like something that belonged at NASA would still have provoked some awe, but today I had other things on my mind.

Right before class began, Thea sat down at my lab table. She raked her eyes over Eli, then turned back to me. "Not bad," she murmured.

My life was literally a tabloid story, but at least Thea Calligaris thought my new bodyguard was hot.

"What do you want?" I asked her under my breath.

"Things I'm not supposed to," Thea mused. "Things I can't have. Anything that I'm told is just out of reach."

"What do you want from me?" I clarified, keeping my voice low enough to prevent anyone but Eli from overhearing.

Class started before Thea deigned to answer, and she didn't speak again until we were let loose on the lab assignment. "Rebecca and I were there when Sir Geeks-a-Lot sank that letter of his in the tub," Thea said lightly. "We know all about the new game." Her expression shifted, and for a split second Thea Calligaris looked almost vulnerable. "It's the first thing in an eternity that has gotten Bex to wake up."

"Wake up?" I repeated. I knew that Thea and Rebecca had a history. I knew that they'd split up in the wake of Emily's death, that Rebecca had withdrawn from everyone and everything.

But I had no idea why Thea expected me to care about either of them now.

"You don't know her," Thea told me, her voice low. "You don't know what Emily's death did to her. If she wants to help Xander with this? I'm going to help *her*. And I just thought that you might want to know that we know about you-know-who." *About Toby.* "We're in this. And we're not telling anyone."

"Is that a threat?" I asked, my eyes narrowing.

"Literally the opposite of a threat." Thea gave an elegant little shrug, like she really didn't care whether I trusted her or not.

"Fine," I said. Thea was Zara's niece by marriage. That Toby was alive wasn't a secret I would have trusted her with, but Xander had—which made no sense, because Xander didn't even *like* Thea.

Deciding it was useless to engage further, I focused first on my lab work, then on what we'd found in Toby's room the night before. *The cipher disk. The poem.* Was there something else in the room we were supposed to find and decode?

Beside me, Thea placed her tablet flat on the table. I glanced at it and realized that she'd done the same search that Xander had the day before, for "A Poison Tree." I took that to mean that Xander had told her—and presumably Rebecca—exactly what we'd found.

I'm going to kill him, I thought, but then my eyes caught on one of the results that Thea's search had turned up: *fruit of the poisonous tree doctrine.*

CHAPTER 11

On the way home from school, I did a search of my own. The fruit of the poisonous tree doctrine was a legal rule that said that evidence obtained illegally was inadmissible in court.

"You're thinking." Jameson was beside me in the car. Some days, he and Xander caught a ride in my bulletproof SUV. Other days, they didn't. Xander wasn't there now.

"I'm always thinking," I replied.

"That's what I love about you, Heiress." Jameson had a habit of tossing out words that should matter like they didn't at all. "Care to share those thoughts?"

"And tip my hand?" I shot back. "So you can get there first and double-cross me?"

Jameson smiled. It was his slow, dangerous, heady smile, designed to elicit a reaction. I didn't give him one.

When we got to Hawthorne House, I retreated to my wing and waited fifteen minutes before I locked my hand around a candlestick on my fireplace mantel and pulled. That motion released a latch, and the back of the stone fireplace popped up just enough that I could fit my hands underneath and lift it upward. Oren had disabled this passageway back when there was a threat on the estate, but after that threat was resolved, it hadn't stayed disabled for long.

I stepped into the secret passageway to find Jameson waiting for me. "Fancy meeting you here, Heiress."

"You," I told him, "are the most annoying person on the face of the planet."

His lips quirked upward on one side. "I try. Headed back to Toby's wing?"

I could have lied, but he would have known I was lying, and I didn't want to wait. "Just try not to get caught by the Laughlins," I told him.

"Don't you know by now, Heiress? I never get caught."

Taking a deep breath, I stepped past the brick debris and made a beeline for Toby's study. I ran my fingers along the edges of the books, going through them shelf by shelf.

We'd checked every volume in here, but only for hidden compartments.

"Care to tell me what you're looking for?" Jameson asked.

The day before, I'd noticed the variety of books Toby Hawthorne read. Comic books and pulp horror. Greek philosophy and law volumes. Without a word to Jameson, I pulled one of the legal books off the shelf.

It took Jameson less than a minute to figure out why. "Fruit of the poisonous tree," he murmured behind me. "Brilliant."

I wasn't sure if he was talking about me—or Toby.

The book's index directed me to the entry for the fruit of the poisonous tree doctrine. As I reached the page in question, my heart sped up. There it was.

Certain letters in certain words were blacked out. The notations went on for pages. Every once in a while, there would be a punctuation mark that had been struck through—a comma, a question mark. I didn't have a pen or paper, so I used my phone to record the letters, painstakingly typing them in one by one.

The result was a string of consonants and vowels with no meaning. *For now.*

"You're thinking." Jameson paused. "You know something."

I was going to deny it, but I didn't, for one simple reason. "I found a cipher disk yesterday," I admitted, "but it was set at neutral. I don't know the code."

"Numbers." Jameson's reply was immediate and electric. "We need numbers, Heiress. Where did you find the cipher?"

My breath caught in my throat. I walked over to the clock, the one I'd taken apart the day before. I turned it over and stared at its face: the hour hand frozen at twelve and the minute hand at five.

"The fifth letter of the alphabet is *E*," Jameson said behind me. "The twelfth is *L*."

Without another word to him, I ran for the cipher disk in my room.

CHAPTER 12

Jameson followed me. Of course he did. All I cared about was getting there first.

Arriving back in my suite, I pulled the cipher disk out of my desk drawer. I matched the fifth letter on the outer wheel to the twelfth letter on the inner. *E* and *L*. And then, with Jameson standing behind me, his hands on the desk on either side of me, our bodies far too close, I began decoding the message.

S-E-C-R-E-

Partially through the first word, breath whooshed out of my lungs, because this was going to work. *Secrets.* That was the first word. *Lies.*

Beside me, Jameson grabbed a pen, but I grabbed it back from him. "My room," I told him. "My pen. My cipher disk."

"If you want to get technical, Heiress, it's all yours. Not just this room or that pen."

I ignored him and transposed letter after letter, until the entire message was decoded. I went back and added spaces and line breaks, and what I was left with was another poem.

One that I could only assume was a Toby Hawthorne original.

Secrets, lies,
All I despise.
The tree is poison,
Don't you see?
It poisoned S and Z and me.
The evidence I stole
Is in the darkest hole.
Light shall reveal all
I writ upon the ...

I looked up. Jameson was still leaning over me, his face so close to mine that I could feel his breath on my cheek. Pushing my chair back into him, I stood. "That's it," I told him. "It ends there."

Jameson read the poem aloud. "*Secrets, lies, all I despise. The tree is poison, don't you see? It poisoned S and Z and me.*" He paused. "S for Skye, Z for Zara."

"*The evidence I stole,*" I picked up, then paused. "Evidence of *what?*"

"*Is in the darkest hole,*" Jameson continued. "*Light shall reveal all I writ upon the* ..." He trailed off, and in the back of my head, something clicked.

"There's a word missing," I said.

"And it rhymes with *all*."

An instant later, Jameson was in motion—and so was I. We ran back, through corridor after corridor, to Toby's abandoned wing. We came to a stop just outside the door. Jameson looked at me as he stepped over the threshold.

Light shall reveal all I writ upon the ...

"Wall," Jameson whispered, like he'd lifted the word directly from my thoughts. He was breathing hard—hard enough to make me think that his heart was pounding even faster than mine.

"Which wall?" I asked, stepping up beside him.

Slowly, Jameson turned, three hundred and sixty degrees. He didn't answer my question, so I threw out another one.

"Invisible ink?"

"Now you're thinking like a Hawthorne." Jameson closed his eyes. I could practically feel him vibrating with energy.

My entire body was doing the same. *"Light shall reveal all."*

Jameson's eyelids flew open, and he turned again, until we were facing each other. "Heiress, we're going to need a black light."

CHAPTER 13

As it turned out, we needed more than one black light—and the member of the Hawthorne family in possession of seven of them was Xander. The three of us lined Toby's suite with them. We turned the overhead lights off, and what I saw took me nearly to my knees.

Toby hadn't written *a* message on the wall of his bedroom. He'd written tens of thousands of words across all the walls in the suite. Toby Hawthorne had kept a diary. His whole life was documented on the walls of his wing of Hawthorne House. He couldn't have been more than seven or eight when he'd started writing.

Jameson and Xander fell silent beside me as the three of us read. The tone of Toby's writing started off completely at odds with everything else we'd found—the drugs, the message we'd decoded, "A Poison Tree." That Toby had been seething with anger. But Young Toby? He sounded more like Xander. There was an unbridled energy to everything he wrote. He talked about conducting experiments, some of them involving explosions. He adored his older sisters. He spent entire days disappearing into the walls of the House. He worshipped his father.

What changed? That was the question I asked myself as I read faster and faster, speeding through Toby's twelfth year, his thirteenth, his fourteenth, his fifteenth. Shortly after his sixteenth birthday, I came to the exact moment when everything changed.

All that entry said was: *They lied.*

It took months—maybe years—before Toby actually put into words what that lie was. What he'd discovered, why he was angry. When I got to that confession, my entire body went leaden.

"Avery?" Xander stopped what he was doing and turned to look at me. Jameson was still reading at warp speed. He must have already read the secret that had turned me to stone, but his laser focus had remained uncompromised. He was on the hunt—and my body felt like it was shutting down.

"You okay there, champ?" Xander asked me, coming to put a hand on my shoulder. I barely felt it.

I couldn't take another step. I couldn't read another word. Because the lie that Toby Hawthorne had referenced, the secrets he mentioned in his poem?

They had to do with who he was.

"Toby was adopted." I turned to look at Xander. "Nobody knew. Not Toby. Not his sisters. *No one.* Your grandmother faked a pregnancy. When Toby was sixteen, he found something. Proof. I don't know what." I couldn't stop talking. I couldn't slow down. "They adopted him in secret. He wasn't even sure it was legal."

"Why would anyone keep an adoption a secret?" Xander sounded truly baffled.

That was a good question, but I could barely process it, because all I could think, over and over again, was that if Toby Hawthorne wasn't biologically related to the Hawthorne family, then he didn't share one ounce of their DNA.

And neither would his child.

"His handwriting..." I choked out the words. It was on the

walls, all around me—and now that I was looking for it, I recognized something I should have noticed the moment the writing had changed from a childish scrawl.

From the time he was twelve or thirteen, Toby Hawthorne had started writing in an odd fashion—a very distinctive mix of print and cursive. I'd seen that handwriting before.

I have a secret, I could hear my mother telling me less than a week before she died. *About the day you were born.*

CHAPTER 14

Late into the night, I sat in the massive leather chair behind Tobias Hawthorne's desk, staring at my birth certificate, at the signature the billionaire had highlighted. The name was my father's, but the handwriting was the same as the writing on the walls of Toby's wing.

A distinctive mix of print and cursive.

Toby Hawthorne signed my birth certificate. I couldn't say those words out loud. All I could do was think about Ricky Grambs. By the age of seven, I'd been done letting him hurt me—but at six, I thought he hung the moon. He would breeze into town, pick me up, swing me around. He'd call me his girl and tell me that he'd gotten me a present. I'd fish through his pockets, and whatever I found there—a pen, loose change, a restaurant mint—I got to keep.

It took me years to realize that every piece of treasure he ever gave me was trash.

My vision blurred, and I blinked back tears, staring at that signature: Ricky's name but Toby's writing.

I have a secret about the day you were born. I could hear my mom, as clearly as if she were in the room with me. *I have a secret.*

It was a game we had played my whole life. She was wonderful at guessing my secrets. I'd never guessed hers.

Now it was right there in front of me. Highlighted. "Toby Hawthorne signed my birth certificate." It hurt to talk. It hurt to remember every game of chess I'd played with Harry.

Ricky Grambs hadn't picked up the phone when my mother died. But Toby? He'd shown up within days. And if Toby was adopted, if he wasn't biologically a Hawthorne, then the DNA test that Zara and her husband had run meant *nothing*. It no longer ruled out the simplest solution to the question of why Tobias Hawthorne had left his fortune to a stranger.

I wasn't a stranger.

Why had "Harry" sought me out right after my mother's death? Why had a Texas billionaire visited the New England diner where my mother worked when I was six years old? Why had Tobias Hawthorne left me his fortune?

Because his son is my father. Everything else—my birthday, my name, the entire puzzle the Hawthorne brothers and I had thought we'd solved—it was exactly what Jameson had called it down in the tunnel: misdirection.

I stood up, unable to stay in one place a moment longer. I hadn't needed a father in a very long time. I'd learned to expect nothing. I'd stopped letting it hurt. But now all I could think about was that, yes, Harry used to scowl when I outmaneuvered him on the chess board, but his eyes had gleamed. He'd called me *princess* and *horrible girl*, and I'd called him *old man*.

A jagged breath caught in my throat. I walked forward, toward the double doors that separated the office from its balcony. I burst through them, and they ricocheted back.

"Toby Hawthorne signed my birth certificate." My voice was rough in my throat, but I had to say the words out loud. I had to hear them to believe them. I gulped in air and tried to take what I'd just said to its logical conclusion, but I couldn't.

I physically couldn't say the words. I couldn't even think them.

Down below, I saw movement in the pool. *Grayson*. His arms cut through the water in a brutal, punishing breaststroke. Even from a distance, I could see the way his muscles pulled against his skin. No matter how long I watched him, his pace never changed.

I wondered if he was swimming to get away from something. To silence the thoughts in his mind. I wondered how it was possible that watching him made breathing easier and harder at the same time.

Finally, he pulled himself out of the pool. As if guided by some kind of sixth sense, his head angled up. *Toward me.*

I stared at him—through the night, through the space between us. He looked away first.

I was used to people walking away. I was good at not expecting anything from anyone.

But as I retreated back inside the office, I found myself staring at my birth certificate again.

I couldn't make this not matter. I couldn't make Toby—*Harry*—not matter. Even though he'd lied to me. Even though he'd let me live in my car and buy *him* breakfast, when he came from one of the richest families in the world.

He's my father. The words came. Finally. Brutally. I couldn't unthink them. Every sign pointed to the same conclusion. I forced myself to say it out loud. "Toby Hawthorne is my father."

Why didn't he tell me? Where is he now?

I wanted answers. This wasn't just a mystery that needed solving or another layer to a puzzle. It wasn't a *game*—not to me.

Not anymore.

CHAPTER 15

We need to talk." Jameson found me hidden away in the archive (prep school for *library*) the next day. Until now, he'd kept his distance within the walls of Heights Country Day.

Not that anyone but Eli was around to see us.

"I have to finish my calculus homework." I avoided looking directly at him. I needed space. I needed to think.

"It's E-day." Jameson pulled up a seat next to mine. "You have plenty of free time."

The modular scheduling system at Heights Country Day was complicated enough that I hadn't even memorized my own schedule. But Jameson apparently had.

"I'm busy," I insisted, annoyed at the way I always felt his presence. The way he *wanted* me to.

Jameson leaned back in his chair, balancing it on two legs, then let the front legs drop down and leaned to whisper directly into my ear. "Toby Hawthorne is your father."

———◆———

I followed Jameson. Eli, who couldn't possibly have heard Jameson's whisper, followed me—out of the main building, across the quad, down a stone path to the Art Center. Inside, Jameson strode past studio after studio, until we ended up in what a sign informed me was the Black Box Theater: an enormous square room with black walls, a black floor, and stage lights built into a black ceiling. Jameson flipped a series of switches, and the overhead lights turned on. Eli took up a position by the door, and I followed Jameson to the far side of the room.

"What I said in the archive," Jameson murmured. "It was just a theory." The room was built for acoustics, built for voices to carry. "Tell me I'm wrong."

I glanced back at Eli and chose my words carefully in response. "I found a hidden compartment in your grandfather's desk. There was a copy of my birth certificate."

I didn't say Toby's name. I wouldn't, not with an audience.

"And?" Jameson prompted.

"The name was my father's." I lowered my voice so much that Jameson had to step closer to hear it. "The signature wasn't."

"I knew it." Jameson started pacing, but he turned back toward me before he got too far away. "Do you realize what this means, Heiress?" he asked, his green eyes alight.

I did. I'd said it out loud once. It made sense—more sense than anything else had made since I arrived for the reading of the will. "There could be other explanations," I said hoarsely, even though I didn't really believe that. *I have a secret.* My mom hadn't invented that game out of nowhere. My whole life, she'd been telling me there was something I didn't know.

Something big.

Something about me.

"It makes perfect sense—*Hawthorne* sense." Jameson couldn't contain himself. If I would have let him, he probably would have picked me up and twirled me around. "Twelve birds, one stone, Heiress. Whatever happened twenty years ago, the old man intended to use you to pull his prodigal son back onto the board now."

"Doesn't seem like it worked," I said, the words bitter on my tongue. I was the biggest news story in the world. I had no idea where Toby was, but the same couldn't be said in reverse.

If he is my father, then where is he? Why isn't he here?

As if that thought had beckoned him toward me, Jameson came closer. "Let's call off the bet," he said softly.

I whipped my head up to look at him. I searched for a tell on his face, something to let me know what angle he was playing.

"This is big, Heiress." If he'd been anyone else, his voice might have sounded gentle—but the Jameson Hawthorne I knew wasn't gentle. "Big enough that neither of us needs extra motivation now. Neither of us is going to solve this alone."

There was something undeniable about the way he said the word *us*, but I resisted the pull of it. "I'm at the center of this." It would have been so easy to let myself get sucked back in. To let myself feel like we really were a team. "You need me."

That was what this was about. The gentle voice. *Us.*

"And you don't need anyone?" Jameson stepped forward. Despite every warning screeching in the back of my brain, when he reached out to touch me, I didn't pull back.

The past twelve hours had turned my entire world upside down. I needed...*something*. It didn't have to mean anything. There didn't have to be feelings involved. "Fine," I said, my voice rough in my throat. "Let's call off the bet."

I expected him to kiss me then—to take advantage of my moment of weakness, to push me back against the wall and wait for my head to angle up toward his, wait for a *yes*. He looked like he wanted to. *I* wanted it.

But instead, Jameson took a step back and cocked his head to the side. "How would you feel about getting some air?"

———————

Two minutes later, Jameson Hawthorne and I were on *top* of the Art Center. This time, Eli didn't get a chance to position himself in the doorway before Jameson locked him out.

My bodyguard knocked on the door to the roof, then pounded.

"I'm fine," I yelled back, watching as Jameson walked over to stand at the very edge of the roof. The toes of his dress shoes hung over the edge. The wind picked up. "Be careful," I said, even though he didn't know the meaning of the word.

"You know something funny, Heiress? My grandfather always said that Hawthorne men have nine lives." Jameson turned back to me. "*Hawthorne men,*" he repeated, "*have nine lives.* He was talking about Toby. The old man knew his son had survived. He knew that Toby was out there. But he never did more than drop hints until he left that message for Xander."

"Find Tobias Hawthorne the Second," I said quietly.

After holding my gaze for a moment longer, Jameson disappeared behind a nearby column and came back with what appeared to be a roll of Astroturf and a bucket of golf balls. He set the bucket down, then rolled out the turf. He disappeared a second time, then came back with a golf club and snatched a ball from the bucket. He laid the ball on the turf and lined up his shot.

"I come up here," he said, looking out at the picturesque woods on the back side of the campus, "to get away." His feet shoulder width apart, he swung the club back, then took his shot. The golf ball soared off the roof of the Art Center and into the woods. "I'm not saying that I think you're overwhelmed, Heiress. I'm not saying that I think you're hurting. I'm just saying"—he held the golf club out to me—"sometimes it feels good to smack the hell out of something."

I stared at him, incredulous, then smiled. "This has got to be against the rules."

"What rules?" Jameson smirked. When I didn't move to take the club, he got another ball and lined up another shot. "Allow me to let you in on a Hawthorne trade secret, Heiress: There are no rules that matter more than winning." He paused, just for a moment. "I don't know who my father is. Skye was never what one would call *maternal*. The old man raised us. He made us in his own image." Jameson swung, and the ball went soaring. "Xan has his mind. Grayson got the gravitas. Nash has a savior complex. And I..." Another ball. Another shot. "I don't know when to give up."

Jameson turned back to me and held the club out once more. I remembered Skye telling me that the word to describe Jameson was *hungry*.

I took the club from his hand. My fingers brushed his.

"I'm the one who doesn't give up," Jameson reiterated. "But Xander's the one the old man asked to find Toby."

On the other side of the door to the roof, Eli was still banging. *I should put him out of his misery.* I looked at Jameson. *I should walk away.* But I didn't. This was the closest Jameson had come to opening up to me about what it was like growing up Hawthorne.

I walked over to the bucket of golf balls and tossed one onto the turf. I'd never held a golf club before. I had no idea what I was doing, but it looked satisfying. Sometimes, it *did* feel good to smack the hell out of something.

The first time I swung, I missed the ball.

"Head down," Jameson told me. He stepped up behind me and adjusted my grip, his arms wrapping around mine, guiding them from shoulder to fingertips. Even through my uniform blazer, I could feel the heat of his body.

"Try again," he murmured.

This time, when I swung back, Jameson swung, too. Our bodies moved in sync. I felt my shoulders rotating, felt him behind me, felt every inch of contact between us. The club connected with the ball, and I watched it soar.

A rush of emotion built up inside me, and this time I didn't push it down. Jameson had brought me up here to let go.

"If Toby's my father," I said, louder than I'd meant to, "where has he been all my life?"

I turned to face Jameson, well aware that we were standing far too close. "You know the way your grandfather's mind operated," I told him fiercely. "You know his go-to tricks. What are we missing?"

We. I'd said *we.*

"Toby 'died' years before you were born." Jameson always looked at me like I had the answer. Like I *was* the answer. "It's been twenty years since the fire on Hawthorne Island."

I felt my thoughts fall in sync with his. It had been twenty years since the fire. Twenty years since Tobias Hawthorne had revised his will to disinherit his entire family. And just like that, I had an idea.

"In the last game we played," I told Jameson, my heart thudding, "there were clues embedded in the old man's will." My pulse jumped, and it had nothing—almost nothing—to do with the way he was *still* looking at me. "But that wasn't the old man's only will."

Jameson knew exactly what I was saying. He saw what I saw. "The old man changed his middle name to Tattersall right after Toby's supposed death. And right after that, he wrote a will disinheriting the family."

I swallowed. "You're always saying he had favorite tricks. What do you think the chances are that the old will is part of *this* puzzle?"

CHAPTER 16

Wind whipping in my hair, I called Alisa from the roof to ask about the will.

"I'm unaware of any special copies of Mr. Hawthorne's prior will, but McNamara, Ortega, and Jones certainly has an original on file that you could view."

I knew exactly what Alisa meant when she said "special," but just because there wasn't an equivalent to the Red Will didn't mean that this was a dead end. Not yet.

"How soon can I see it?" I asked, my eyes still on Jameson's.

"I need you to do two things for me first."

I scowled. When I'd asked to see the Red Will, Alisa had leveraged my request to put me in a room with a team of stylists. "Not another makeover," I groaned. "Because this is about as made over as I get."

"You're perfectly presentable these days," Alisa assured me. "But I will need you to clear some time in your schedule for an appointment with Landon right after school."

Landon was a media consultant. She handled PR—and prepping me to talk to the press.

"Why do I need to meet with Landon right after school?" I asked suspiciously.

"I'd like you interview-ready within the next month. We need to be sure that we're the ones controlling the story, Avery." Alisa paused. "Not your father."

I couldn't say what I wanted to say, which was that Ricky Grambs *wasn't* my father. It wasn't *his* signature on my birth certificate.

"Fine," I said sharply. "What else?" Alisa had said "two things."

"I need you to recover your senses and let your poor bodyguard onto that roof."

<hr>

After school, I met with Landon in the Oval Room.

"Last time we met, I taught you how not to answer questions. The art of answering them is a bit more complicated. With a group of reporters, you can ignore questions you don't want to answer. In a one-on-one interview, that ceases to be an option."

I tried to at least look like I was paying attention to what the media consultant was saying.

"Instead of ignoring questions," Landon continued, her posh British accent pronounced, "you have to redirect them, and you must do so in a way that ensures that people are interested enough in what you're saying that they fail to notice when you take a detour directly toward one of your preordained talking points."

"My talking points," I echoed, but my thoughts were on Tobias Hawthorne's will.

Landon's deep brown eyes didn't miss much. She arched an eyebrow at me, and I forced myself to focus.

"Lovely," she declared. "The first thing you need to decide is what you want people taking away from any given interview. To do that, you will need to formulate a personal theme, exactly six talking points, and no fewer than two dozen personal anecdotes that will humanize you *and* redirect any category of question you might receive toward one of your talking points."

"Is that all?" I asked dryly.

Landon ignored my tone. "Not quite. You'll also need to learn to identify 'no' questions."

I could do this. I could be a good little heiress celebrity. I could refrain from rolling my eyes. "What are 'no' questions?"

"They're questions that you can answer in a single word, most typically *no*. If you can't spin a question around to a talking point, or if talking too much will make you look guilty, then you need to be able to look the interviewer in the eye and, without sounding the least bit defensive, give her that one-word answer. *No. Yes. Sometimes.*"

The way she said those words sounded *so* sincere—and she hadn't even been asked a question.

"I don't have anything to feel guilty about," I pointed out. "I haven't done anything wrong."

"That," she said evenly, "is exactly the kind of thing that is going to make you sound defensive."

———◆———

Landon gave me homework, and I left our session determined to ensure that Alisa held up her end of the bargain. An hour later, Oren, Alisa, Jameson, and I were on the way to the law firm of McNamara, Ortega, and Jones.

To my surprise, Xander was sitting out front when we got there. "Did you tell him we were coming?" I asked Jameson as the two of us stepped out of the SUV.

"I didn't have to," Jameson murmured back, his eyes narrowing. "He's a Hawthorne." He raised his voice loud enough for Xander to hear it. "And he'd better not have me bugged."

The fact that surveillance technology was even a possibility here said a lot about their childhood.

"It's a wonderful day for looking at legal documents," Xander replied cheerfully, sidestepping the comment about having Jameson bugged.

Neither Alisa nor Oren said a word as the five of us entered the building and rode the elevator up. When the doors opened, my lawyer led me to a corner office, where a document was lying on the desk. *Déjà vu.*

Alisa gave the three of us an Alisa Look. "I'll leave the door open," she announced, taking up a position next to Oren, right outside the door.

Jameson called after her, amused. "Would you close the door if I promised very sincerely not to ravish your client?"

"Jameson!" I hissed.

Alisa glanced back and rolled her eyes. "I've literally known you since you were in diapers," she told Jameson. "And you have *always* been trouble."

The door stayed open.

Jameson cut his eyes toward me and gave a little shrug. "Guilty as charged."

Before I could reply, Xander vaulted past us to get to the will first. Jameson and I crowded in beside him. All three of us read.

> I, *Tobias Tattersall Hawthorne, being of sound body and mind, decree that my worldly possessions, including all monetary and physical assets, be disposed of as follows:*
>
> *In the event that I predecease my wife, Alice O'Day Hawthorne, all my assets and worldly possessions shall be bequeathed unto her. In the event that*

Alice O'Day Hawthorne predeceases me, the terms of
my will shall be as follows:

 To Andrew and Lottie Laughlin, for years of loyal
service, I bequeath a sum of one hundred thousand
dollars apiece, with lifelong, rent-free tenancy granted
in Wayback Cottage, located on the western border
of my Texas estate.

Xander tapped his finger against that sentence. "Sounds familiar."
The bit about the Laughlins had appeared in Tobias Hawthorne's
more recent will as well. Going on instinct, I scanned the will in
front of us for other similarities. Oren wasn't mentioned in this one,
but Nan was, under the exact same terms as Tobias Hawthorne's
later will. Then I came to the part about the Hawthorne daughters.

 To my daughter Skye Hawthorne, I leave my com-
pass, may she always know true north. To my daugh-
ter Zara, I leave my wedding ring, may she love as
wholly and steadfastly as I loved her mother.

The wording there was familiar, too, but in his final will, Tobias
Hawthorne had also left his daughters money to cover all debts
accrued as of his date of death, and a onetime inheritance of fifty
thousand dollars. In this version, he really *had* left them nothing
except trinkets. Nash, the only Hawthorne grandson who'd been
born before this will was written, wasn't mentioned at all. There
was no provision allowing the Hawthorne family to continue living
in Hawthorne House. Instead, the rest of the will was simple.

 The remainder of my estate, including all properties,
monetary assets, and worldly possessions not other-

wise specified, is to be liquefied and the proceeds split
equally among the following charities...

The list that followed was long—dozens in total.

Attached to the back of Tobias Hawthorne's will was a copy of his wife's will, containing nearly identical terms. If she died first, everything went to her husband. If he predeceased her, their assets went to charity—with the same bequests to the Laughlins and Nan, and nothing left to Zara and Skye.

"Your grandmother was in on it," I told the boys.

"She died right before Grayson was born," Jameson said. "Everyone says the grief over Toby killed her."

Had the old man told his wife that their son was still alive? Had he known—or even suspected—the truth back when this will was written?

I returned my attention to the document and read it again from the top. "There are only two major differences between this will and the last one," I said when I was done.

"You aren't in this one." Xander ticked off the first. "Which, barring time travel, makes sense, given that you weren't born until three years after it was written."

"And the charities." Jameson was in laser-focus mode. He didn't so much as spare a glance for his brother—or for me. "If there's a clue in here, it's in that list."

Xander grinned. "And you know what that means, Jamie."

Jameson made a face that suggested that he did, in fact, know what that meant.

"What?" I asked.

Jameson sighed theatrically. "Don't mind me. This is what I look like when I'm preparing to be painfully bored and predictably annoyed. If we want the rundown on the charities on this list, there's an efficient way of getting it. Prepare yourself for a lecture, Heiress."

That was the exact moment when I realized what he was talking about—and who had the information we needed. The member of the Hawthorne family who knew its charitable works intimately. Someone I'd already told about Toby. "Grayson."

CHAPTER 17

The Hawthorne Foundation looked exactly as it had the last time I'd been there. The walls were still a light silver-gray—the color of Grayson's eyes. Massive black-and-white photographs still hung all around the room. Grayson's handiwork.

This place *was* Grayson—but this time Jameson and Xander were there as a buffer between us.

"If he says the phrase *effective altruism*," Xander warned me with mock solemnity, "run."

I snorted back laughter. A door opened and shut nearby, and Grayson strode into the room. His gaze settled on me for a second or two before he looked past me to his brothers.

"To what do I owe the honor, Jamie? Xan?"

Xander opened his mouth, but Jameson beat him to speaking. "I invoke the ancient rite of *On Spake*."

Xander looked startled, then delighted.

"The what?" I said.

Grayson narrowed his eyes at his brother, then answered my question. "Anagram it."

It took me less than three seconds. "No speak."

"Exactly," Jameson said. "Once I begin telling him what I have to say, my dearest, darling older brother here can't say a single word until I finish."

"At which point, if I choose, I can invoke the sacred rite of *Taeb Nwod*." Grayson dusted an imaginary speck off the cuff of his suit. "I believe those rules expired when I was ten."

"I recall no such expiration!" Xander volunteered.

I did a little mental rearranging of the words Grayson had spoken and then shook my head. "Beatdown? You've got to be kidding me."

"It's a friendly beatdown," Xander assured me. "A *brotherly* beatdown." He paused. "More or less."

"Well?" Jameson gave Grayson a look.

In reply, Grayson took off his suit jacket and laid it on a nearby desk, presumably preparing for part two of this little ritual. "Whatever you have to tell me, Jamie, I'm all ears."

"We went to see the will the old man wrote right after Toby 'died.'" Jameson took his time with what he had to say—because he could. "Yes, I know you think asking to see the will was a bad idea. No, I don't have any particular objection to bad ideas. Long story short, we found a list of charities. We need you to look through them and see what, if anything, you notice."

Grayson arched an eyebrow.

"He can't talk until I cease *On Spake*," Jameson told me. "Let's just cherish the sound of silence for another moment."

A vein in Grayson's forehead pulsed. "Come on," I told Jameson.

He blew out a long breath. "Cease *On Spake*."

Grayson began cuffing the sleeves of his dress shirt.

"You two aren't actually going to fight, are you?" I asked warily. I turned to Xander. "They're not actually going to fight, are they?"

"Who can say?" Xander replied merrily. "But perhaps you and I should wait outside in case this gets ugly."

"I'm not going anywhere," I insisted. "Jameson, this is ridiculous."

"Not my call, Heiress."

"Grayson!" I said.

He turned to look at me. "I really would prefer you wait outside."

CHAPTER 18

Your brothers are idiots," I told Xander, pacing back and forth in front of the building. Oren, who stood a few feet away, looked somewhat amused.

"It's fine," Xander assured me. "This is just what brothers do."

I highly doubted that.

From inside the building, there was silence.

"By tradition, the first blow is Gray's," Xander offered helpfully. "He usually goes for a leg sweep. Classic! But he'll circle Jameson first. They'll circle each other, really, and Gray will go into warnings-and-orders mode, which will cause Jamie to mock him, so on and so forth, until the first blow is struck."

There was a thud from inside. "And after that?" I asked, my eyes narrowing.

Xander grinned. "We have an average of three black belts apiece, but it usually devolves into wrestling. One of them will pin the other. Argue, argue, bicker, bicker, and voilà."

Given that Grayson had made it very clear that he thought pulling at the strings of Toby's disappearance was a bad idea, I had a guess or two about what that argument might sound like.

"I'm going back in," I muttered, but before I could, the door to the building opened.

Jameson stood there, looking only slightly worse for the wear. He didn't seem injured. A little sweaty, maybe, but not bleeding or bruised. "I take it there was no beatdown?" I said.

Jameson grinned. "What would make you think that?" He glanced over at Oren. "If you wait out here, you have my word that she'll be perfectly safe inside. It's secure."

"I know." Oren stared Jameson down. "I designed the security on this building myself."

"Can you give us a minute, Oren?" I asked. My head of security shot a hard look in Jameson's direction, then Xander's, and then nodded. Xander and I followed Jameson back inside.

"Don't worry," Jameson murmured as Grayson came into view. "I took it easy on him."

Like Jameson, Grayson appeared unharmed. As I watched, he slipped his suit jacket back on. "You two are idiots," I muttered.

"Be that as it may," Grayson replied, "you want my help."

He wasn't wrong. "Yes, we do."

"I told you this was a bad idea, Avery." Grayson's focus was on me and me alone. It was intense. I wasn't used to people being protective of me. But right now, *protection* wasn't what I wanted—or needed—from him.

"While you and Jameson were playing WWF like eight-year-olds," I said, "did he happen to tell you that Toby was adopted?" I swallowed and looked down because this next part was harder to say. "Did he tell you about my birth certificate?"

"Your what?" Xander said immediately.

Grayson stared at me. He was just as capable as any Hawthorne of reading between the lines. Toby was adopted. I'd mentioned my birth certificate. Everyone in this room knew why this search mattered to me now.

"Here's a picture I took." I held my phone out to Grayson. "Those are the charities listed in the will your grandfather wrote shortly after Toby's disappearance."

Grayson managed to take the phone from me without our fingers so much as brushing. Beside me, I could feel Jameson's stare, just as palpable as his brother's.

"There are very few surprises on this list." Grayson looked up from the phone just in time to catch me watching him read. "Most of these organizations have received regular support—or, at the very least, a sizable onetime donation—from the Hawthorne Foundation."

I forced myself to pay attention to what Grayson was saying, not the way his silvery eyes settled on mine as he talked. "You said 'few surprises,'" I pointed out. "Not none."

"Off the top of my head, I see four organizations that I don't recognize. That doesn't mean we haven't given to them before...."

"But it's a start." Jameson's voice buzzed with a familiar energy—familiar to me, almost certainly familiar to his brothers.

"The Allport Institute," Grayson rattled off. "Camden House. Colin's Way. And the Rockaway Watch Society. Those are the only four organizations on this list that I haven't seen in the foundation's records."

Immediately, my brain started cataloging what Grayson had said, playing with the words and the letters, looking for a pattern. "Institute, house, way, watch," I tried out loud.

"Watch, house, institute, way." Jameson scrambled the order.

"Four words," Xander offered. "And four names. Allport, Camden, Colin, Rockaway."

Grayson stepped between the two of us and past Jameson—and

kept on walking. "I'll leave you three to it," he said. Near the doorway, he paused. "But, Jamie? You're wrong." And then Grayson said something in a language I deeply suspected was Latin.

Jameson's eyes flashed, and he responded in the same language.

I glanced at Xander. The youngest Hawthorne's eyebrows—well, eyebrow, really, since he'd burned the other one off—skyrocketed. He clearly understood what had just been said but volunteered no translation.

Instead, he tugged me toward the doorway—and the SUV parked outside. "Come on."

CHAPTER 19

On the drive back to Hawthorne House, Jameson, Xander, and I buried ourselves in our phones. I assumed that their missions were the same as mine: to research the four charities that Grayson had identified.

My intuition was that they might not actually *be* charities, that Tobias Hawthorne might have made them up as part of the puzzle, but a series of internet searches quickly dispelled that theory. The Allport Institute, Camden House, Colin's Way, and the Rockaway Watch Society were all registered nonprofits. Sorting out the details of each one took longer.

The Allport Institute was a research facility based in Switzerland, dedicated to studying the neuroscience of memory and dementia. I scrolled through the staff page, reading each of the scientists' bios. Then I clicked on some news coverage about the institute's latest clinical trials. *Short-term memory loss. Dementia. Alzheimer's. Amnesia.*

I sat with that for a moment. *Is this a clue? To what?* I glanced out the window and caught sight of Jameson's reflection in the glass. His hair could never quite decide which way to lie, and even caught up in thought, his face was always in motion.

When I finally managed to turn my attention back to my phone, the next search term I typed in wasn't one of the charities. It was my best approximation of the words that Grayson had said to Jameson back at the foundation.

Est unus ex nobis. Nos defendat eius. As I'd suspected, it was Latin. An online translator told me that it meant *It is one of us. We protect it.* Jameson's response, *Scio*, meant *I know*. It only took me one more search to realize that the same translation would hold if *it* was replaced with *she. She is one of us. We protect her.*

Maybe I should have bristled at that. Three weeks ago, I probably would have, but three weeks ago, I never would have dreamed that they would come to see me as one of them.

That I could *be* one of them, not just an outsider looking in.

Trying not to let that thought consume me, I forced myself to move on to the next charity on my list. Camden House was an in-patient rehabilitation center for substance abuse and addiction, focused on the "whole person." The website was full of testimonials. The staff was full of doctors, therapists, and other professionals. The grounds were beautiful.

But the website didn't provide any answers.

An institute for memory research in Switzerland. An addiction treatment facility in Maine. I thought about the pills and powder that we'd found in Toby's room. What if Tobias Hawthorne had used his will—and these four charities—to tell a story? *Maybe Toby was an addict. Maybe he was a patient at Camden House. As for the Allport Institute...*

I didn't get the chance to finish that thought before we pulled through the gates of the estate. As we wound our way up the long drive, I snuck a look at the boys. Xander was still fixated on his phone, but Jameson was staring straight ahead. The moment we stepped out of the car, he took off.

So much for working on this *together*.

"Oh, look," Xander said, nudging me in the side. "There's Nan. Hello, Nan!"

The boys' great-grandmother glared at Xander from the porch. "And just what have you been up to?" she asked him sharply.

"Nonsense and mischief," he replied solemnly. "Always."

She scowled, and he bounded up onto the porch and kissed the top of her head. She swatted at him. "Think you can sugar me up, do you?"

"Perish the thought," Xander replied. "I don't *have* to sugar you up. I'm your favorite!"

"Are not," Nan grunted. She poked him with her cane. "Go on with you. I want to talk to the girl."

Nan didn't ask if I wanted to talk. She just waited for me to approach, then took my arm for balance. "Walk with me," she ordered. "In the garden."

She said nothing for at least five minutes as we made our way, at a snail's pace, through a topiary garden. Dense bushes had been shaped into sculptures. Most were abstract, but I saw a topiary elephant and couldn't keep an incredulous look from settling over my face.

"Ridiculous," Nan scoffed. "All of it." After a long moment, she turned to me. "Well?"

"Well, what?" I said.

"What have you done to find my boy?" Nan's harsh expression trembled slightly, and her grip on my arm tightened.

"I'm trying," I said quietly. "But I don't think Toby wants to be found."

If Toby Hawthorne had wanted to be found, he could have returned to Hawthorne House at any time in the last twenty years. *Unless he doesn't remember.* That thought hit me out of nowhere.

The Allport Institute focused on memory research—Alzheimer's, dementia, and *memory loss*. What if *that* was the story Tobias Hawthorne was telling in the will? What if his son had lost his memory?

What if Harry didn't *know* he was Toby Hawthorne?

The thought that he might not have lied to me nearly took me to my knees. I forced myself to slow down. I was leaping to conclusions. I didn't even know for certain that the four charities had been chosen to tell a story.

"Have you ever heard of Camden House?" I asked Nan. "It's a treatment center for—"

"I know what it is." Nan cut me off, her voice gruff.

There was no easy way to ask this next question. "Did your daughter and son-in-law send Toby there?"

"He wasn't an addict," Nan spat. "I know addicts. That boy was just... confused."

I wasn't about to bicker with her about words. "But they sent him to Camden House, for his *confusion*?"

"He was angry when he left and angry when he got back." Nan shook her head. "That summer..." Her lip quivered. She didn't finish what she was saying.

"Was that the summer of the fire?" I asked softly.

Before Nan could reply, a shadow fell across the two of us. Mr. Laughlin stepped onto the garden path. He was holding a pair of shears. "Everything okay here?" He scowled, and I thought about Mrs. Laughlin calling me cruel.

"Everything's fine," I said, my voice tight.

Mr. Laughlin looked toward Nan. "We talked about this, Pearl," he said gently. "It isn't healthy." Clearly, he knew what I'd told Nan about Toby. And clearly, he didn't believe me any more than his wife did.

After a long silence, Mr. Laughlin turned back to me. "I made some repairs in the House." A muscle in his jaw tightened. "To one of the older wings. When things fall into disrepair around here…" He gave me a look. "People get hurt."

I understood then that *one of the older wings* was code for *Toby's*. I wasn't sure what the groundskeeper meant by repairs until I made my way back into Hawthorne House and went to check.

Toby's wing had been bricked up again.

CHAPTER 20

On the way from Toby's wing to mine, I found myself glancing back over my shoulder every hundred feet. As I stepped into my hall, I heard Libby's voice: "Did you know about this?"

"You're going to have to be a bit more specific, darlin'." That was Nash, obviously. I could see his silhouette in the doorway to my sister's room.

"Your lawyer girlfriend. These papers. Did you know?"

I couldn't see Libby at all, so I had no idea how she was looking at Nash or what kind of papers she was holding.

"Sweetheart, I wouldn't let Alisa hear you refer to her as my anything."

"Don't call me sweetheart."

This didn't feel like a conversation I had any business overhearing, so I crept for the door to my room, opened it, and slipped inside. Closing the door behind me, I flipped on my light. A breeze caught my hair.

I turned to see that one of the massive windows on my far wall was open. *I didn't leave that window open.* A breath caught in my throat, and I felt the drum of my heart in every inch of my body. I'd had nightmares like this before: First you notice one thing that's off, and then—

Blood. The muscles in my throat tightened like a vise. *There's blood.* Panic flooded my body like a shot of adrenaline straight to the heart. *Get out. Get out get out get—*

But I couldn't move. All I could do was stare in horror at the white bedsheet lying under my open window, drenched in blood. *Move. You have to move, Avery.* Sitting on top of the white sheet, there was a heart.

Human?

And through the heart—*a knife.* My lungs felt like they were locked. My body didn't listen no matter how many times I told it to run. *There's a knife. And a heart. And—*

I let out a low gurgling sound. I still couldn't run, but I managed to stumble backward.

I tried to scream, but no sound came out. I felt the way I had in the Black Wood, in the sights of someone who wanted me dead. *I have to get out of here. I have to—*

"Breathe, kid." Nash was there suddenly. He placed a hand on each of my shoulders. He bent down, putting his face even with mine. "In and out. That's a good girl."

"My room," I wheezed. "There's a heart in my room. A knife—"

A dangerous expression flickered across Nash's face. "Call Oren," he told Libby, who had appeared beside us. When Nash turned back to me, his expression was gentle. "In and out," he said again.

I sucked in a frantic breath and tried to look at my room, but the eldest Hawthorne brother sidestepped and blocked me from seeing a damn thing except for his face. He was suntanned and had a five o'clock shadow. He was wearing his trademark cowboy hat. His gaze was steady.

I breathed.

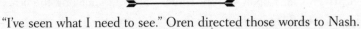

"I've seen what I need to see." Oren directed those words to Nash. "It's a cow heart, not human. Knife is a steak knife, same brand they keep in the kitchens here."

My mind went to the List. Would-be stalkers. *Threats.*

"The linens are Hawthorne linens," Oren continued.

"Inside job?" Nash asked, his jaw tightening. "One of the staff?"

"Likely," Oren confirmed. He turned to me. "Upset anyone lately?"

I managed to get ahold of myself. "I might have upset the Laughlins." I thought about Mrs. Laughlin calling me cruel. About her husband, warning me about people getting hurt.

"You think the Laughlins did this?" Libby asked, her eyes wide.

"Not a chance in the world." Nash's reply was firm. He glanced at Oren. "More likely, someone on the staff got wind that Mr. and Mrs. L are in a tizzy about something and took that to mean it's gloves off."

Oren digested that. "Can you get someone in here to clean this up?" he asked Nash.

Nash responded by making a call. "Mel? I need a favor."

I recognized the maid who showed up a few minutes later. Mellie had a habit of looking at Nash like he hung the moon.

"Can you take care of this for me, darlin'?" Nash asked, gesturing toward the mess.

Mellie nodded, her dark brown eyes fixed on his. Alisa had told me once that Mellie was "one of Nash's." I had no idea how many of the household staff the oldest Hawthorne brother had saved—or how many of "my" people saw me as a villain who'd stolen Nash's inheritance.

"I need you to talk to folks for me," Nash told Mellie. "Make it clear: This ain't open season. I don't care who's looking the other way or why. Hands off. You got me?"

Mellie laid a hand on Nash's arm and nodded. "Of course."

CHAPTER 21

There will be some changes to your security protocol on the estate until we get this figured out," Oren told me after everyone else had left. "But before we talk about those, we need to talk about the Laughlins. More specifically, we need to talk about *how* you upset them."

I grappled for a way to respond without giving too much away. "Jameson, Xander, and I were messing around in Toby's wing."

Oren folded his arms over his chest. "I know. I also know *why*."

Oren had access to the security system—and one of his men had been in the Black Box that afternoon. *What exactly did Eli overhear?*

My head of security laid it out for me. "Tobias Hawthorne the Second. You think he's alive."

"I *know* he is."

Oren was silent for a long moment. "Have I told you how I came to be in Mr. Hawthorne's employ?"

I had no idea where that question had come from. "No."

"I was career military, ages eighteen to thirty-two. I would have stayed in until I hit twenty years, but there was an incident." The way Oren said the word *incident* sent ice down my spine. "Everyone in my unit was killed except me. By the time Mr. Hawthorne found me a year later, I was in bad shape."

I couldn't picture Oren out of control. "Why are you telling me this?"

"Because," Oren said, "I need you to understand that I owe Mr. Hawthorne my life. He gave me a purpose. He dragged me back into the light. And the last thing he asked of me was that I stay on to head *your* security team." Oren let that sink in. "Whatever I have to do to keep you safe," he continued, his voice low, "I will do it."

"Do you think there's a threat?" I asked him. "A real one? Are you worried about whoever left that heart?"

"I'm worried," Oren replied, "about what you and the boys are doing. About the ghosts you're digging up."

"Toby's alive," I said fiercely. "I knew him. I think he's—"

"Stop," Oren ordered.

My father, I finished silently. "Grayson would kill me for telling you this," I said. "He thinks that if it gets out that Toby's alive—"

Oren finished my sentence for me. "The repercussions could be deadly."

"What?" That hadn't been what I was going to say. At all.

"Avery," Oren said, his voice low, "right now the family believes that there is no effective way of challenging the will—no way of getting ahold of the fortune that Mr. Hawthorne left to you. Zara and Constantine would much rather deal with you inheriting and the law firm holding the reins than with the fortune passing to *your* heirs, and that's assuming that your death wouldn't count as defaulting on the terms of the will and revert the entire fortune to charity. Mr. Hawthorne always thought ten steps ahead. He tied their fortunes to yours. He made you as safe as he could. But if the will isn't ironclad? If there's another heir..."

Someone might decide that killing me is worth it? I didn't say that out loud.

"You need to lie low," Oren told me. "Whatever it is you and the boys are up to—stop."

➤————◄

I couldn't stop. That night, with security posted right outside my door, I resumed the search I'd started conducting that afternoon.

The Allport Institute was a center for memory research. Camden House was an addiction treatment facility—and, based on my conversation with Nan that afternoon, Toby had been a patient there. A new search on the Rockaway Watch Society told me that Rockaway Watch was a small coastal town directly across from Hawthorne Island. *Kaylie Rooney was from Rockaway Watch.* It took me a good fifteen minutes to put it together, but once I did, the neurons in my brain started firing painfully fast.

There was a story here—one that started with Toby angry and addicted, one that involved the fire and the young people who'd died there. *What about the Allport Institute?* Had Toby lost his memory after the fire? Was that why he'd never returned home?

With laser focus to rival Jameson's, I did a search for the last remaining charity on Grayson's list: Colin's Way. I'd verified earlier that it existed, but I hadn't dug deep. This time I did a once-over of the website. The first thing I saw on the landing page was a picture of a bunch of elementary schoolers playing basketball. I clicked on a tab labeled *Our Story* and read.

> *Colin's Way provides a safe after-school environment
> for kids between the ages five and twelve. Founded
> in memory of Colin Anders Wright (pictured at
> right), we are in the business of Playing, Giving, and
> Growing—so all children have a future.*

It took me a second to place the name. Like Kaylie Rooney, Colin Anders Wright had died on Hawthorne Island twenty years earlier. *How soon did Colin's family create a charity in his memory?* I wondered. It must have been nearly immediate, for Colin's Way to have been included in Tobias Hawthorne's twenty-year-old will. I searched for news articles within a month of the fire with the search term *Colin's Way* and found a half dozen articles.

Right after the fire, then. I toggled back to the Colin's Way website and dug through the media section—through years, then decades, until I hit the first press clipping available—a press conference of some kind.

I hit Play on the video. There was a family on-screen: a woman with two young children, standing behind a man. At first I thought they were husband and wife, but it soon became clear that they were siblings.

"This is a horrific tragedy, one from which our family will never recover. My nephew was an incredible young man. He was intelligent and driven, competitive but kind. There is no telling what good he would have done in this world had the actions of others not robbed him of that opportunity. I know that if Colin were here, he would tell me to let go of the anger. He would tell me to concentrate on what matters. And so, along with his mother, his siblings, and my wife, who could not be here today, I am proud to announce the formation of Colin's Way, a charity that will channel my nephew's competitive and giving spirit to bring the joy of athletics, teamwork, and family to underprivileged children in our communities."

There was something about the man's voice that stuck with me, something jarring. Something familiar. When the camera zoomed in closer, I noticed his eyes.

Ice blue, bordering on gray. Once he ended his speech, reporters called out for his attention. "Mr. Grayson!"

"Mr. Grayson, over here!"

A ticker bar ran across the bottom of the screen. Feeling dazed and borderline dizzy, I read the name of Colin Anders Wright's uncle: *Sheffield Grayson*.

CHAPTER 22

The next morning, Jameson called to me from the other side of my fireplace, and I pulled the candlestick on the mantel to trigger the release.

"Did you find what I found?" he asked me. "Two of the four charities have connections to victims of the fire. I'm still piecing together the rest, but I have a theory."

"Does your theory involve Toby having been a patient at Camden House and potentially losing his memory after the fire?" I asked.

Jameson leaned toward me. "We're brilliant."

I thought about the rest of what I'd discovered. He hadn't mentioned Sheffield Grayson.

"Heiress?" Jameson leaned back and assessed me. "What is it?"

It was obvious to me that he hadn't looked up anything about Colin's Way beyond the charity's namesake. Obvious that he hadn't seen the video I'd seen. Without a word, I pulled it up for him on my phone. I handed it over. As Jameson watched, I finally found my voice.

"His eyes," I said. "And his last name is Grayson. I know that Skye never told you anything about your fathers, but you all have last names as first names. Do you think..."

Jameson handed the phone back. "Only one way to find out." He came to stand right behind me. "We could go out your door, like normal people, but one of Oren's men is stationed outside, and I doubt anyone on your security team would sign off on you going to visit my mother."

Going to visit a woman who'd tried to have me killed was a bad idea. I knew that. But Grayson was nineteen, which meant that he'd been conceived twenty years ago—not long after the fire on Hawthorne Island. What were the chances that was a coincidence? There was no such thing in Hawthorne House. And right now, the only person who could answer our questions was Skye.

"Oren isn't going to be happy about this," I told Jameson.

He smiled. "We'll be back before anyone realizes we're gone."

◆━━━━━━◆

Jameson knew the secret passageways like the back of his hand. He got us to the massive indoor garage unseen. He pulled a motorcycle off a rack on the wall and solved the puzzle box where the keys were kept. The next thing I knew, he was wearing a helmet and holding a second one out to me.

"Do you trust me, Heiress?" Jameson had donned a leather jacket. He looked like trouble. The good kind.

"Not even a little," I replied, but I took the helmet from his outstretched hand, and when he climbed onto the motorcycle, I climbed on behind him.

CHAPTER 23

Skye Hawthorne was staying at a luxury hotel—a hotel I *owned*. It was the kind of place that had caviar on the room-service menu and offered in-room spa services. I had no idea how Skye was paying for a room, or if she was paying. The idea that *this* was her punishment for an attempt on my life was infuriating.

"Easy," Jameson murmured beside me as he knocked on the door. "We need her to talk."

Talk first, I thought. *Have security remove her from the premises later.*

Skye opened the door wearing a crimson silk robe that brushed the tips of her toes and flowed around her as she moved. "Jamie." She smiled at Jameson. "Shame on you for not visiting your poor mother until now."

Jameson gave me the briefest of warning looks, a clear *Let me handle this.*

"I'm an awful son," Jameson agreed, dialing his level of charm up to meet Skye's. "Horrid, really, so preoccupied with the person you tried to have killed that I've barely spared a thought for how difficult getting caught must have been for you."

I hadn't breathed a word to Jameson about what his mother had done, but he knew Skye had moved out. It probably hadn't taken him long to figure out that Grayson had *forced* her out—and why.

"What has your brother been telling you?" Skye demanded, without specifying which brother she was talking about. "And you believe him? Believe *her*—"

"I believe," Jameson said smoothly, "that I've found Grayson's father."

That got an eyebrow arch out of Skye. "Was he lost?" The victim act melted off her like snow in the sun.

"Sheffield Grayson." I said the name, forcing Skye's gaze to flit toward me. "His nephew died in the fire on Hawthorne Island, along with your brother, Toby."

"I haven't the faintest idea what you're talking about."

"And I have no idea why you think lying to me is a good idea, when I could have you kicked out of this hotel," I shot back. I'd intended to let Jameson handle this. Really. It just hadn't worked out that way.

"You?" Skye sniffed. "This hotel has been in my family for decades. You are under quite the delusion if you think—"

"That the management will care more about the feelings of the new owner than about yours?"

"Aren't you just adorable?" Skye retreated into the room. "Don't just stand there," she called back. "You're letting in a draft."

With a glance at Jameson, I crossed the threshold—and found myself almost immediately joined by Oren and Eli. Apparently, I'd been under closer guard than I'd realized.

Skye gave every appearance of being delighted at the appearance of my security team. "It appears we have a party." She sat down on a chaise longue and stretched out her legs. "Let's get down to business, shall we? I have something you want, and I would like a few assurances, starting with how very welcome I will be to stay in this penthouse indefinitely."

Like hell, I thought.

"Counteroffer," Jameson interjected before I could reply. "If you answer our questions, I won't tell Xander what you did." He flopped down on a sofa next to Skye's chaise. "I'm sure Nash has put two and two together. I figured it out quickly enough. But Xan? For all he knows, this is just another little trip of yours. I'd hate to have to tell him about your murderous impulses."

"Jameson Winchester Hawthorne, I am your mother. I brought you into this world." Skye reached for a nearby glass of champagne, and I noticed that there was a second glass beside it.

She wasn't here alone.

"However," she continued with a heavy sigh, "because I am in such a generous mood, I suppose I will answer a question or two."

"Is Sheffield Grayson Gray's father?" Jameson wasted no time.

Skye took a sip. "Not in any way that signifies."

"Biologically," Jameson pressed.

"If you must know," Skye said, staring at him over the rim of her glass, "then, yes, technically Sheff is Grayson's father. But what does a little biology matter? I'm the one who raised you all."

Jameson snorted. "By some definitions."

"Does Sheffield Grayson know that he has a son?" I asked, my mind full of Grayson, wondering what this would mean for him.

Skye gave an elegant little shrug. "I haven't the faintest idea."

"You never told him?" Jameson asked.

"Why would I?"

I stared at her. "You got pregnant on purpose." Nash had told me as much.

"You were grieving," Jameson said softly. "So was he."

The softness seemed to get to Skye in a way that nothing else had. "Toby and I were so close. Sheff practically raised Colin. We understood each other, for a time."

"For a time," Jameson repeated. "Or for a night?"

"Honestly, Jamie, what does it matter?" Skye was getting impatient now. "You boys never wanted for anything. My father gave you the world. The staff spoiled you. You all had each other, and you had me. Why wasn't that enough?"

"Because," Jameson said, his voice rough, "we didn't really have you."

Skye set her glass down. "Don't you dare rewrite history. What do you think it was like for me? Son after son—and every single one of you preferred my father."

"They were children," I said.

"Hawthornes are never children, darling," Skye told me archly. "But let's not argue. We're family, Jamie, and family is so very important. Don't you agree, Avery?"

Something about that question and the way she'd said it was deeply unsettling.

"In fact," Skye continued, "I'm considering having another child. I'm young enough, still. Healthy. My sons have turned their backs on me. I deserve something of my own, don't I?"

Something, I thought, my heart aching for Jameson. *Not someone.*

"You never told Sheffield Grayson that he had a son." I returned to the issue at hand. The sooner I could get Jameson out of here, the better.

"Sheff knew who I was," Skye said. "If he'd wanted to follow up, he could have. It was a test of sorts: If I didn't matter enough to chase—then what use were they to me?"

They. I registered her word choice. She wasn't just talking about *Grayson*'s father.

Skye leaned back against the chaise longue. "Frankly, I suspect that Sheff knows exactly what came of our time together." She met Jameson's eyes. "This family is prominent enough that any of the men I slept with would have to live under a rock not to know that they had a son."

She was telling him that *his* father—whoever he was—knew.

"We're done here," I said, standing up. "Come on, Jameson."

He didn't move. I laid a hand on his shoulder. After a moment, he reached up to touch my fingers. I let him. Jameson Hawthorne didn't like being vulnerable. He didn't like needing people any more than I did.

"Come on," I told him again. We'd gotten what we came for: confirmation.

"Won't you stay a bit longer?" Skye asked. "I'd love to introduce you to my new friend."

"Your friend," Jameson repeated, his eyes going to the second glass of champagne.

"Your little heiress knows him," Skye said, taking a sip of champagne. She waited for that comment to land, waited for confusion to really sink in before she smiled and went for the jugular. "Your father is such a *lovely* man, Avery."

CHAPTER 24

S kye Hawthorne. And Ricky. Skye Hawthorne was sleeping with Ricky.

He's not my father. I clung to that as Oren and Eli ushered us away from Skye's suite. *Ricky Grambs is not my father.* He also wasn't a "lovely man." Skye Hawthorne was caviar and champagne, and Ricky was throwing-up-cheap-beer-in-motel-bathrooms. He didn't have two dimes to rub together. But he did have a claim—however tenuous—to me.

I felt like I was going to be sick. *In fact*, I could hear Skye saying with a billion-dollar twinkle in her eyes, *I'm considering having another child.* Was that her plan? Get pregnant with my half-sibling? *Not mine.* That thought wasn't as comforting as it should have been, because any child of Ricky's would be *Libby's* half-sibling—and I would do anything for Libby.

"What were you thinking?" Oren snapped when we were sequestered safely in an elevator. "A woman who tried to have you killed is sleeping with a man who stands to inherit if you die—and you ditched your protection detail to *put yourself in a room with her.*"

I'd never thought of Ricky as one of my heirs, but I was too young for a will. His name was on my birth certificate.

"Why didn't you know?" I shot back at Oren before I could rein in the storm of emotions churning in my gut. "They're both on your list, aren't they? How could you not know that they…" I trailed off, sucking in a breath that I couldn't bring myself to let out.

"You did know," Jameson concluded. Oren didn't deny it. The second the elevator door opened, Jameson pulled me out. "Let's get out of here, Heiress."

Eli stepped to block him. Oren broke Jameson's hold on my arm. I could feel the exact moment when the other people in the lobby noticed us. The moment they recognized me.

"She's not going anywhere but school," Oren told Jameson quietly. His expression looked perfectly pleasant. My head of security knew how not to make a scene.

Jameson crooked his head to look at me. He *excelled* at making scenes. There was an invitation in his green eyes—and a promise. If I went with him, he'd find a way to make us both forget what had just happened.

I wanted that. But girls like me didn't always get what we wanted. I looked down. "Jameson." My voice was quiet. People were staring. Out of the corner of my eye, I saw someone lift a phone and snap our picture.

"On second thought," Jameson said grandly, "Oren's right. Play it safe, Heiress." The look he gave me then was one I felt through every square inch of my body. "For now."

CHAPTER 25

Eli stuck to my side all day. Anytime I tried to get space, amber-ringed blue eyes stared me down. At one point, he informed me that Oren had tightened all security protocols—not just at Country Day but also on the estate. I wasn't going *anywhere* without an escort.

When Oren came to collect us that afternoon, Alisa was in the back seat of the SUV. The first thing she did after I buckled myself in was hand me a tablet. I looked down at the screen and saw a photograph, one that had been taken at the hotel. Jameson's eyes were dark and glittering, and I was staring at him the way a thousand other girls had probably stared at Jameson Hawthorne.

Like he mattered.

The headline read *Tensions Grow Between Heiress and Hawthorne Family.*

"This is not the message we want to be sending," Alisa told me. "I've already arranged for damage control. There's a memorial fundraiser at Country Day tomorrow evening. You and the Hawthorne brothers will be in attendance."

Some teenagers got grounded. I got sentenced to black-tie galas.

"Fine," I said.

"I'll also need your signature on this." Alisa handed me a three-page form. I flashed back to the conversation I'd overheard between Libby and Nash, then read the bold print on the form: **Petition for Emancipation of Minor**.

"Emancipation?" I said.

"You're seventeen. You have permanent housing and substantial income. Your legal guardian is willing to consent, and you have the most powerful law firm in the state behind you. We're not anticipating any difficulties here."

"Libby consented?" I asked. She hadn't sounded happy about the papers to me.

"I can be very persuasive," Alisa said. "And with Ricky in the picture, this is the right move. Once you're emancipated, he has no standing to try anything in the courts."

"And," Oren added from the front seat, "you'll be able to sign a will."

Once I was emancipated, Ricky would have nothing to gain from my death.

Alisa handed me a pen. As I read through the form, I thought about Libby. Then I thought about Ricky, about Skye—and I signed.

"Excellent," Alisa declared. "Now, there's just one final matter that needs your attention." She handed me a small square of paper with a number written on it.

"What's that?" I asked.

"It's your friend Max's new phone number."

I stared at her. "What?"

Alisa laid her hand lightly on my shoulder. "I got her a phone."

"But her mother—"

"Will never know," Alisa said briskly. "That probably makes me a very bad influence, but you need someone. I understand that,

Avery. And you don't want that someone to be a Hawthorne. Whatever's going on with you and Jameson—"

"There's nothing going on between us."

That got me an Alisa Look and then some. "First the roof, then the hotel." She paused. "Call your friend Max. Let her be your person. Not one of them."

CHAPTER 26

Y ou glorious beach." An hour later, Max answered her new phone sounding downright upbeat.

"You got the phone."

"It is the most beautiful thing I have seen in my bobforsaken life. Hold on a second. I have to turn on the shower."

A second later, I could hear running water. "You're not actually in the shower, are you?"

"My parents don't need to overhear me talking to you on my new burner phone," Max replied. "This is some double-oh-seven-level shift right here, Ave. I'm motherfaxing James Bond, motherfaxers! And yes, I am in the shower. Stealth, thy name is Max."

I snorted. "I've missed you." I paused then, thinking of our last couple of conversations. Max had accused me of making our friendship all about me. She hadn't been wrong. "I know that I haven't been—"

"Don't," Max cut me off. "Okay?"

"Okay." I hesitated for a second or two. "Are we...okay?"

"That depends," Max replied. "Anyone try to kill you lately?"

After I'd been shot at, Max had wanted me to get out, but

leaving Hawthorne House meant giving up the inheritance. To get the money, I had to stay for a year—Alisa had made that very clear.

"Your silence on the issue of people trying to kill you is deeply disturbing."

"I'm fine," I told Max. "It's just..."

"Just?"

I tried to decide where to start. "Someone left a bloody cow heart in my bedroom. With a knife."

"Avery!" Max sighed. "Tell me everything."

"So, to summarize," Max said, "the dead uncle? Not dead, might be your father. Hot boys are also tragic, everyone wants a piece of your fine ash, and the woman who tried to have you killed is foxing your father?"

I winced. "That pretty much covers it."

"You know what I'd like for my birthday?" Max asked calmly.

Max's birthday. It's tomorrow. "A little less drama?"

"Functional life-sized re-creations of the top-three most lovable droids in the *Star Wars* universe," Max corrected. "And a little less drama."

"How are you?" I asked. That was the question I'd failed to ask way too many times before.

"Delightful," Max replied.

"Max."

"Things here have been...fine."

"That sounds like a lie," I said. Max's ex had sent compromising photos of her to her parents when she broke up with him for trying to sell information on me to the press.

Her life definitely wasn't *fine* right now.

"I'm thinking of going on a mission trip," Max told me. "Maybe a long one."

Max's parents were religious. So was Max. It wasn't just something she did for their benefit—but I'd never heard her talking about mission trips before.

How bad are things at home? At school? "Is there anything I can do?" I asked.

"Yes," Max replied seriously. "You can tell your sorry excuse for a father to stick his head up his asp and eat ship. And ducks. Ducks and ship, in that order."

There was a reason Max was my best friend. "Anything else?"

"You could tell me what Jameson Hawthorne's abs feel like," Max suggested innocently. "Because I saw that picture of the two of you, and my psychic senses are telling me that you have communed with those abs."

"No!" I said. "There has been absolutely no communing."

"And why is that?" Max pressed.

"I have a lot going on right now."

"You always have a lot going on," Max told me. "And you don't like wanting things." She sounded oddly serious. "You're really good at protecting yourself, Avery."

She wasn't telling me anything I didn't know. "So?"

"You're a billionaire now. You have an entire team of people to protect you. The world is your motherfaxing oyster. It's okay to want things." Max turned off the shower. "It's okay to go after what you want."

"Who says I want anything?" I asked.

"My psychic senses," Max replied. "And that picture."

CHAPTER 27

I wasn't surprised to find Eli positioned outside my door. After the incident with the heart, I could probably expect a personal security escort—even on the estate—for the foreseeable future. I was, however, surprised to find Grayson standing beside Eli. He was wearing a black suit with an immaculate white dress shirt and no tie, and my mind went to the way he'd looked cuffing his sleeves, preparing to fight.

Whatever hushed conversation Eli and Grayson had been having ceased the second I stepped out into the hall.

"You didn't tell me that someone left a bloody heart in your room." Grayson was Not Pleased—and no one did Not Pleased like Grayson Hawthorne "Why?"

It was clear from his tone that Grayson expected an answer. As a general rule, when Grayson Hawthorne demanded something, the world obliged.

"When would I have told you?" I asked. "I haven't seen you since it happened. With very few exceptions, you've been doing an excellent job of avoiding me all week."

"I'm not avoiding you," Grayson said, but he couldn't even say the words without looking away.

In the back of my mind, I could hear Max telling me that I didn't like wanting things. It was annoying when she was right.

"You went to see my mother." Grayson didn't phrase that sentence as a question.

I glared at Eli, who apparently had a very big mouth.

"Hey," Eli said, holding up his hands. "I didn't tell him."

"Oren?" I asked Grayson, scowling. "Or Alisa?"

"Neither," Grayson replied, and he brought his gaze back to mine. "I saw a picture of you at the hotel. I'm more than capable of making inferences myself."

I tried not to read too much into that last sentence, but I couldn't help thinking about the *inference* that Max had made about that picture of Jameson and me. Was that why Grayson was acting like this?

You're the one who stepped back, I thought. *This is what you wanted.*

"If you needed something from Skye," Grayson said, his voice strained, "all you had to do was tell me."

I remembered then *what* I'd needed from Skye. What she'd confirmed. Suddenly, nothing else mattered.

"Have you seen Jameson today?" I asked Grayson, a muscle in my stomach twisting. "He skipped school. Did he...come find you?"

"No." Grayson's jaw tightened. "Why?"

Jameson hadn't told Grayson about his father, but it didn't feel right for me to do it. "We figured something out." I looked down. "About the charities in the will."

"You don't stop." Grayson shook his head. His arms stayed by his sides, but I saw the thumb on his right hand rubbing the back of his forefinger—a small loss of control that made me think he might be on the verge of a bigger one. "And neither," he continued, "does Jameson." He turned then, tension visible in his neck and jaw, even as his voice remained deadly calm. "If you'll excuse me, I need to have a word with my brother."

CHAPTER 28

I followed Grayson. Eli followed me. To Grayson's credit, he gave up trying to lose me pretty quickly. He let me trail him all the way to the third floor, through a series of twisting hallways, up a small wrought-iron staircase, to an alcove. There was an antique sewing machine in the corner. The walls were covered with quilts. Grayson lifted one to reveal a crawl space.

"If I told you to go back to your room, would you?" he asked.

"Not a chance in this world," I said.

Grayson sighed. "About ten feet in, you'll find a ladder." He held the quilt back and waited, his chin tilted downward, his eyes on mine. The world might bend to the will of Grayson Hawthorne—but I didn't.

Leaving Eli behind, I made my way through the crawl space on all fours. I could feel and hear Grayson behind me, but he didn't say a word until I started to climb the ladder. "There's a pull-down door at the top. Be careful. It sticks."

I pushed down the urge to turn back and look at him and managed to get the door open and climb through, blinking when harsh sunlight hit my eyes. I'd expected an attic—not the roof.

Looking around, I climbed out onto a small, flat area, about five feet by five feet, nestled among the grand angles of the Hawthorne House roofline. Jameson was leaning back against the roof, his face aimed skyward, like he was sunbathing.

In his hand, he held a knife.

"You kept that?" Grayson stepped onto the roof behind me.

Jameson, eyes still closed, twirled the knife in his hand. The handle on the blade parted in two, revealing a compartment inside. "Empty." Jameson opened his eyes and pressed the compartment closed. "This time."

Grayson's mouth settled into a firm line. "I invoke—"

"Oh no," I said fiercely. "Not this again. No one is invoking anything!"

Jameson caught my gaze. His green eyes were liquid and shadowed. "Did you tell him?" he asked me.

"Tell me what?" Grayson said sharply.

"Well, that answers that." Jameson pushed himself into a standing position. "Heiress, before we start spilling secrets, I'm going to need you to promise me a plane."

"A plane?" I gave him an incredulous look.

"You have several." Jameson smiled. "I want to borrow one."

"Why do you need a plane?" Grayson asked suspiciously.

Jameson waved away the question.

"Fine," I told him. "You can take one of my planes." Yet another sentence I never thought I'd say.

"Why," Grayson repeated through gritted teeth, "do you need a plane?"

Jameson looked back at the sky. "Colin's Way was founded in memory of Colin Anders Wright." I wondered if Grayson could hear the undertone in Jameson's voice. Not quite sadness, not quite regret—but *something*. "Colin was one of the victims of the fire on Hawthorne Island. The charity was founded by his uncle."

"And?" Grayson was getting impatient.

Jameson looked suddenly toward me. *He can't say it. He can't be the one who tells him.*

I pressed my lips together and took a breath. "That uncle's name is Sheffield *Grayson*."

Absolute silence greeted that statement. Grayson Hawthorne wasn't a person who showed much emotion, but in that moment, I felt every subtle shift of his expression in the pit of my stomach.

"That's why you went to see Skye," Grayson said. His voice was tight.

"She confirmed it, Gray." Jameson ripped the bandage off. "He's your father."

Grayson went quiet again, and Jameson moved suddenly, tossing the knife at him. Grayson's hand whipped up to catch it by the handle.

"There is no way that the old man didn't know," Grayson said harshly. "For twenty years, he included Colin's Way in his will." A muscle in Grayson's throat tightened. "Was he trying to make a point to Skye?"

"Or was he leaving her a clue?" Jameson countered. "Think about it, Gray. He left a clue for us in the newer will. Maybe that was an old trick, one he'd used before."

"This isn't just a *clue*," Grayson said, his voice low and harsh. "This is my..." He couldn't say the word *father*.

"I know." Jameson crossed to stand in front of his brother, lowering his forehead until it touched Grayson's. "I know, Gray, and if you let this be a game, it doesn't have to hurt."

I was overcome with the feeling that I shouldn't be there, that I wasn't supposed to see the two of them like this.

"Nothing has to matter," Grayson replied tightly, "unless you let it."

I turned to go, but Grayson caught my movement out of the corner of his eye. He pulled away from Jameson and turned to me. "This Sheffield Grayson might know something about the fire, Avery. About Toby."

He'd just had his world shattered with a revelation about his father, and he was thinking about me. About Toby. About that signature on my birth certificate.

He knew I wasn't going to stop. "You don't have to do this," I told him.

Grayson's grip tightened over the handle of the knife. "Neither one of you is going to leave this alone. If I can't stop you, I can at least make sure that someone with a modicum of common sense oversees the process."

In a flash, Grayson tossed the blade back to Jameson, who caught it.

"I'll arrange for the plane." Jameson smiled at his brother. "We leave at dawn."

CHAPTER 29

That *we* didn't include me. To inherit, I had to live in Hawthorne House for a year. I wasn't sure I *could* travel, and even if there was a way, I couldn't insert myself into this. Grayson had a right to meet his father without me tagging along. He had Jameson, and I couldn't shake the feeling that this was something they needed to do together.

Without me there.

So I went to school the next day and kept my head down and waited. In between classes, I kept checking my phone, kept expecting an update. That they'd landed in Phoenix. That they'd made contact—or that they hadn't. *Something.*

"I could ask you where my brothers are." Xander fell in next to me in the hallway. "And what they're up to. Or..." He flashed me a ridiculous smile. "I could beckon you to the dark side through the overwhelming power of my charisma."

"The dark side?" I snorted.

"Would it help if I brooded?" Xander asked as we came to the door of my next class. "I can brood!" He scowled fiercely, then grinned. "Come on, Avery. This is *my* game. They're *my* knuckleheaded, notably less charismatic brothers. You have to deal me in."

115

He followed me into the classroom and helped himself to the seat next to mine.

"Mr. Hawthorne." Dr. Meghani shot him an amused look. "Unless I'm mistaken, you are not in this class."

"I'm free until lunch," Xander told her. "And I *need* to make meaning."

In any other school, that never would have flown. If he'd been anyone other than a Hawthorne, it might not have here, either, but Dr. Meghani allowed it. "Last class," she lectured at the front of the room, "we talked about white space in the visual arts. Today, I want you working in small groups to conceptualize the equivalents in other art forms. What serves the function of white space in literature? Theater? Dance? How can meaning be made—or emphasized—through purposeful gaps or blanks? When does *nothing* become *something*?"

I thought about my phone. About the lack of communication from Jameson and Grayson.

"I expect two thousand words on that topic and a plan of artistic exploration by the end of next week." Dr. Meghani clapped her hands together. "Get to work."

"You heard the woman," Xander said beside me. "Let's get to work."

I snuck another glance at my phone. "I'm waiting to hear from your brothers," I admitted, keeping my voice low and trying to look like I was deeply pondering the true meaning of art.

"About?" Xander prompted.

Dr. Meghani passed by our table, and I waited until she was out of earshot before continuing. "Does the name Sheffield Grayson mean anything to you?" I asked Xander.

"Indeed it does!" he replied jauntily. "I created a database of major donors for all the charities on our list. The name Sheffield Grayson appears on that list precisely twice."

"For Colin's Way," I said immediately. "And..."

"Camden House."

I filed that away for future reference. "Have you seen a picture of Sheffield Grayson?" I asked Xander quietly. *Do you know who he is to your brother?*

In response, Xander did an image search and then sucked in a breath. "Oh."

Xander somehow persuaded Dr. Meghani that I intended to approach my essay by comparing white space in nature to white space in the arts, and she authorized us to spend the rest of the class period outside. When we reached the perimeter of the wooded acreage just south of the baseball diamond, Xander stopped. So did I—and four feet away, so did Eli.

"What are we waiting for?" I asked.

Xander pointed, and I saw Rebecca coming toward us from about a hundred yards away.

"I'm starting to understand why you call your side the dark side," I muttered.

"The old man had a soft spot for Rebecca," Xander told me. "Bex knew him pretty well, and I don't think he expected me to do this alone."

I gestured to myself. "You're not alone."

"And you're on my team? Not Jamie's?" Xander gave me a look. "Not Gray's?"

"Why do there have to be teams?" I asked.

"It's just the way they are. Hawthornes, I mean." Rebecca came to a stop in front of me. When I turned to look at her, she looked down. "You said you have news?" she asked Xander.

"Let's wait for Thea," Xander suggested.

"Thea?" I grumbled.

"She's delightfully Machiavellian, and she hates to lose." Xander was absolutely unapologetic. "I like what that does to my odds."

"She's also Zara's niece," I couldn't help pointing out. "And she hates you and your brothers."

"*Hates* is a strong word," Xander hedged. "Thea just loves us in a somewhat negative and occasionally vitriolic way."

"Thea isn't coming," Rebecca said, interrupting the back-and-forth between Xander and me.

"She isn't?" Xander raised his lone eyebrow.

"I just..." Rebecca took a breath, and the wind caught in her dark red hair. "I can't, Xan. Not today."

What's today?

"What's the new lead?" Rebecca asked, her expression begging Xander not to press her further. "What do we know?"

Xander gave a slight nod, and then he cut to the chase. "One of our persons of interest is Grayson's father. Jamie and Gray are, I assume, making contact. Until we find out what they find out, our only option is following up on my other lead."

"What other lead?" I asked.

"Camden House," Xander said definitively. "Cross-referencing its major donors to the victims on Hawthorne Island led to two matches. David Golding's family are platinum-level supporters. Colin Anders Wright's uncle gave a onetime, but very generous, donation. And though I haven't identified any direct donations from my grandfather, I have a theory."

"Toby was a patient there," I cut in. "Nan told me as much."

"I'm almost positive that all three of the boys did a stint at Camden House," Xander said. "I think that's where they met."

I thought about the news coverage of the fire. The suggestion that there had been a wild party that had spun out of control. The way that the tragedy had been blamed, again and again, on Kaylie

Rooney, when the three upstanding young men had been partying straight out of rehab.

"If the boys met at Camden House," Rebecca said slowly, "then..."

"Exactly! Then...*what*?" Xander bounced from one foot to the other.

"This tells us something about their state of mind that summer," I said. "Leading up to the fire."

"The fire," Rebecca repeated, "and their deaths." She closed her eyes tight, and when she opened them, she shook her head and began backing away. "I'm sorry, Xan. I want to play this game. I want to help you. I want to be able to do this with you, and I will, okay? Just not today."

CHAPTER 30

It took me longer than it should have to piece together that when Rebecca had said earlier in the week that Emily's birthday was Friday—today—she hadn't been lying. Neither had Thea when she'd said that there was a memorial fundraiser.

The *same* fundraiser that Alisa was planning that I would attend.

"I booked you a session with Landon for this afternoon. She had limited availability, so we may have to double up with hair and makeup."

I buckled my seat belt and narrowed my eyes at Alisa as Eli settled into the front passenger seat. "You failed to mention that tonight's memorial was for Emily Laughlin."

"Did I?" Alisa didn't sound even the least bit guilty. "Country Day is building a new chapel in her honor."

I heard a cough from the driver's seat and realized that Oren wasn't the one driving. This man had lighter, longer hair. I'd almost gotten used to Eli shadowing me at school, but this was the first time since the will had been read that Oren had willingly let me out of his sight while I was in transit. "Where's Oren?" I asked.

"Otherwise occupied," the driver replied. "There was a situation."

"What kind of situation?" I pressed. No response. I looked at Alisa, but she just shrugged and redirected the conversation.

"You wouldn't happen to know why Jameson and Grayson took one of your jets, would you?"

> ———————◄

Back at Hawthorne House, we found Oren waiting at the door with the *situation* he'd been dealing with.

"Max?" I was stunned to see her. We hadn't been together in person in more than a year, but there Max was, her black hair tied up in messy buns on either side of her head.

She beamed at me, then shot the world's most aggrieved look in Oren's direction. "Finally! Avery, will you tell Monsieur Bodyguard over here that I'm not a security risk?"

My shock started to wear off. "Max!" I took a step toward her, and that was all Max needed to launch herself at me. She hugged me. Hard. "What are you doing here?" I asked.

She shrugged. "I told you that I was considering a mission trip. I am here to bring the love of God to these poor, backward billionaires. It's an ugly job, but someone's got to do it."

"She's joking," I told Oren. "Probably." I studied Max a little more closely. As glad as I was to see her, I also knew her parents wouldn't have approved this trip. She was already on thin ice with them.

And that was when I realized: "Today's your birthday, too."

"Too?" For a split second, I saw raw emotion behind Max's eyes, but then she shook it off. "I'm eighteen." Max was legally an adult. Had her parents kicked her out, or had she left on her own? "Got a spare bedroom?" she asked me, all bravado.

I squeezed her hand. "I probably have forty."

Max offered me her brashest, most invincible Maxine Liu smile. "So what does a girl have to do around here to get a tour?"

Ten minutes into Max's tour, my phone rang. I looked down at the screen. "Jameson," I reported.

Max gave me a look. "Don't mind me." She beamed. "Pretend I'm not even here."

I answered the call. "What's going on? Is everything okay?"

"Other than the fact that my stick-in-the-mud brother utterly refuses to play Drink or Dare while we wait?" Jameson had a way of making everything sound like a joke—and dark humor at that. "Things are just peachy."

"Drink or Dare?" I asked. "No—don't answer that. What exactly are you waiting on?"

There was a beat of silence on the other end of the line. "Sheffield Grayson has security that rivals ours. There's no getting near the man unless he wants you to."

The muscles in my chest tightened. "And he doesn't want Grayson near him." I ached, just thinking about that. "Is he okay?"

Jameson did not answer that question. "Grayson has business cards—and yes, I mocked him mercilessly for that. He wrote our hotel information on the back of one and left it with the guard at the gate to the Grayson estate."

The less serious Jameson sounded, the more I ached for him, too. "And so you wait," I said quietly.

There was a brief silence on the other end of the line. "And so we wait."

There was a heaviness in Jameson's tone. The fact that he'd let me hear it was shocking.

"Don't worry, Heiress." Jameson fell back into banter. "I *will* prevail on the Drink or Dare front if we have to wait around much longer."

When I hung up the phone, Max practically pounced on me. "What did he say?"

———————

"So the boys you want to fax took your private jet to Arizona in hopes that the mystery father of one of said boys knows something about a tragic and deadly fire, lo these many years ago."

"That about covers it," I told Max. "Except I don't want to fax anyone."

"Only in your mind and only with your eyes," Max said solemnly.

"Max!" I said, and then I turned the tables on her. "You want to tell me what you're doing here? We both know you're not okay."

Max looked up at the twenty-foot ceiling. "Maybe I'm not. But I *am* standing in the middle of a bowling alley *in your house*. This place is unbelievable!"

If she wanted a distraction, she'd come to the right place.

"Now, is there anything else about the Bonkers Life of Billionaire Avery that you left out?"

I knew better than to press her if she didn't want to talk. "There is one more thing," I said. "Remember Emily?"

"Died and left a thousand broken pieces in her wake?" Max said immediately. "Loss reverberates through all the players in her tragedy to this day? Yes, I remember Emily."

"Tonight, I'm going to a fundraiser in her honor."

CHAPTER 31

Where are you with developing your talking points and your theme?" Landon asked. Apparently, she had no qualms whatsoever about quizzing me while my face was being contoured and my hair aggressively moussed.

"You have a theme?" Max piped up beside me. "Is it *smash the patriarchy*? I hope it's smash the patriarchy."

"I like it," I told Max. "Why don't you come up with some talking points?"

"Hold still." Firm hands grabbed my chin.

Landon cleared her throat. "I don't think that would be prudent," she told me, glancing delicately at Max.

"Patriarchy smashing is *always* prudent," Max assured her.

"Look up," the makeup artist commanded. "I'm going to get started on your eyes."

That sounded way more ominous than it should have. Doing my best not to blink, I gritted my teeth. "Why don't you just save us all a lot of time and effort and tell me what you want me to say?" I asked Landon.

"We need to communicate that you are relatable, grateful for the tremendous opportunity you've been given, on good terms with the Hawthorne family, and exceedingly unlikely to throw multiple billion-dollar industries into chaos." She let a second pass, then continued. "But *how* you communicate those things is up to you. If I write the script, it will sound like a script, so you need to do the work here, Avery. What can you authentically say about this whole experience?"

I thought about Hawthorne House, about the boys who lived here, about the secrets built into the very walls. "It's incredible."

"Good," Landon replied. "And?"

My throat tightened. "I wish my mom were here."

I wished that she could see me. I wished that I'd had money—any money—when she'd gotten sick. I wished that I could ask her about Toby Hawthorne.

"You're on the right track," Landon told me. "Truly. But for the time being, it would be best to avoid bringing up your mother."

If I'd been able to, I would have stared at her, but instead, my chin was tilted roughly back, and I found myself staring at the ceiling.

Why doesn't she want me talking about my mom?

Two hours later, I was bedecked in a knee-length dress made of lavender silk, with an impossibly delicate black lace wrap. Instead of heels, I wore knee-high boots—black, suede, and not comfortable in the least. *Preppy with an edge*, my signature look.

I was still thinking about Landon—and my mother.

"I did some research." Max waited until the two of us were alone to share. "Looks like there's a tabloid that keeps writing stories about your mom."

"Saying what?" I asked. My heart rate ticked up. The dress I'd been told to wear was tight enough that I was almost certain you could *see* my heart beating. *Does the press suspect that she lied about who my father is?* I pushed down the thought.

"The tabloid claims your mom was living under a fake name." Max handed me her phone. "So far, no one else has picked up the story, so it's probably bullship, but..."

"But Landon doesn't want me talking about my mom," I finished. I closed my smoky eyes, just for a second. "She didn't have any family," I told Max when I opened them. "It was just her and me." I thought of every ridiculous guess I'd ever made in a game of I Have A Secret. I'd gone down the secret-agent-living-under-a-false-identity route more than once.

"It might make sense," Max said. "Wasn't Toby living under a fake name, too?"

That raised a whole sea of questions that I'd been avoiding: How exactly had my mom come to be involved with Tobias Hawthorne's son? Had she known who he really was?

A sharp knock at the door broke into my thoughts. "Are you ready?" Alisa called.

"Are we sure I can't skip this?" I called back.

"You have five minutes."

I turned back to Max. "We wear the same size," I said.

"And that is of interest why?" Max asked, her brown eyes dancing.

I led her over to my closet, and when I threw open the doors, she literally gasped at the sight beyond. "Get dressed, birthday girl. There's no way I'm going to this thing on my own."

CHAPTER 32

The biggest indoor space at Heights Country Day was called the Commons. It was part lounge, part meeting space, and tonight it had been transformed. Gold curtains lined the sides of the room. The furniture had been replaced with dozens of circular tables covered with silk tablecloths in a deep midnight purple. *Emily's favorite color.* Near the front of the room, two enormous pictures sat on golden easels. One was an architect's sketch of the new chapel. The other was a photograph of Emily Laughlin. I tried not to stare at it—and failed.

Emily's hair was strawberry blond, with just enough of a natural wave to make her look a little unpredictable. Her skin was unbearably clear, her eyes all-knowing. She wasn't as beautiful as Rebecca, but there was something about the way she smiled....

I couldn't help thinking that maybe it was a good thing that Jameson and Grayson weren't here. They'd loved her, both of them. *Maybe they still do.*

Beside me, Xander bumped his shoulder into mine. Alisa had given him strict orders to stay close to me, just like she'd reluctantly assigned Nash as Libby's escort tonight. Part of the damage control we were supposed to do was conveying that I was on good terms with the Hawthorne family—easier said than done, given that Xander and Nash weren't the only Hawthornes in attendance.

On the far side of the room, I caught sight of Zara and Constantine, mingling.

"We need to work the room," Alisa murmured directly into the back of my head. She began herding Xander and me toward a string quartet, and that was the exact moment when I spotted Skye Hawthorne. She was laughing freely, surrounded by admirers—some male, some female.

"The couple on the left are Christine Terry and her husband, Michael," Alisa murmured. "Third-generation oil money. Not people you want as enemies."

I translated that to mean: *not people we want laughing with Skye.*

"I'll introduce you," Alisa told me.

"Help me," I mouthed at Max.

"I would," she whispered, "but there's a waiter who just walked by, and he's carrying shrimp!"

Ten seconds later, I was shaking hands with Christine Terry. "Skye here was telling us you're not much of a football fan," her husband declared, jovial and loud. "Any chance you feel like parting with the Lone Stars?"

"You'll have to forgive my husband," Christine told me. "I keep telling him there's a time and a place for business."

"And a time and place for football!" Michael boomed.

"Avery's not looking to part with any assets at the moment," Alisa said evenly. "I don't know what could have given anyone that idea."

By *anyone*, she meant Skye, but the boys' murderous mother was a Hawthorne to her bones—and thoroughly undaunted. "Darling Avery here is a Libra," Skye cooed. "Ambivalent, people-pleasing, and cerebral. We can all read between those lines." She paused, then extended a hand to her right. "Isn't that right, Richard?"

She couldn't have timed his appearance better if she'd tried. *Richard*—which was 100 percent not Ricky's given name—wrapped an arm around Skye's waist. She'd dressed the deadbeat in an expensive tailored suit. Looking at him, I tried to remind myself that he was nothing to me.

But when he smiled, I still felt seven years old and about three inches tall.

I tightened my grip on Xander, but he stepped away from me suddenly. About a dozen yards away, I saw the Laughlins. Mr. and Mrs. Laughlin looked distinctly uncomfortable in formal wear. Rebecca was standing beside them, and next to her was a woman in her forties or fifties who looked eerily like Emily would have if she'd lived to grow older.

As I watched, the woman—who I could only assume was the girls' mother—downed a large glass of wine in one gulp. Rebecca's eyes met Xander's, and a second later, he was gone, leaving me to his mother's mercies.

"Have I introduced you to Avery's father?" Skye asked the group, her gaze settling on Christine Terry. "I have it on good authority that he'll be filing for custody of our little heiress very soon."

⊷————⊶

Forty minutes later, when I saw Ricky heading for the bar, I tasked Max with distracting Alisa so I could corner him alone.

"Why the long face, Cricket?" Ricky Grambs smiled as I came to stand beside him. He was the kind of drunk who had effusive praise for everyone. I should have expected the charm offensive. The fact that he'd called me by a nickname shouldn't have mattered.

"Don't call me Cricket. My name is Avery."

"It was supposed to be Natasha," he declared grandly. "Did you know that?"

My throat tightened. He was a deadbeat. He'd always been a

deadbeat. Based on what I'd discovered, he probably wasn't even my father. So why did talking to him hurt?

"Your mom had a middle name all picked out, so I was going to choose your first. I've always liked the sound of the name Natasha." The bartender approached, and Ricky Grambs didn't miss a beat. "One more for me," he said, then winked. "And one for my daughter."

"I'm underage," I said stiffly.

His eyes sparkled. "You have my permission, Cricket."

Something inside me snapped. "You can shove your *permission* up your—"

"Smile," he murmured, leaning toward me "For the press."

I glanced back and saw a photographer. Alisa had dragged me to this party to tell a story, not make a scene.

"You really should smile more, pretty girl."

"I'm not that pretty," I said quietly. "And you're not my father."

Ricky Grambs accepted a bottled beer from the bartender. He lifted it to his lips, but not before I saw his bulletproof charm waver.

Does he know that I'm not his? Is that why he's never cared? Why I never mattered?

Ricky recovered. "I may not have been there as much as either of us would have liked, Ladybug, but I was never more than a phone call away, and I'm here now to make things right."

"You're here for the money." It took everything in me not to yell. Instead, I lowered my voice enough that he had to lean forward to hear it. "You're not going to get a dime. My legal team will bury you. You refused to take custody when Mom died. You think a judge won't see through your sudden interest now?"

He stuck his chin out. "You weren't alone after your mom. My Libby took good care of you." He clearly expected credit for that, when he'd never done a damn thing for Libby, either.

"You never even signed my birth certificate," I gritted out. I half expected him to deny it.

Instead, he gulped the rest of the beer and placed the empty bottle on the bar. I stared him down for a second or two, then picked up the bottle, turned, and walked toward Alisa, who was *still* trying to get around Max.

I handed my lawyer the beer bottle. "I want a DNA test," I murmured.

Alisa stared at me for a moment, then schooled her face into a perfect pleasant expression. "And I want you to go find a half dozen items to bid on in the silent auction."

I accepted the terms of her deal. "Done."

CHAPTER 33

I had no idea how a silent auction worked, but Max, high on shrimp and her victory in distracting Alisa, quickly caught me up on what she'd managed to glean. "There's a sheet beneath each item. Bidders write down their names and their bids. If you want to outbid someone, you write your name below theirs." Max strode over to what appeared to be a teddy bear and upped the high bid by two hundred and fifty dollars.

"Did you just bid eight hundred dollars for a teddy bear?" I asked her, aghast.

"A *mink* teddy bear," Max told me. "Pearl Earrings over there is stalking this auction." My best friend nodded to a woman who looked to be in her seventies. "She wants that bear and doesn't care if she has to slice a motherfaxer's neck to get it."

Sure enough, a few minutes later, the woman glided by the teddy bear and scrawled down another bid.

"I'm a philanthropist," Max declared. "So far, I've cost the people in this room ten thousand dollars!"

All things considered, she really should have been the heiress. With a shake of my head, I circled the room, looking at the items on auction. Art. Jewelry. A designated parking space. The farther I walked, the bigger ticket the items became. Designer purses. A Tiffany sculpture. A private chef dinner for ten. A yacht party for fifty.

"The real big-ticket items are in the live auction," Max told me. "From what I've gathered, you donated most of them."

This was unreal. This life was never going to stop being unreal.

"Personally," Max said, adopting a snooty accent, "I think you should bid on the tickets to the Masters at Augusta. *With housing.*"

I looked her dead in the eye. "I have no idea what that means."

She grinned. "Neither do I!"

Alisa had told me to bid, so I circled the room again. There was a basket of high-end makeup. Bottles of wine and scotch with high bids that nearly made my eyes bulge out of their sockets. Backstage passes. Vintage pearls.

None of this was me.

Eventually, I saw a grandfather clock. The description said it had been carved by a retired Country Day football coach. It was simple but perfect. Across the room, Alisa nodded at me. I gulped and upped the current high bid by what the page informed me was the minimum.

I felt nauseous.

"It's for a good cause," Max assured me. "Sort of."

This school didn't need a new chapel any more than *I* needed a bronzed sculpture of a cowboy on the back of a wild, bucking bull, but I bid on that, too. I bid on a baking lesson with a local pastry chef for Libby and doubled down on the mink teddy bear for Max. And then I saw the photograph.

I knew, before I even looked down, that it was one of Grayson's.

"He does have an eye."

I turned to find Zara standing beside me.

"Are you going to bid on it?" I asked her.

Zara Hawthorne-Calligaris arched a brow at me. Then, without

133

a word, she went to up the bid that I had placed on the grandfather clock.

"Well, *ship*," Max whispered beside me. "I'm pretty sure she just challenged you to a rich-people duel."

"Easy there, slugger." Xander appeared beside me.

"Where have you been?" I asked him, annoyed.

"I was helping Rebecca with her mom." Xander's voice was uncharacteristically quiet. "She doesn't do well with wine."

I didn't get a chance to probe that statement further before Alisa came over to escort us to our table. "Plated dinner," she told me. "Followed by the live auction."

I managed to sit, eat my salad with the correct fork, and not spill anything on the silk tablecloth. Then things took a turn for the worse. A loud crashing sound broke through the din of polite chit-chat. Everyone in the room turned to see Rebecca, beautiful and wan, trying to help her mother back to her feet. The easels holding the picture of Emily and the architect's sketch had been knocked over. Rebecca's mother yanked her arm out of her daughter's grip and stumbled again.

Suddenly, Thea was there, kneeling between Rebecca and her mom. Thea said something to the distraught woman, and even from across the room, I could see the expression on Rebecca's face, like she'd just remembered a thousand things she'd been trying desperately to forget.

Like this moment and the way Thea reached for her might destroy her in the best and worst possible way.

A moment later, Libby was there, trying to help Rebecca's mom to her feet, and the grieving woman exploded.

"*You.*" She pointed a finger at Libby. My sister was dressed in a black cocktail dress. Her blue hair had been ironed silky straight. Instead of a necklace, she wore a black ribbon tied around her neck.

She looked about as sedate as Libby ever looked, but Rebecca's mother was sneering at her like she was monstrous. "I saw you with him. That Hawthorne boy." She managed to stand. "Never trust a Hawthorne," she slurred. "They take *everything*."

"Mom." Rebecca's whisper cut through the room. Her mother dissolved in sobs. Libby became aware of the number of people staring at her and fled. I ran after her and ignored Alisa when she tried to call me back. As I passed Rebecca, Thea, and Rebecca's mom, I heard the drunk woman whimpering the same words, over and over again.

"Why do all my babies die?"

CHAPTER 34

I made it outside to Libby and found Nash already there. "Hey now, darlin'," he murmured. "Come back inside. You didn't do anything wrong."

Libby lifted her head up and looked past him to me. "Sorry, Ave. When I saw her go down, I went on autopilot." Before our lives had gotten turned upside down, Libby had been an orderly at a nursing home. She grimaced. "This is exactly what Alisa meant when she told me not to cause a scene tonight."

"She told you what now?" Nash said, his voice low and dangerous.

Libby shrugged.

"You had no way of knowing that Rebecca's mom was going to explode like that," I told Libby, then I cut a glance toward Nash, who sighed.

"She's the Laughlins' daughter. Grew up on the estate. It was before my time—she's got about fifteen years on Skye. From what I've gathered, the relationship between Mr. and Mrs. L and their daughter has always been a bit tense. After they lost Emily..." Nash shook his head. "She blamed my family."

Both Jameson and Grayson had been there the night Emily died.

"She said all her babies die," I murmured. Belatedly, I processed the fact that she'd been looking right at Rebecca—her living daughter—when she'd said it.

"Miscarriages." Nash said quietly. "She and her husband were older when they started trying for kids. Mrs. Laughlin mentioned once that they'd lost multiple babies before they had Emily."

If I thought about any of this for too long, I was going to start feeling even sorrier for Rebecca Laughlin. "Are you okay?" I asked Libby instead.

She nodded and looked toward Nash. "Could you give us a minute?"

With one last look at my sister, Nash sauntered off, and Libby turned back to me. "Avery, what did you say to Dad earlier?"

I wasn't going to have this conversation with her. "Nothing."

"I get it," Libby told me. "You hate him, and you have every right to. And, yes, the thing with Skye is kind of weird, but—"

"Weird," I repeated. "Libby, she tried to have me killed!" It took me a full three seconds to realize what I'd done.

Libby stared at me. "What? When?" *Libby knew Skye moved out—but she didn't know why.* "Have you told the police?" she demanded.

"It's complicated," I hedged. I was trying to figure out how to explain my promise to Grayson, but Libby didn't give me more than a second.

"And I'm not," she said quietly, her chin jutting out.

At first, I wasn't sure what she was saying. "What?"

"I'm not complicated," Libby clarified. "That's what you think. It's what you've always thought. I'm too optimistic and too trusting. I never went to college. I don't think the way you think. I give people too many chances. I'm naive—"

"Where is this coming from?" I asked.

Blue hair fell into Libby's face as she looked down. "Forget it," she said. "I signed the emancipation papers. Pretty soon, you officially won't have to listen to me. Or Dad. Or anyone." Her voice caught. "That's what you want, right?"

I hadn't *asked* to be emancipated. That was all Alisa, but I recognized that it was probably the right move. "Lib, it's not like that." Before I could say anything else, my phone rang.

It was Jameson.

I looked back up from the screen to Libby. "I have to take this," I told her. "But..."

Libby just shook her head. "You do what you have to do, Ave— and I'll try not to cause any more scenes."

CHAPTER 35

H ello?"

For a moment, there was silence on the phone. "Avery?"

I recognized that low, rich voice in a heartbeat. *Not Jameson.* "Grayson?" He'd never called me before. "Did something happen? Are you—"

"Jameson dared me to call."

Nothing—literally nothing—about that sentence made sense. "Jameson what?"

"Jameson when, Jameson where, Jameson *who*?" That was Jameson, in the background, his voice taking on a musical lilt, his tone almost philosophical.

"Am I on speakerphone?" I asked. "And is Jameson *drunk*?"

"He shouldn't be," Grayson said, sounding truly disgruntled. "He doesn't really turn down dares."

Grayson wasn't slurring his words. His speech wasn't slow. His voice coated me, surrounded me—but it occurred to me suddenly that *Grayson* might be drunk.

"Let me guess," I said. "You're playing Drink or Dare."

"You're really good at guessing things," drunk Grayson said. "Do you think the old man knew that about you?" His tone was hushed and almost confessional. "Do you think that he knew that you were...you?"

I heard a thud in the background. There was a long pause, and then one of them—I was betting on Jameson—started cracking up.

"We have to go," Grayson said with a great deal of dignity, but when he went to hang up the phone, he must have hit the wrong button, because I could still hear the two of them.

"I think we can both agree," Jameson said, "that it's time for Drink or Dare to give way to Drink or Truth."

A better person probably would have hung up right then, but I turned the volume on my phone all the way up.

"What did you say to Avery," I heard Jameson ask, "the night we solved the old man's puzzle?"

Grayson hadn't said anything to me that night. But the next day, after he'd sent Skye on her way, he'd had plenty to say. *I will always protect you. But this...us...It can't happen, Avery.*

"Because right after that," Jameson continued, "she took to the tunnels with me."

Grayson started to say something—what, I couldn't quite hear—but then he cut off. "The door," Grayson said, clear as day. He sounded dumbfounded.

Someone's at the door, I realized. And then I heard some more muffled sounds. And then I heard Grayson's father.

At first, I couldn't entirely make out the words being exchanged, but at some point, either the conversation moved closer to the phone, or the phone moved closer to the conversation, because suddenly, I hear every word.

"You obviously aren't surprised to see me." That was Grayson. He'd sobered up quickly.

"I've built three different companies from the ground up. You don't achieve what I have achieved without an eye to potential eventualities. Potential risks. Frankly, young man, I expected Skye to tell you about me years ago."

A knot in my stomach twisted. Poor Grayson. His father saw him as a *risk*.

"You were married when I was conceived." Grayson's tone was neutral—almost dangerously so. "Still are. You have children. I can't imagine that you are happy at my intrusion on your life, so let's keep this short, shall we?"

"Why don't you cut to the chase and tell me why you're really here?" That was a demand. An order. "You were recently cut out of the family fortune. Financially speaking, you may have found that you have certain…needs."

"You think we're here for money?" That was Jameson.

"I've found that the simplest explanation is most often the correct one. If you're here for a payout—"

"I am not."

My entire body felt tense. I could see Grayson in my mind's eye, every muscle in his body taut, but his expression even and cool. *Bribe. Threaten. Buyout.* Grayson had been raised to be formidable. There was a reason he'd already mentioned the man's wife.

"For reasons I won't be sharing with you," I heard him say, "I am looking into what happened twenty years ago on Hawthorne Island."

The pause that greeted those words told me that Sheffield Grayson hadn't been expecting that. "Are you, now?"

"My sources have led me to believe that the press coverage of the tragedy is, shall we say…incomplete."

"What sources?"

I could practically *hear* Grayson smile. "I'll make you a deal. You tell me what the news stories left out, and I'll tell you what my sources have said about Colin."

At the mention of his nephew's name, Sheffield Grayson's voice went too low for me to hear. Whatever he'd said, Grayson reacted defensively.

"My grandfather was the most honorable man I know."

"Tell that to Kaylie Rooney," Sheffield's voice was audible again, booming. "Who do you think spoon-fed that story to the press? Who do you think quashed anything the least bit unflattering to his family?"

Grayson's response was garbled. Had he turned away?

"Toby Hawthorne was a little punk." That was Sheffield again. "No regard for the law, for his own limitations, for anyone but himself."

"And Colin wasn't like that?" Jameson was needling the man. It worked.

"Colin was going through a rough patch, but he would have come out of it. I would have *dragged* him out of it. He had his whole life ahead of him."

Again, the response was garbled.

"The Rooney girl never even should have been there!" Sheffield exploded. "She was a criminal. Her parents? Criminals. Cousins, grandparents, aunts, and uncles? *Criminals.*"

"But the fire wasn't her fault." Grayson's voice was louder now, clearer. "You've implied as much already."

"Do you know how much I paid to private detectives to get real answers?" Sheffield snapped. "Probably only a fraction of what your grandfather paid the police to bury their report. The fire on Hawthorne Island wasn't an accident. It was arson—and the person who purchased the accelerant was your uncle Toby."

CHAPTER 36

When the line went silent, I said Grayson's name, then Jameson's. Again. And again. Nobody heard me. I hung up and called back, but nobody picked up.

No matter how many times I called, no one picked up.

I was worried—about Grayson, about the barely controlled anger I'd heard in his father's voice. Beneath that worry, my gut was churning for different reasons. *What did you do, Harry?*

If the fact that Toby Hawthorne had survived the fire had been public knowledge, would his father have been able to bury this scandal? Would the police have been so easy to buy off—assuming they *had* been bought off—if this weren't a tragedy with no survivors?

If he set that fire... I couldn't think much past that, so I thought about Tobias Hawthorne instead. Why had the billionaire disinherited his entire family after the fire on Hawthorne Island? Why use his will to point to what had happened there, when he'd apparently paid good money to cover it up?

"Avery." Alisa's heels hit the pavement with a rapid *click, click, click* as she approached me. "You need to get back inside. The live auction is about to start."

I made it through the rest of the evening. As Max had promised, most of the items in the live auction had been donated by...me. A weeklong stay in a four-bedroom house on Abaco, in the Bahamas. Two weeks in Santorini, Greece, private plane included. A castle in Scotland to be used as a wedding venue.

"How many vacation homes do you *have*?" Max asked me on the way home.

I shook my head. "I don't know."

"You could actually look at the binder I gave you," Alisa suggested from the front seat.

I barely heard her, but that night, after I'd placed another six fruitless phone calls and spent hours turning the conversation with Grayson's father over in my head, I slipped out of bed and walked to my desk. The binder in question was just sitting there. Alisa had given it to me weeks ago, as a primer on my inheritance.

I flipped through it until I found myself staring at a villa in Tuscany. A thatched cottage in Bora-Bora. A literal castle in the Scottish Highlands. This was *unreal*. Page after page, I drank in the pictures. Patagonia. Santorini. Kauai. Malta. Seychelles. A flat in London. Apartments in Tokyo and Toronto and New York. Costa Rica. San Miguel de Allende...

I felt like I was having some kind of out-of-body experience, like it was impossible to feel what I was feeling and still be flesh and blood. My mom and I had dreamed of traveling. Stashed in my enormous closet, in a ratty bag from home, was a stack of blank postcards. Mom and I had imagined going to those places. I'd wanted to see the world.

And the closest I'd ever come was postcards.

A ball of emotion rising in my throat, I flipped another page—and I stopped breathing. The cabin in this photograph looked like it had been built into the side of a mountain. The snow-covered roof was A-line, and dozens of light fixtures lit up the brown stone like lanterns. *Beautiful.*

But that wasn't what had robbed the breath from my lungs. Every muscle in my chest tightened as I lifted my fingers to the text at the top of the page, where the details of the home were written. It was in the Rocky Mountains, ski in/ski out, eight bedrooms—and the house had a name.

True North.

CHAPTER 37

T o my daughter Skye Hawthorne, I leave my compass, may she always know true north." The next morning, I paced in front of Max, unable to contain myself. "The part about the compass and true north was in both of Tobias Hawthorne's wills. The older one was written twenty years ago. The clues in that will couldn't have been meant for the Hawthorne grandsons—not originally." If there was a connection between that line in the will and the home I'd inherited in Colorado, that message had been meant explicitly for Skye. "This game was for Tobias Hawthorne's daughters."

"Daughters, plural?" Max inquired.

"The old man left Zara a bequest, too." My mind raced as I tried to recall the exact wording. *"To my daughter Zara, I leave my wedding ring, may she love as wholly and steadfastly as I loved her mother."*

What if that was a clue, too?

"One piece of the puzzle is at True North," I said. "And if there's another one, it must have something to do with that ring."

"So," Max said gamely, "first, we go to Colorado, and then we steal ourselves a ring."

It was tempting. I wanted to see True North. I wanted to go

there. I wanted to experience even a fraction of what that binder told me my new world had to offer. "I can't," I said, frustrated. "I can't go anywhere. I have to stay here for a year to inherit."

"You go to school," Max pointed out. "So, obviously, you don't have to stay holed up at Hawthorne House twenty-four hours a day." She grinned. "Avery, my billionaire friend, how long do you think it would take us to fly by private jet to Colorado?"

➤————————◄

I called Alisa, and she arrived within the hour.

"When the will says that I have to live in Hawthorne House for a year, what does that mean exactly? What constitutes *living* at Hawthorne House?"

"Why do you ask?" Alisa replied, blinking.

"Max and I were looking at the binder you gave me. At all of those vacations homes."

"Absolutely not." Oren spoke from the doorway. "It's too risky."

"I agree," Alisa said firmly. "But since I have a professional obligation to answer your question: The will's appendix makes it clear that you may spend no more than three nights per month away from Hawthorne House."

"So we *could* go to Colorado." Max was delighted.

"Out of the question," Oren told her.

"Given what's at stake here, I concur." Alisa gave me the Alisa Look to end all Alisa Looks. "What if circumstances prevented you from returning on time?"

"I have school on Monday," I argued. "Today's Saturday. I'd only be gone for one night. That gives us plenty of leeway."

"What if there's a storm?" Alisa countered. "What if you're injured? One thing goes wrong, and you lose everything."

"So do you."

I looked back to the doorway and saw a stranger standing there.

A brown-haired woman wearing khaki slacks and a simple white blouse. Belatedly, I recognized her face. *"Libby?"* My sister had dyed her hair a sedate medium brown. I hadn't seen her with a natural human hair color since...*ever*. "Is that a French braid?" I asked, horrified. "What happened?"

Libby rolled her eyes. "You make it sound like I was kidnapped and forcibly braided."

"Were you?" I asked, only half joking.

Libby turned back to Alisa. "You were just telling my sister that you can't *allow* her to do something?"

"Go to Colorado," Max clarified. "Avery owns a house there, but her keepers here think traveling is too big a risk."

"It's not really their decision, is it?" Libby looked down at the ground, but her voice was steady. "Until Avery's emancipated, *I* am her guardian."

"And I control her assets," Alisa replied. "Including the planes."

I cut a glance at Max. "I guess we could fly commercial."

"No," Alisa and Oren responded in unison.

"Did it ever occur to you that Avery needs a break?" Libby stuck out her chin. "From..." Her voice caught in her throat. "All of this?"

I felt a stab of guilt, because I wasn't overwhelmed by *all of this*. I was doing fine here. *But Libby isn't.* I could hear it in her tone. When I'd inherited, she lost everything. Her job. Her friends. Her freedom to walk outside without a bodyguard. "Libby—"

She didn't let me get more than her name out of my mouth. "You were right about Ricky, Ave." She shook her head. "And Skye. You were right, and I was just too stupid to see it."

"You aren't stupid," I said fiercely.

Libby fingered the end of her French braid. "Skye Hawthorne asked me who I thought a judge would think is more respectable: the new and improved Ricky or me."

148

That was why she'd dyed her hair. That was why she was dressed the way she was. "You didn't have to do this," I said. "You don't—"

"Yes," Libby cut in softly. "I do. You're my sister. Taking care of you is *my* job." Libby turned back to Alisa, her eyes blazing. "And if *my* sister needs a break, you and that billion-dollar law firm can damn well find a way to give her one."

CHAPTER 38

O ren and Alisa agreed to a weekend at True North. Fly out this morning, fly back Sunday evening—one night away. Oren would bring a six-man team. Alisa was coming along to get some "candid shots" that Landon could slip to the press. Our itinerary gave me a little less than thirty-six hours to find whatever Tobias Hawthorne had left for his daughter at True North—without ever tipping Alisa off that I was looking.

On the way to the airport, I texted Jameson. Again. I told myself that I didn't need to worry about him and Grayson. That they were probably drunk or hungover or following a new lead without me. I told them where I was going—and why.

A few minutes later, I got a text back. Not from Jameson—from Xander. *Meet you at the plane.*

"Okay," I muttered. "He definitely has some kind of surveillance on Jameson's phone."

Max arched an eyebrow at me. "Or yours."

><>———————<><

"I do solemnly swear that I'm not surveilling anyone who doesn't share at least twenty-five percent of my DNA." In Xander's world, that passed for a greeting. "And in other excellent news, Rebecca and Thea will both be joining us on this lovely jaunt to Colorado."

Max shot a sideways glance at me. "Are we happy 'Rebecca' and 'Thea' are coming?" She punctuated the names with air quotes, like she suspected they were aliases, even though I had definitely mentioned both of them to her.

"We're resigned," I told Max, shooting Xander a look.

He'd told me once that Grayson and Jameson had a history of teaming up during the old man's games. They'd also had a habit of double-crossing each other, but to Xander, the fact that his brothers had gone to meet Sheffield Grayson without him probably seemed like just another team-up.

I couldn't really blame him for stacking *his* team.

"Maxine." Xander offered my best friend his most charming Xander Hawthorne smile. "There's nothing I admire more than a woman who makes liberal use of air quotes. May I ask: What are your feelings on robots that sometimes explode?"

━━━━◆━━━━

The interior of the jet—*my private jet*—had luxury seating for twenty and looked more like a high-end business lounge than a vehicle. Security sat near the front, and behind them, Alisa and Libby sat in leather chairs opposite a granite-topped table. Nash, who'd tagged along, was stretched out across two seats on the other side of that table, facing Libby and Alisa. *Awkward.* But at least the tension was likely to keep the three of them busy, which let those of us under the age of nineteen get down to business in the back of the plane.

Two extra-long suede sofas stretched out, with another granite table between them. Max and I sat on one side of the table. Xander, Rebecca, and Thea sat on the other. A platter of baked goods rested on the table between us, but I was more focused on Xander's "team." Something about the way Rebecca's body angled toward Thea's made me think about the expression I'd glimpsed on Rebecca's face the night before at the auction.

"We don't know *what* we're looking for." Xander kept his voice low enough that the adults at the front of the plane couldn't hear us. "But we know the old man left it for Skye. It will be in or very near to the cabin, and it will probably have Skye's name on it."

"Do we have anything else to go on?" Rebecca asked. "Any particular wording in the prior clue?"

"Very good, young Padawan." Xander bowed toward her.

"No *Star Wars* references," Thea shot back. "Listening to you talk geeky gives me a migraine."

"You knew I was quoting from *Star Wars*." Xander gave her a triumphant look. "I win!"

"Sorry," Rebecca told Max and me. "They're just like this."

I got the distinct sense that I was getting a view into what all three of them had been like *before*. Rebecca's phone rang then, and she looked down. Deep-red hair covered her alabaster face. I could almost *see* her shrinking into herself.

"Everything okay?" I asked. I wondered if her mother was the one calling.

"It's fine," Rebecca said from behind a wall of hair.

She wasn't fine. That wasn't a secret. I'd known it since that night in the tunnels, when she'd confessed. I'd just been trying very hard not to care.

A determined expression on her face, Thea made a grab for the ringing phone. "Rebecca's phone," she answered, pressing it to her ear. "Thea speaking."

Rebecca's head whipped up. "Thea!"

"Everything's fine, Mr. Laughlin." Thea held out a hand to ward off Rebecca's attempts to grab the phone from her. "Bex just nodded off. You know how she gets on planes." Thea twisted to block Rebecca again. "Sure, I'll tell her. Take care. Bye."

Thea hung up the phone and angled her face toward Rebecca. "Your grandfather says to have a good trip. He'll take care of your mom. Now..." Thea tossed the phone down on the table and turned back to the rest of us. "I believe Rebecca asked about the wording of the clue."

Max poked me in the side. "When you fly private, you can talk on the phone!"

I didn't respond, because I'd just realized how quiet Xander was being. He hadn't answered Rebecca's original question, so I did. "A compass. The clue that pointed us toward True North was in the part of Tobias Hawthorne's will where he left Skye his compass."

"Oh," Thea said innocently. "Like the antique compass Xander's hiding in his pocket?"

Xander scowled at her. Max reached for the pastry platter and beaned Xander with a croissant. "Holding out on us?" she demanded.

"I see our budding friendship has reached its croissant phase," Xander told her. "I am pleased."

"You're also hiding things," I accused. "You have the compass the old man left Skye?"

Xander shrugged. "A Hawthorne always comes prepared." And this was *his* game.

"Can I see it?" I asked. Xander reluctantly handed me the compass. I opened it and stared at the face. The design was simple; it didn't look expensive.

A phone buzzed—not Rebecca's this time. Mine. Looking down, I realized that Jameson had finally texted back.

His text was exactly three words long: *Meet you there.*

CHAPTER 39

I stared out the window as the jet began its descent. From a distance, all I could see was mountains and clouds and snow, but soon I could make out the tree line. A month ago, I'd never even been on a plane. Now I was flying private. No matter how focused I tried to stay on the task at hand, I couldn't help wanting to lose myself in the vastness of the sight out that window.

I couldn't shake the feeling that this life was never meant for me.

>———————>

We landed at a private airstrip. It took half an hour—and three enormous SUVs—to make the drive to True North, which was nestled higher up on the mountain, far away from the resort town below.

"The house has ski-in/ski-out access," Alisa informed Max and me on the drive. "It's private, but there's a trail that will take you to the lodge below."

As True North came into view, it hit me that the photos hadn't done it justice. The A-line roof was white with snow. The house was massive but somehow still looked like an extension of the mountain.

"I called ahead to have the caretaker open up the house," Alisa said as she, Oren, Max, and I stepped out onto the snow. "We should be stocked with food. I took the liberty of having appropriate attire delivered for you girls."

"*Fox me*," Max whispered, awed, as she took in the sight in front of us.

"It's beautiful," I told Alisa.

A soft smile crossed my lawyer's lips, and her eyes crinkled at the edges. "This property was one of Mr. Hawthorne's favorites," Alisa told me. "He always seemed different up here."

A second, identical SUV parked next to ours, and Libby stepped out, followed by Nash and more of Oren's men. A half dozen strands of Libby's hair had fought their way free of her French braid and blew wildly in the mountain wind.

"I understand that Grayson and Jameson will be joining us," Alisa said, deliberately turning away from Nash and my sister. "Whatever you do," she cautioned, "do not let any of the Hawthornes challenge you to a Drop."

CHAPTER 40

The inside of the house matched the outside perfectly. The living room ceiling stretched up two stories, with giant beams visible in the rafters. The floors were wood, the walls wood-paneled, and everything—the furniture, the rugs, the light fixtures—was oversized. Fur throws draped the enormous leather sofa—softer than anything I'd ever felt.

A fire crackled in a stone fireplace, and I walked toward it, mesmerized.

"There are four bedrooms on this floor, two at basement level, and two up." Alisa paused. "I've put you in the biggest bedroom on this floor."

I turned away from the fire and tried to make my next question sound natural. "Actually...which bedroom was Skye's?"

>———◄

The stairway to the third floor was lined with family photographs. It looked almost...*normal*. The frames weren't expensive. The photos were snapshots. There was one of a much younger Grayson, Jameson, and Xander with their heads sticking out of a tent. Another of what appeared to be a chicken fight between all four brothers. One of Nash with his arms around Alisa. And farther up the wall there were photos of Tobias Hawthorne's children.

Including Toby.

I tried not to stare at pictures of Toby Hawthorne at twelve and fourteen and sixteen, searching for some kind of resemblance to myself. I failed. There was one photo in particular—it was impossible for me to look away. Toby was standing between teenage girls I assumed to be Zara and Skye. It had obviously been taken at True North. All three of them were on skis. All three were smiling.

And I thought that maybe Toby's smile looked a bit like mine.

At the top of the stairs, Max and I deposited our bags in the room that we'd been told was once Skye's. With a glance back over my shoulder, I closed the door.

"Look for hidden compartments," I told Max as I examined a wooden chest. "Secret drawers, loose floor panels, false backs to the furniture—that kind of thing."

"Sure," Max said, drawing out the word as she watched me making quick work of the wooden chest. "Absolutely. That is a thing I know how to do."

It wasn't that I expected to hit payload immediately, but after searching Toby's wing, I knew how to look. I didn't find anything of note until I ventured into the closet. There were clothes hanging on the racks and sweaters folded on the shelves. None of them looked like things I would expect Skye to wear now. I went through the items one by one and eventually came to the ski jacket that Skye had been wearing in the picture on the stairs. How old had she been when she wore this? Fifteen? Sixteen?

Had these clothes been hanging in this closet that long?

A thump sounded on the other side of the closet wall, and then I heard a creak. Parting the clothes, I saw a crack of light at the back of the closet and found the source. There, cut directly into the wall, was a small door. I pushed, and the wall moved, allowing me to step into a narrow passageway beyond.

The passageway smelled like cedar. I felt around for the walls, then managed to locate a light switch. The moment I turned it on, I saw a pair of eyes.

Someone stepped toward me.

I scrambled back, meeting the eyes—and stifling a scream as I recognized them. "Thea!"

"What?" she said with a small smirk. "Feeling jumpy?" Beyond her, I could see Rebecca standing near a second doorway, identical to the one behind me.

"Whose room is that?" I asked.

"It used to be Zara's," Rebecca murmured. "I'm staying here tonight."

Thea turned to shoot her a meaningful look. "Good to know."

Pushing past them, I explored Zara's room and found a closet nearly identical to Skye's. The clothes on the racks tended more toward icy-blue tones, but like Skye's closet, this one looked like it had been frozen in time.

"I found something." Thea announced, back in the passageway. "And you're welcome."

I backtracked. Rebecca followed me, and Max squeezed into the passageway from the other side. It was a tight fit, but I managed to kneel next to Thea, who was holding a wooden board in her hands.

One of the floorboards, I realized as she set it aside to reach into the compartment she'd bared.

"What is it?" I said as she withdrew an object.

"A glass bottle?" Max leaned into Thea to get a better look. "With a message inside. A message in a motherfaxing bottle! Now we're cooking."

"Motherfaxing?" Thea arched a brow at Max, then stood and sauntered past me, back into Zara's room. She tipped the bottle upside down on a nearby desk, and with some jiggling, a small piece of paper fell out. As Thea attempted to unroll it, I noted that it was yellowed with age.

"I'm guessing that's pretty old," Max said.

I thought about Tobias Hawthorne's will. "Like, twenty years?" But when Thea finished unraveling the paper, the writing I saw on the missive wasn't Tobias Hawthorne's. It was cursive, with the occasional embellishment, neat enough that it could have passed for a font.

Feminine.

"I don't think this is what we came here to find," I said. Had I really thought it would be that easy? Still, I read the message. We all did.

You knew, and you did it anyway. I will never forgive you for this.

"Did what?" Thea queried. "Knew what?"

I stated the obvious out loud. "These rooms were Zara's and Skye's."

"In my experience, Zara isn't what I'd call the forgiving type." Thea looked toward Rebecca. "Bex? Any thoughts? You know the Hawthorne family as well as anyone."

Rebecca didn't reply immediately. I thought about the picture I'd seen of Zara, Skye, and Toby smiling. Had the three of them been close once?

The tree is poison, don't you see? Toby had written. *It poisoned S and Z and me.*

"Well?" I asked Rebecca. "Did you ever overhear any arguments between Zara and Skye?"

"I overheard a lot of things growing up." Rebecca gave a little shrug. "People paid attention to Emily, not me."

Thea put a hand on Rebecca's shoulder. For a moment, Rebecca leaned into Thea's touch.

"I don't know who did what to whom," Rebecca said, looking down at that hand. "But I do know…" She took a step back from Thea. "Some things are unforgivable."

Why did I get the feeling that she wasn't still talking about Zara and Skye?

"People aren't perfect," Thea told Rebecca. "No matter how hard they try. No matter how much they hate showing weakness. People make mistakes."

Rebecca's lips parted, but she didn't say anything.

Max raised her eyebrows, then turned to me. "So," she said loudly. "Mistakes."

I turned back to look out the window again and focus on the task at hand. *What "mistake" poisoned the relationship between Zara and Skye?*

CHAPTER 41

I was staring out the largest ground-floor window when a new SUV pulled up outside. Jameson stepped out first, then Grayson. Both of them were wearing sunglasses. I wondered if they were hungover.

I wondered if either one of them had slept the night before, after that conversation with Grayson's father.

><

It took me fifteen minutes to get one of them alone. Jameson and I ended up on a balcony. My breath visible in the air, I caught him up on what I'd found. He listened, quiet and still.

Neither one of those was an adjective I associated with Jameson Hawthorne.

When I finished, Jameson turned his back on the mountain view and leaned against the snow-covered railing. He was still dressed for Arizona. His elbows were bare, but he acted like he couldn't even feel the cold. "I have something to tell you, too, Heiress."

"I know."

"Sheffield Grayson believes that Toby set the fire on Hawthorne Island." Jameson's eyes were still hidden behind sunglasses. It made it difficult to tell what, if anything, he was feeling.

"I know," I repeated. "Grayson forgot to hang up the phone last night. I didn't hear everything, but I got the gist. The last thing I heard was that Toby had purchased accelerant. Then the phone went dead. I tried to call you both. Repeatedly. But nobody answered."

Jameson didn't say anything for a full four or five seconds. I wasn't sure he was going to reply to what I'd just said at all.

"The bastard made it clear that he wants nothing to do with Gray. He said that Colin was the closest thing he'll ever have to a son." Jameson swallowed, and even though his eyes were still masked by the sunglasses, I could feel the way those words had affected him.

I didn't want to think about the impact they might have had on Grayson.

"For once, Skye wasn't lying." Jameson's voice was low. "Grayson's father has always known about him."

I was used to Jameson flirting and rattling off riddles, balancing precariously on the edges of rooftops and throwing caution to the wind. He didn't let things matter. He didn't let them hurt.

If I took off those sunglasses, what would I see?

I stepped toward him. The door to the balcony opened. Alisa looked at me, looked at Jameson, looked at the foot of space between us, and then gave me a pointed smile. "Ready to hit the slopes?"

No. I couldn't say that. I couldn't tip my hand that the reason we were here had nothing to do with wanting a winter getaway. Whatever our plan for searching the rest of the house, we had to be subtle.

"I..." I searched for an appropriate response. "I don't know how to ski."

Grayson appeared in the doorway behind Alisa. "I'll teach you."

Jameson stared at him. So did I.

CHAPTER 42

That True North was "ski in/ski out" meant we had direct access to the slopes. All you had to do was step out the back door, pop on your skis, and *go*.

"There's an easy trail here," Grayson told me after he'd showed me the basics. "If we take it long enough, we'll hit the busier ski areas on the mountain."

I glanced back at Oren and one of his men—not Eli. This man was older. Oren had called him the team's arctic specialist. Because every Texas billionaire needed an arctic specialist on their security team.

I wobbled on my skis. Grayson reached out to steady me. For a moment, we stood there, his body bracing mine. Then, slowly, he stepped back and took my hands, pulling me forward on the very slight incline near the house, skiing backward as he did.

"Show me your stop," he said. *Always issuing orders.* But I didn't complain. I turned my toes inward and managed to stop without falling...barely.

"Good." Grayson Hawthorne actually smiled—and then he caught himself smiling, like it was forbidden for his lips to do *that* in my vicinity.

"You don't have to do this," I told him, lowering my voice to avoid being overheard. "You don't have to teach me anything. We can tell Alisa I chickened out. I'm not here to ski."

Grayson gave me a look—a know-it-all, never-wrong, do-not-question-me kind of look. "No one is going to believe *you* chickened out of anything," he said.

From the way he'd phrased that, you would have thought I was fearless.

It took me all of five minutes to lose a ski. The trail was still relatively private. Other than my bodyguards, it was like Grayson and I were alone on the mountain. He zipped to retrieve my ski with the ease of someone who'd been skiing from the time he could walk. Returning to my side, he dropped the ski in the snow, then took my elbows in his hands.

This afternoon was the most he'd touched me—ever.

Refusing to let that mean anything, I popped the ski back on and repeated what I'd told him earlier. "You don't have to do this."

He let go of my arms. "You were right." That had to be a first: Grayson Hawthorne admitting someone else was right about *any-thing*. "You said that I've been avoiding you, and I have. I promised I'd teach you what you need to know to live this life."

"Like skiing?" I could see myself in the reflection of his ski goggles, but I couldn't see his eyes.

"Like skiing," Grayson said. "To start."

We made it to the bottom, and Grayson taught me how to get on a ski lift. Oren went on the lift in front of us; the other guard on the one behind.

That left me alone with Grayson: two bodies, one lift, our feet dangling as we ascended the mountain. I caught myself sneaking glimpses at him. He'd pulled his goggles down, so I could make out all the lines of his face now. I could see his eyes.

After a few seconds, I decided I wasn't about to spend the entire ride in silence. "I heard your conversation with Sheffield," I told Grayson quietly. "Most of it, anyway."

Down below, I could see skiers making their way down the mountain. I looked at them instead of Grayson.

"I'm starting to understand why my grandfather disinherited his children." Grayson didn't sound quite like himself—the same way Jameson hadn't. The difference was, the night before had made Jameson more reserved, and it seemed to have had the opposite effect on his brother. "If Toby set that fire, if my grandfather had to cover it up, and then Skye—" He cut off abruptly.

"Skye what?" I said. We passed over a patch of snow-kissed trees.

"She sought Sheffield Grayson out, Avery. The man blamed our family for his nephew's death. He slept with her out of spite. God knows why Skye did it, but I was the result."

I looked at him in a way that forced him to look back at me. "You don't get to feel guilty about that," I said, my voice steady. "Pissed?" I continued. "Sure. But not guilty."

"The old man disinherited the entire family around the time I was conceived." Grayson steeled himself against that truth even as he said it. "Was Toby really the straw that broke the camel's back—or was I?"

This was Grayson Hawthorne, showing weakness. *You don't always have to bear the weight of the world—or your family—on your shoulders.* I didn't say that.

"The old man loved you," I said instead. I wasn't sure about much when it came to billionaire Tobias Hawthorne, but I was sure of that. "You and your brothers."

"We were his chance to do something right." Grayson's voice was taut. "And look how disappointed he was in the end—in Jameson, in me."

"That's not true," I said, aching for him. For *them.*

Grayson swallowed. "Do you remember the knife Jameson had up on the roof?" The question caught me by surprise.

"The one with the hidden compartment?"

Grayson inclined his head. I couldn't see the muscles in his shoulders or neck, but I could picture them beneath his ski jacket, tensing. "There was one puzzle sequence my grandfather constructed years ago. The knife was part of it."

For reasons I couldn't even pinpoint, the muscles in my own throat tightened. "And the glass ballerina?" I asked.

Grayson looked at me like I'd just said something very unexpected. Like *I* was unexpected. "Yes. To win the game, we had to shatter the ballerina. Jameson, Xander, and I got the next part wrong. We fell for the misdirection. Nash didn't. He knew the answer was the shards." There was something in the way he was looking at me. Something I didn't even have a word for. "My grandfather told us that as you amass the kind of power and money he had—things get broken. *People.* I used to think that he was talking about his children."

"*The tree is poison,*" I quoted softly. "*Don't you see? It poisoned S and Z and me.*"

"Exactly." Grayson shook his head, and when he spoke again, the words came out rough. "But I'm starting to believe we missed the point. I've been thinking about the things—and people—that *we* have broken. All of us. Toby and the victims of that fire. Jameson and me and..."

He couldn't say it, so I said it for him. "Emily. It's not the same, Grayson. You didn't kill her."

"This family breaks things." Grayson's tone never wavered. "My grandfather knew that, and he brought you here anyway. He put you on the board."

Grayson wanted me safe, and I wasn't. Having inherited the Hawthorne fortune, I might never be *safe* again.

"I'm not the glass ballerina," I said firmly. "I'm not going to shatter."

"I know you won't." Grayson's voice was almost hoarse "So I'm not going to avoid you anymore, Avery. I'm not going to keep telling you to stop doing the things that I know you can't and won't stop doing. I know what Toby is to you—what he means to you." Grayson's breath was heavy. "I know, better than anyone, why you can't stop."

Grayson had met his father. He'd looked him in the eyes and discovered what he meant to the man. And, yeah, the answer to that question was *nothing*—but he knew why I couldn't just leave the mystery of Toby alone.

"So you're in this?" I asked Grayson, my heart skipping a beat.

"Yes." He said the word like a vow. It hung in the air between us, and then he swallowed. "As your friend."

Friend. The word had edges. This was Grayson pulling back, keeping me at arm's length. Pretending that he got to make the rules.

It would have stung if I'd let it, but I didn't. "Friends," I repeated, fixing my gaze on the end of the lift, which was quickly approaching.

"Slide forward in your seat," Grayson told me. *All business.* "Tilt the tips of your skis up. Lean forward, and *go.*"

The chair gave me a little push, and I zoomed forward, fighting to keep my balance. I didn't need Grayson Hawthorne to do *this.*

Through sheer force of will, I kept my skis underneath me and managed to stop.

See? I don't need you to hold me up. I turned back toward my *friend* Grayson, a smile spreading across my face, fully prepared to gloat—and that was when I saw the paparazzi.

CHAPTER 43

Oren and the arctic specialist got me back to True North in impressive time. Eli and another guard were waiting outside when we got there.

"Do a sweep of the perimeter," Oren told his men. "If anyone needs a reminder that this is private property, feel free to provide it."

"I guess that's it for skiing," I said. In theory, that was a good thing. I now had an excuse to stay at True North, to do what I'd come to do. *Less time on the mountain with Grayson.*

Pressing that thought down, I took my skis off. Grayson did the same, and we headed inside, but before we made it to the back door, a clump of snow fell down from the roof, right at our feet.

I looked up just in time to see Jameson dropping. He landed beside me on skis, no poles in sight.

"Nice entrance," Grayson told him dryly.

"I try." Jameson smiled, and then he brandished an object in his hands. It took me a second to realize that it was a picture frame.

Why is he holding a picture frame? This was Jameson Hawthorne. We'd come here for a reason. I knew why. My heart jackrabbited. "Is that...," I started to say.

Jameson shrugged. "What can I say? I really am just that good."

He lazily placed the frame in my hand, then turned to grab a pair of ski poles leaning against the side of the house. "And I challenge *you*," he told Grayson, "to a Drop."

➤———◀

The picture in the frame was one I'd seen on the stairs, of all three of Tobias Hawthorne's children. Jameson hadn't provided any information before taking off, but as I walked down the interior stairs toward the basement, I turned the frame over in my hands and saw the image carved into the back.

The face of a compass.

I was so engrossed in what I was looking at that I almost ran into Rebecca. And Thea. *Thea and Rebecca*, I realized, taking a step back. The former had the latter pressed up against the wall of the stairwell. Rebecca's hands were on the sides of Thea's face. Thea's hair looked like it had been torn from its ponytail.

They were kissing.

The last words I'd heard them exchange rang in my ears. *Some things are unforgivable. People aren't perfect.*

Thea noticed me but didn't pull back from the kiss until Rebecca's green eyes went almost comically wide, and even then Thea took her sweet time stepping back.

"Avery." Rebecca sounded mortified. "This isn't—"

"Any of your business," Thea finished, her lips lifting up on the ends.

I sidestepped both of them. "Agreed." This star-crossed—and probably ill-advised—make-out session was not my concern.

The frame in my hand was. So I made my way down the rest of the staircase, a woman on a mission. On the lower level, I found Max on Xander's shoulders, inspecting the blades of a fan.

"He's very tall," Max told me approvingly. "And he's only dropped me once!"

Thea and Rebecca came into the room behind me. Xander shot them a look, but I stayed on task.

"Jameson gave me this." I held up my bounty and sat down on an oversized suede chair. "A picture frame from the stairwell." I placed it facedown on my lap. "Look at the back."

Max dismounted, and everyone crowded around me.

"Take the back off the frame," Xander said immediately.

I looked up at him. "We're going to need a screwdriver."

Four minutes later, all five of us were sequestered in the third-floor room that had once belonged to Skye. I removed the final screw and lifted the back off the frame. Beneath it, behind the picture of Toby, Zara, and Skye, I found a piece of notebook paper folded in half. Inside, there was another picture.

This photo had clearly been taken around the same time as the one that had been on display in the frame. Zara and Skye were wearing the same jackets. They both looked to be teenagers. Zara had one arm around Skye and the other around a boy who looked slightly older than either of them. He had shaggy hair and a killer smile.

I turned the picture over. There was no caption on the back. Max bent to pick up the piece of paper that had been folded over the photo.

"Blank," she said.

"For now," Xander corrected.

Max didn't get the implication right away. She wasn't used to the Hawthornes and their games. "Invisible ink?" Rebecca asked, before I could. "On either the picture or the paper it was wrapped in?"

"Almost certainly," Xander replied. "But do you know how many different kinds of invisible ink there are?"

"A lot?" Thea said dryly.

Xander blew out a long breath. "My guess is that this is only half a clue. The old man left half to Skye and half to—"

"Zara," I finished. "The ring." Carefully, I took the blank page from Max. I had no idea how we were supposed to use a ring to make writing appear on this page, but I could see the logic in what Xander was saying. It was Hawthorne logic.

Tobias Tattersall Hawthorne logic.

He gave himself that middle name as a signal that he intended to leave them all in tatters. He used that name to sign a will and buried clues in the will for his daughters. I'd known that this game hadn't originally been meant for us. I'd known we were here to find Skye's clue. But now I had to wonder.

"What do you think this picture would mean to Skye?" I asked, holding up the photo that had been hiding behind Tobias Hawthorne's smiling children. Skye, Zara, and a guy. "Who is he?" I asked, and then I thought about the message we'd found in the bottle hidden under the floorboards in the passage between Skye's room and Zara's.

You knew, and you did it anyway. I will never forgive you for this.

"My psychic senses," Max announced, "are now attuned to that picture, and I'm getting some pretty clear messages about communing and abs."

They fought over a boy, I thought. The same way Jameson and Grayson had over Emily Laughlin.

"Jameson just gave you this?" Xander flopped down on the bed. "He found it and just *gave* it to you?"

I nodded. I could tell it bothered Xander that he hadn't been the one to find the clue.

"And where is Jameson now?" Xander asked, sounding a little more mutinous than I'd ever heard him.

I cleared my throat. "He challenged Grayson to something called a Drop."

"Without me?" Now Xander sounded downright offended. "He gave *you* this and challenged *Grayson* to a Drop?" Xander bounded to his feet. "That's it. The gloves are coming off. No more Mr. Nice Xander. Avery, can I see that picture?"

I handed him the photograph of Zara, Skye, and the boy with the shaggy hair. A second later, Xander was on his way out the door.

"Where are you going?" Rebecca and I called after him in unison.

Max jogged to catch up. "Where are *we* going?" she corrected.

Xander glowered at us—though it wasn't a terribly convincing glower. "To the lodge."

CHAPTER 44

Somehow I talked Alisa into okaying another little venture: one last photo op. Oren wasn't thrilled, but I got the distinct feeling this wasn't his first time securing a trip to the lodge at the base of the mountain.

"My grandfather outlawed the Drop when I was around twelve," Xander announced in the SUV on the way down. "Too many broken bones."

"Because that's not concerning or anything," Max said cheerfully.

"Hawthornes," Thea scoffed.

"Be nice." Rebecca gave her a look.

"It's just a friendly game of ski-lift chicken," Xander assured us. "You ride the lift up, until someone calls 'drop.' And then you"— Xander shrugged—"drop."

"As in jump off the lift?" I stared at him.

"The first person to call is the challenger. If the other person declines, the challenger has to drop. If the other person accepts the challenge, they drop and get a fifteen-second head start in the race."

"The race?" Max and I said in unison.

"To the bottom," Xander clarified.

"That is the single dumbest thing I've ever heard in my life," I told Xander.

"Maybe," Xander replied stubbornly. "But as soon as we've finished at the lodge, I've got winner."

>————◄

At the lodge, we were escorted through the main dining room to a private alcove overlooking the slopes beyond. Two of Oren's men took position at the door while my head of security stayed glued to me.

"You sit," Alisa told me. "You sip on hot chocolate. We get a few pictures—and we get you out."

That was her plan. We had our own. Namely, identify the boy in the photo. Xander seemed to think that some of the staff at the lodge had worked here for decades. Given how tight security was on me, I wasn't holding my breath that I'd be able to do this myself, but Max and Xander were a different story.

So were Thea and Rebecca.

Oren let the four of them venture off to the bathroom with a single guard. When they came back ten minutes later, that bodyguard looked like he had developed a migraine.

"These two," Max told me, nodding toward Thea and Rebecca, "are *really* useful in getting information out of people."

"Thea's better at flirting," Rebecca murmured.

Thea met Rebecca's eyes. "And you're a very quick learner."

"What did they find out?" I asked Max and Xander.

"The guy in the photo used to work on the mountain." Max was clearly relishing this. "He was a ski instructor, early twenties. Very big with the ladies."

"Did you get a name?" I asked.

Xander was the one who provided that answer. "Jake Nash."

Jake. My brain whirred. *Nash.*

175

CHAPTER 45

In the wake of that bombshell, Xander went to find Jameson and Grayson. Hours later, all three brothers returned from the slopes, looking scraped up and worse for the wear. Jameson eased himself into a wingback chair.

"Don't bleed on that," Grayson ordered.

"Wouldn't dream of it," Jameson retorted. "What are your thoughts on vomiting in that vase?"

"You're an idiot," Grayson replied.

"You're all idiots," I corrected. They turned to look at me. I was wearing a pair of thick winter pajamas, part of the True North wardrobe Alisa had ordered for me. "Did Xander tell you what we found?"

"What *I* found, Heiress," Jameson corrected me, then smiled. "I know about the picture. The page with what we can assume is likely a message of some kind, written in invisible ink."

Grayson studied me for a moment, then turned to Xander. "What *else* did you find?"

"For the record," Xander said grandly, hobbling over to sit on the fireplace, "I won the Drop." He looked down at his feet. "And

I might have neglected to mention that the guy in that photo is Nash's father."

That statement had the exact effect it was supposed to—on Jameson and Grayson. But I wasn't surprised. After what we'd learned at the lodge, it was the logical conclusion. All four of the Hawthorne brothers had last names as first names. Grayson's father was Sheffield *Grayson*. The guy in the picture—the guy Zara had her arm around—was Jake *Nash*.

You knew, the note in the closet had read, *and you did it anyway.*

"Are you going to tell Nash?" I asked the boys.

"Tell me what?"

I turned to see Nash in the doorway, Libby beside him. "Tell him what?" She narrowed her eyes at the silence that followed. "Come on, Ave," Libby groaned. "No more secrets."

She was the reason I'd gotten to come here, and she had no idea why.

Across from me, Grayson stood. "Nash, might we have a moment outside?"

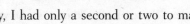

Alone with Libby, I had only a second or two to make a decision about what I was going to tell her. Looking at that plain brown hair, knowing everything she'd given up for me, it was a surprisingly easy decision to make.

I told her everything. About Harry and who he really was. About what we'd found in Toby's wing. About my birth certificate and the charities in the will and why I'd wanted to come to True North.

"I know this is a lot," I said.

Libby blinked four or five times. I waited for her to say something. Anything. "What are Grayson and Jameson telling Nash out there?" she asked finally.

There was no reason to hold back now, so I answered the question.

"So Nash's father...," she said.

"Is probably Jake Nash," I confirmed.

"And your father...," Libby looked at me and swallowed.

My father is Toby Hawthorne.

"It makes sense," I said quietly. Unable to look her directly in the eye, I let my gaze travel to a massive window nearby. "Toby's the one who signed my birth certificate, and we met for the first time right after Mom died. I think he was checking up on me. I think he meant for us to meet." I paused. "I think Tobias Hawthorne knew everything."

"And that's why he left you the money." Libby could read between the lines as well as I could. "If your dad isn't Ricky," she said slowly, "then you and I aren't really..."

"If you say we aren't sisters, I will flying-tackle you right here, right now." I was fully prepared to do it, too, but Libby seemed to decide not to tempt me.

"Have you tried to find him?" she asked me instead. "Toby?"

I looked down. "Before I even knew who he was. Alisa's people couldn't find a trace of him."

Libby snorted. Audibly. "Or so Alisa Ortega claims. Does *she* know who he is?"

I looked up at her. "No."

"So how much do you think your lawyer prioritized looking for a random homeless guy you used to play chess with?" Libby's hands made their way to her hips. "Have *you* tried to find him? Forget the puzzles. Forget the clues. Have you actually looked for the man?"

When she put it that way, I felt a little ridiculous. From inside Tobias Hawthorne's game, everything I'd done made perfect sense.

But from an outside perspective? We were going about all of this in the most roundabout way possible.

"You saw how hard it was to talk Oren and Alisa into letting me come here," I said. "There's no way they'll let me jet off to New Castle to pick up Toby's trail."

"Do you want me to go?" The question was tentative, but Libby got over her hesitation pretty quickly. "I could take a trip home. No one would question why I might want to. I can bring security with me."

"The paparazzi will follow you," I warned. "You're news by association."

Libby ran a hand over her French braid and grinned. "I blend now. I'm not sure the paparazzi would even recognize me."

All I could think in that moment was that I should have told her the truth days ago. What was wrong with me that I went to such lengths to keep the people who mattered most at a distance?

"It's settled, then," Libby declared. "You'll fly back to Hawthorne House, and I'll take the other plane to Connecticut."

"Correction, darlin'." Nash strolled back into the room. I couldn't get a read on his expression, on any effect of the bombshell his brothers had just dropped. "*We* will."

CHAPTER 46

That night, a little after midnight, Max nudged me awake.

"What is it?" I blinked at her, and after a few seconds' delay, my fight-or-flight instincts kicked in. "Is everything okay?"

"Everything's fine," Max told me. She smiled wickedly. "*Very* fine." She nudged me again. "Jameson Hawthorne is in the hot tub."

I narrowed my eyes at her, then rolled over in bed and pulled the covers over my head.

She pulled them back down. "Did you hear me? Jameson Hawthorne is in the hot tub. This is a DEFCON-faxing-one situation."

"What is it with you and Jameson?" I asked.

"What is it with *you* and Jameson?" Max retorted.

For reasons I couldn't begin to explain, I didn't toss her out of my bed. I answered her question. "He doesn't want me," I told Max. "Not really. He wants the mystery. He wants to keep me close until he can use me. I'm a part of the puzzle to him."

"But...," Max prompted, "would you *like* to be used by him?"

I thought about Jameson: the way his eyes gleamed when he knew something I didn't, the crook of his smile, the way he'd covered my body with his when gunshots went off in the Black

180

Wood—and later cupped my face with his hands when the sound of fireworks sent me plunging into dark memories. The annoying way he called me Heiress. Golfing on the rooftop. My body clinging to his on the back of a motorcycle. The exact tilt of his lips when he'd told me to play it safe—*for now.*

"You like him." Max sounded way too satisfied with herself.

"I might like the way I feel when I'm with him." I chose my wording very carefully. "But it's not that simple."

"Because of Grayson."

I stared at the ceiling and flashed back to the ski lift. "We're friends."

"No," Max corrected. "You and I are friends. Grayson is the physical manifestation of your avoidant attachment style. He won't let himself want you. You don't want to want to be wanted. Everybody stays at arm's length. Nobody gets hurt, and *nobody gets any.*"

Max gave me her most aggrieved best friend look.

"Why do you care?" I asked her. "Since when are you this invested in my love life?"

"Lack of," Max corrected, and then she shrugged. "My life has exploded. My parents won't take my calls. They won't let my brother talk to me, either. You're all I have right now, Ave. I want you to be happy."

"You tried calling your parents?" I didn't want to push her too hard, but I did want to be there for her.

Max looked down. "That's not the point. The point is, *Jameson Hawthorne is in the hot tub.*" She crossed her arms over her chest. "So what are you going to do about it?"

CHAPTER 47

The clothing Alisa had ordered for me included a designer bathing suit: a black bikini trimmed in gold. Narrowing my eyes, I put it on, then quickly covered myself with a floor-length robe, the unspeakably soft kind I imagined they used in high-end spas. The hot tub was on the main level. I'd made it to the back door when I realized that Oren was shadowing me.

"You're not going to tell me to stay inside?" I asked him.

He shrugged. "I have men in the woods." Of course he did.

I put my hand on the doorknob, took a deep breath, and pushed out into the freezing night air. Once the cold hit me, there was no room for hesitation. I made a beeline for the hot tub. It was big enough for eight people, but Jameson was the only one there. His body was nearly completely submerged. All I could see was his face pointed skyward, the lines of his neck, and the barest hint of his shoulders.

"You look like you're thinking." I sat on the side of the hot tub farthest away from him, pulled up my robe, and sank my legs into the water, up to my knees. Steam rose into the air, and I shivered.

"I'm always thinking, Heiress." Jameson's green eyes stayed fixed on the sky. "That's what you love about me."

I was too cold to do anything but shed the robe and slip into the steaming water. My body objected, then relaxed into the sting of the heat. I could feel a flush rising on my face.

Jameson angled his eyes toward mine. "Any guesses what I'm thinking about?" We were separated by four or five feet, but that didn't feel like much—not with the way he was looking at me. I knew what he wanted me to think he was thinking about.

I also knew *him*. "You're thinking about the ring."

Jameson shifted position, the top of his chest rising out of the water. "The ring," he confirmed. "It's the obvious next step, but getting it from Zara could be a challenge."

"You like a challenge."

He pushed off the side and came closer to me. "I do."

This is Max's fault, I thought, my heart beating a merciless rhythm against my rib cage.

"Hawthorne House has a vault." Jameson came to a stop a foot or so away from me. "But even I don't know its location."

It took everything in me to focus on what he was saying—and not his body. "How is that possible?"

Jameson shrugged, the water lapping against his shoulders and chest. "Anything is possible."

I swallowed. "I could ask to see it." I tried my hardest to stop staring and cleared my throat. "The vault."

"You could," Jameson agreed, with one of those devastating Jameson Winchester Hawthorne smiles. "You're the boss."

I looked down. I had to, because suddenly I was very aware of just how little of my body this swimsuit covered. "We just have to find the wedding ring your grandfather left your aunt." I tried to stay detached. "Then, somehow, that ring will help us make invisible ink a little more..."

"Visible?" Jameson suggested. He bent toward me so that he could catch my eye. For three full seconds, neither one of us could look away. "Okay, Heiress," Jameson murmured. "What am I thinking *now*?"

I moved forward. Just like that, our bodies were separated by inches instead of a foot. "Not about the ring," I said. I let my hand float to the surface of the water.

"No," Jameson agreed, his voice low and inviting. "Not about the ring." He lifted one of his hands to mine. We didn't touch, not quite. He let his arm float, a hairbreadth away from my submerged skin. "The question is," Jameson said, throwing down the gauntlet, "what are you thinking about?"

I turned my hand over and it brushed his, electric. "Not the ring." I thought about Max telling me that it was okay to want things. Right now, there was only one thing I wanted.

One thing on my mind.

I moved again through the water. The rest of the space between us vanished. I brought my lips to Jameson's, and he kissed me, hard. My body remembered this. I kissed him back.

It was like the hot tub was on fire, like the two of us were burning, and all I cared about was burning more. His hands found their way to the sides of my face. Mine were buried in his hair.

"This isn't real," I murmured as his lips began to work their way down my neck, toward the surface of the water.

"Feels real to me." Jameson was smiling, but I didn't let it fool me.

"Nothing ever feels real to you," I whispered, but the magical thing was that I didn't care. This didn't have to be real to be right. "This...us..." I let my lips hover over his. "It doesn't have to be anything other than what it is. No messy feelings. No obligations. No promises. No expectations."

"Just this," Jameson whispered, and he pulled my body tight to his.

"Just this." It was better than riding on the back of a motorcycle going a thousand miles an hour or standing on a rooftop fifty stories tall. It wasn't just the rush or the thrill. I felt completely, utterly in control. I felt unstoppable.

Like *we* were unstoppable.

And then, without warning, Jameson froze. "Don't move," he whispered, his breath visible in the air between his lips and mine. "Oren?" Jameson called.

I did the one thing he'd told me not to do. I moved, whirling around to face the forest, my back to him, so that I could see what he was seeing. *A flash of movement. And eyes.*

"I've got her," Oren told Jameson, and just like that, my head of security was pulling me from the hot tub. The freezing air hit me like a truck. Adrenaline shot through me as Oren bit out an order. "Eli, go!"

The younger guard, positioned near the tree line, took off running toward the intruder. I tried to track his movements, like doing that might somehow make me safer. *I'm fine. Oren's here. I'm fine.* So why couldn't I remember how to breathe?

Oren ushered me inside.

"What was that?" I wheezed. "Who was that?" My brain clicked into gear. "Paparazzi? Did he take pictures?" The thought was horrifying.

Oren didn't reply. On some level, I became aware that Grayson had heard the commotion. Someone wrapped a towel around me. Not Jameson. Not Grayson.

It was a full five minutes before Eli came back. "I lost him." He was breathing hard.

"Paparazzi?" Oren asked.

Eli's bright blue eyes narrowed until all I could see was the amber ring around the center. "No. This was a professional."

That statement landed like a bomb. I felt like my own ears were ringing. "A professional what?" I asked.

Oren didn't answer. "Go pack," he told me. "We leave at dawn."

CHAPTER 48

I stared out the plane's window, watching the mountain get smaller and farther away until the jet hit cruising height. I'd barely slept, but I didn't feel tired.

"What did Eli mean, *a professional*?" I said out loud. "A professional *what*?" I turned my attention from the view out the jet's window to Max, who was seated beside me. I'd caught her up to speed—on the security situation *and* the hot tub. "A private detective? A spy?"

"An assassin!" Max said giddily. She read a lot of books and watched a lot of TV shows. "Sorry." She held up a hand and tried to appear a little less enthralled with this latest turn of events. "Assassins, bad. I'm sure the man in the woods wasn't a deadly assassin from an ancient league of deadly assassins. Probably."

Before inheriting, I would have told Max that she was reaching, but *Who would want me dead?* wasn't a dismissive question anymore. It was a question with answers. *Skye.* I thought about confronting Ricky at the gala. Libby had fought with him, too. If she'd told him that I was getting emancipated, if he'd told Skye that their golden ticket was disappearing...

What exactly would they do? *He's one of my heirs. If something happens to me...*

"No one is going to hurt you." Grayson sat opposite me, with Jameson beside him. "Isn't that right, Jamie?" Grayson's tone sharpened. I got the feeling that he wasn't just talking about the man in the woods.

"If I weren't so confident in our brotherly affection for each other," Jameson replied languidly, "I would find that comment a bit pointed."

"Pointed?" Xander repeated in faux horror. "Gray? *Never.*"

"So," I said, before this situation could devolve, "who's up for a friendly game of poker?"

>———————<

"I call." I stared Thea down. She had a good poker face—but mine was better.

Thea laid down her hand: a full house. I laid down mine: the same. But aces were high, and I had them. I went to collect the pot, but Jameson stopped me.

"Not so fast, Heiress. I'm still in. And I have..." He shot me a wicked little smile that made me feel like I was right back in the hot tub. "Nothing." He showed his cards.

"You always did talk a big game," Thea said.

Beside her, Rebecca's phone buzzed. Rebecca looked down at it. This time, when Thea reached for it, Rebecca was faster. "No."

The phone buzzed again. And again. Thea caught a glimpse of the screen, and her expression shifted.

"It's your mom." Thea tried to catch Rebecca's gaze. "Bex?"

Rebecca turned the phone off.

"That wasn't what I meant," Thea said. "Maybe you should see what she wants."

Rebecca seemed to fold in on herself a little. "I'll be home soon enough."

"Bex, your mom—"

"Don't tell me what she needs." Rebecca's voice was soft, but her whole body seemed to vibrate with intensity. "You think I don't know she's not okay? Do you honestly think I need *you* to tell me that?"

"No, I—"

"She looks at me, and it's like I'm not even there." Rebecca stared holes in the table. "Maybe if I were more like Em, maybe if I were better at mattering—"

"You matter." Thea's voice had gone almost guttural.

"You know," Max said awkwardly, "this seems kind of like a private conversation, so maybe—"

"I don't matter enough." Rebecca's voice went brittle. "It's been fun, running around, playing detective, pretending the real world away, but it can't just be like this."

"Like what?" Thea reached for Rebecca's hand.

"Like *this*. The way you find reasons to touch me." Rebecca pulled her hand back from Thea's. "The way I let you. You were my world, and I would have done anything for you. But I begged you not to cover for Emily that night, and you—"

"Don't do this." If Thea were anyone else, she would have sounded like she was begging.

"If I were better at mattering…" Rebecca spoke louder. "If, for once in my life, I'd been enough for anyone—for the girl I *loved*— my sister might still be alive."

Thea had no response. Silence descended again. Painful, awkward, excruciating silence.

Jameson was the one who put Thea out of her misery. "So, Heiress," he said, throwing out a subject change like he was throwing a tarp over a fire. "How are we going to go about getting that ring?"

CHAPTER 49

Once we arrived back at Hawthorne House, I asked Oren to show me the elusive Hawthorne vault. He took me, and only me, to see it. We zigged and zagged through hallways until we reached an elevator. When the elevator door opened, I went to step on, but Oren stopped me. He pressed the call button a second time, holding his index finger flat against it.

"Fingerprint scan," he told me. After a moment, the back wall of the elevator began to slide, revealing a small walkway.

"What happens if someone pries the doors open while the elevator is on a different floor?" I asked.

"Nothing." Oren's lips parted in a very subtle smile. "The passage only opens if the elevator is present."

"Whose fingerprints can open it?" I asked.

"Currently?" Oren returned. "Mine and Nan's."

Not Zara's. Not Skye's. And not mine. In Tobias Hawthorne's will, he'd left all of his wife's jewelry to her mother. At the time of the will's reading, that had seemed trivial, but as we walked toward an honest-to-God vault door—the kind you'd expect to see on a bank vault—it didn't seem so trivial now.

"If everything in the Hawthorne vault belongs to Nan...," I started to say.

"Not everything," Oren cut in. "Nan owns the late Mrs. Hawthorne's jewelry, but Mr. Hawthorne also had an impressive collection of watches and rings, as well as pieces he purchased for artistic and sentimental reasons. Mrs. Hawthorne's jewelry passed to Nan, but many of the museum-quality pieces are yours."

"Museum-quality?" I swallowed. "Am I getting ready to see the crown jewels?" I was only partially joking.

"Of what country?" Oren replied—and he wasn't joking at all. "Anything valued over two million dollars is kept off the premises, in a more secure location."

The vault's lock disengaged. Oren spun the handle on the door and opened it. Holding my breath, I stepped into a steel room lined, ceiling to floor, with metallic drawers. I reached for one at random. When I pulled it out, displays popped up: three of them, each containing a set of tear-drop earrings: diamonds, bigger than any engagement ring I'd ever seen. I opened three or four more drawers and blinked. Repeatedly.

My brain refused to compute.

"Is there something in particular you were looking for?" Oren asked me.

I tore my eyes away from a ruby half the size of my fist. "Wedding ring," I managed. "Tobias Hawthorne's." Oren stared at me for a second or two, then walked over to the far wall. He pulled one drawer, then another, and I found myself staring at a dozen Rolex watches and a pair of varnished silver cuff links.

"Is the ring hidden?" I asked, my fingers wandering toward one of the watches.

"If the ring isn't in that drawer, it isn't here," Oren said. "My guess would be that Mr. Hawthorne had it placed in the envelope that was given to Zara at the reading of the will."

In other words: I was surrounded by a fortune in jewels, but the one thing I needed wasn't here.

CHAPTER 50

You're going to need someone to run interference if you want to search Zara's wing." Grayson had apparently meant it when he promised to help me see this through to the end.

"Gray excels at distraction," Jameson said loftily. "I attribute it to his uncanny ability to be boring and long-winded on cue."

Grayson didn't rise to the bait. "We'll need to make sure Constantine stays clear, too."

"I, too, excel at the art of distraction," Max volunteered. "I attribute it to my ability to channel any or all of my favorite fictional spies on cue."

"Grayson and Max can set up a perimeter." Xander's voice was uncharacteristically muted. "Jameson, Avery, and I will do a sweep of the wing."

Rebecca had split the moment the plane landed. Thea hadn't lingered long once Rebecca was gone. Xander's team had abandoned him, but he wasn't backing down.

He wasn't about to let Jameson and me search for the ring on our own.

"This is a very bad idea." Eli didn't even pretend that he hadn't been eavesdropping.

That's why we waited until Oren was off duty to do it, I thought.

The door to Zara's wing was at least ten feet tall—and locked.

"Do you want to pick it?" Jameson asked Xander. "Or should I?"

Two minutes later, the three of us were in. Grayson and Max stayed behind and took up posts at the far ends on the hall. Eli grumbled as he followed me into the belly of the beast.

A quick inspection told me there were seven doors lining the main hall in Zara's wing. Behind three of them we found bedrooms, each one the equivalent of an entire suite. Two of the three suites were clearly in use.

"Do Zara and her husband sleep in different rooms?" I asked Jameson.

"Don't know," he replied.

"Don't want to know," Xander added cheerily.

I saw men's shoes in one room. The other was immaculate. *Zara's.* There was a marble fireplace near the back of the room. Built-in shelves lined the wall to the left. There were books on the shelves, large, leather-bound volumes. The kind of books a person *displayed*, not the kind they read.

"If I were a person whose bookshelves looked like that," I murmured, "where would I keep my jewelry?"

"A safe," Xander answered, probing a molding on the wall.

Jameson stepped past me, letting his body brush mine. "And that safe," Jameson told me, "is assuredly hidden."

It took ten minutes for our search to hit pay dirt: a remote control taped to the bookshelf, behind one of the leather-bound books. I peeled off the tape and got a better look at the remote, which had only one button.

"Well, Heiress..." Jameson flashed me a smile. "Will you do the honors?"

Looking at that smile, I flashed back to the hot tub. There was no reason for me to be thinking about it. No reason for me to be thinking about Jameson that way right now.

I pushed the button.

As the massive built-in shelves began to move, slowly disappearing into the wall, I stared at what had been hidden behind them. "More shelves," I said, dumbfounded. "And...more books?"

Rows of paperbacks were stacked two deep. Romance. Science fiction. Cozy mysteries and paranormal. I tried to picture Zara reading a romance novel, or a space opera, or the type of mystery that had a cat and a ball of yarn on the cover—and couldn't.

"If we take the books off these shelves, will we find another remote?" Xander postulated. "And *more* shelves? And another remote? And—" Xander cut off.

It took me a second to realize what he'd heard: the sound of high heels clicking against the wood floor.

Zara.

Jameson pulled me into the closet. If it had been hard not to think of the hot tub before, it was impossible now.

"So much for Gray's distraction," he murmured into my neck as he pulled me close, and we disappeared back into the seemingly endless racks of clothes. I stood still, barely breathing and all too aware that he was doing the same behind me.

Xander must have hidden, too, because for several seconds, the only sound in the bedroom was the clicking of Zara's heels. I willed my heart to stop beating so hard and tried to stay focused on tracking Zara's movements—not on the way my body fit against Jameson's.

Not on the fact that I could feel his heart beating, too.

The footsteps stopped directly outside the closet. I felt Jameson's breath on the back of my neck and pushed back the urge to shiver. *Don't move. Don't breathe. Don't think.*

"The bodyguard positioned at the door is a dead giveaway," Zara called, her voice as clear as a bell and sharp as a knife. "You might as well come out."

Jameson pressed a finger to my lips, then stepped out of our hiding place, leaving me hidden in shadow, still feeling the ghost of his touch. "I was hoping we could talk," he told his aunt.

"Of course," Zara replied smoothly. "After all, the proper way of starting a conversation often involves lurking in your conversation partner's closet." She peered past Jameson to the rack of clothes where I was still hiding. "I'm waiting."

After a long moment, I stepped out.

"Now," Zara said. "Explain."

I swallowed. "Your father left you his wedding ring."

"I am aware," Zara replied.

"Twenty years ago, when the old man first revised his will to disinherit you all, he left you the exact same thing," Jameson added.

Zara arched an eyebrow at us. "And?"

"Can we see it?" That was Xander, who had poked his head out of the bathroom. Even though he was the one who'd asked the question, I was the one who received the response.

"Allow me to get this straight," Zara said, staring past Jameson and straight to me. "You, to whom my father left virtually everything, want the one and only thing he left to me?"

"When she puts it that way," Max said, appearing in the doorway, "it does sound like kind of a deck move." Behind her, I could see Eli. He wasn't acting like Zara was a threat.

"Five minutes." Jameson flipped into negotiation mode. "Just give us five minutes with the ring. There must be something you want. Name your terms."

Again, Zara's attention stayed focused on me. "Five million dollars." Her smile didn't come even close to reaching her eyes. "I'll give you lot five minutes with my father's ring," she enunciated, "for the low, low price of five million dollars."

CHAPTER 51

Five million dollars?" I said those words repeatedly as we retreated from Zara's wing to Tobias Hawthorne's study to strategize. "*Five. Million. Dollars.* Does Zara honestly think that Alisa is just going to agree to cut that kind of check?"

The will was still in probate. Even once the estate was settled, I was a minor. There were trustees. I could practically hear my lawyer throwing out terms like *fiduciary duty*.

"She's playing with us." Jameson sounded more pensive than outraged.

Grayson tilted his head to the side. "Perhaps it would be wise to—"

"I can get the money," Xander blurted out. His brothers stared at him.

"You want to pay Zara five million dollars to show us your grandfather's wedding ring?" I said, stunned.

"Wait." Grayson narrowed his eyes. "You have five million dollars?"

Each year on their birthdays, the Hawthorne grandsons had been given ten thousand dollars to invest. Xander had spent years dumping it into cryptocurrency, then sold at just the right time, and *that* money wasn't part of Tobias Hawthorne's estate. It was Xander's—and apparently, his brothers hadn't been aware of it until now.

"Look, ash-hole," Max said, pointing a finger at Xander, "nobody is giving anybody five million dollars. We'll just have to find another way to get the ring."

"You're still a minor," Grayson told Xander, his voice low. "If Skye finds out you have that kind of money..."

"It's in a trust," Xander assured him. "Nash is the trustee. Skye isn't getting near it."

"And you think Nash is going to let you write Zara a check for five million dollars?" I asked incredulously. That seemed about as likely as Alisa letting me access the funds.

"I can be very persuasive," Xander insisted.

"There's another way." Jameson had that look on his face—the one that told me he'd found a way of moving this chess game into three dimensions. "We'll set up a trade."

Grayson's eyes narrowed. "And what, precisely, do you think our aunt would trade for her father's wedding wing?"

Jameson smiled at me as he replied, like he and I were in this together. Like he expected me to anticipate his words. "Her mother's."

———➤————◄———

I didn't know much about the late Alice O'Day Hawthorne, but I did know who had inherited her jewelry. We found Nan in the music room, sitting in a small wingback chair, facing ceiling-to-floor windows that looked out on the pool and the estate beyond.

"Don't just stand there," Nan ordered without ever turning around. "Help an old lady up."

We made our way into the room. Grayson offered his great-grandmother an arm, but she looked past him to me. "You, girl."

I helped her out of the chair. Nan leaned on her cane and examined the five of us. "Who's she supposed to be?" the old woman grunted, nodding toward Max.

"That's my friend Max," Xander replied.

"*Your* friend Max?" I repeated.

"I promised to build her a droid," Xander said cheerily. "We're very close now. But that's beside the point."

"We need your help, Nan." Grayson circled back to the reason we were here.

"You do, do you?" Nan snorted in her great-grandsons' direction, then cut a glance toward me. She was scowling, but the flash of raw hope in her eyes was heartbreaking.

Without meaning to, I thought back to the Laughlins telling me how cruel I was for playing with an old woman. Nan loved Toby. She wanted us to find him.

Here's hoping she wants that badly enough to give us the ring. I took a deep breath.

"We found a message that your son-in-law left for Skye, right after Toby disappeared." *Message* was probably stretching it a little, but it was less complicated than the truth. "We think the old man left a similar message for Zara and that together they might somehow lead us to Toby."

"But to get what we need from Zara," Jameson interjected, "we need to offer her something in return."

"And what might that something be?" Nan's eyes narrowed.

Jameson looked at Grayson. Neither one of them actually wanted to say it.

"We need your daughter's wedding ring," I told her evenly. "So that we can trade it for your son-in-law's."

Nan harrumphed. "Zara always was a strange, quiet little thing."

"I feel a story coming on." Xander rubbed his hands together. "Nan tells the best stories."

Nan swiped at him with her cane. "Don't you try to butter me up, Alexander Hawthorne."

"Is that what I'm doing?" Xander asked innocently.

Nan scowled, but she couldn't resist a captive audience. "Zara was a shy, bookish child. Not like my Alice, who loved attention. I remember when Alice was pregnant with Zara, how giddy she was at the thought of having a little girl of her own to spoil." Nan shook her head. "But Zara never took much to spoiling. It drove my Alice up the wall. I used to tell her that the girl was just sensitive, that all she needed was some toughening up. I told her Skye was the one to worry about. That child came out of the womb tap-dancing."

I thought about the picture of Toby, Zara, and Skye. They'd looked so happy—before Toby had found out about the secrets and lies, before Skye had gotten pregnant with Nash, before Zara had gone from quiet and bookish to the cold, hypercontrolled force she was now.

"About that ring," Jameson said, turning on the charm. "The old man left Zara the same bequest in multiple wills: his wedding ring, *may she love as wholly and steadfastly as I loved her mother.* That ring is a clue."

"Not much of one. Steadfastly?" Nan grunted. "Wholly? Leaving his own daughter nothing but a damned wedding ring? Tobias never was as subtle as he liked to think."

It took me a second to understand what she was implying. *He left Zara his wedding ring and a message about being steadfast in love to make a point.*

"Constantine is Zara's second husband." Grayson didn't miss much. "Twenty years ago, when Toby disappeared, Zara was married to someone else."

"She was having an affair." Xander didn't phrase that as a question.

Nan turned back toward the window and stared out at the estate. "I'll give you Alice's ring," she said abruptly. She began walking slowly toward the doorway, and I saw Eli standing just outside. "When you give it to her, you tell Zara that she'll get no judgment from me. She's toughened up just fine, and we all do what we have to do to survive."

CHAPTER 52

Alice Hawthorne's wedding ring wasn't what I'd pictured. The diamond, singular, was small. The bands, which had been soldered together, were thin and made of gold. I'd been expecting platinum and a stone the size of my knuckle, but this wasn't ostentatious.

It looked like it had cost a few hundred dollars at most.

"You should take it to her." Jameson looked from the ring to my face. "Alone, Heiress. Zara clearly sees this as an issue between her and you."

I saw something inside the band then. **8-3-75.** *A date*, I thought. *August third, nineteen seventy-five. Their wedding date?*

"Avery?" Grayson must have seen something on my face. "Is everything okay?"

I took my phone out and snapped a picture of the inside of the ring. "Time to make a trade."

➤————————◄

"Nan just...gave it to you?" Zara somehow managed not to choke on those words. "Legally. She transferred its ownership to *you*."

I got the feeling that this could go south very quickly, so I reiterated why I was here. "Nan gave me this ring to trade *you* for your father's ring."

Zara's eyes closed. I wondered what she was thinking, what she was *remembering*. Finally, Zara reached for a delicate chain around her neck and pulled a thick silver band out from underneath her lacy dress-shirt. She closed her fist over it, then opened her eyes. "My father's ring," she agreed hoarsely, "in exchange for my mother's."

Her hands shook as she undid the clasp on the chain. I handed her Alice Hawthorne's ring, and she handed me the old man's. Unable to resist the impulse, I turned the ring in my hand, looking for an inscription, and there it was—another date. **9-7-48**.

"His date of birth?" I asked, taking a stab in the dark.

Zara didn't have to glance down at the ring to know what I was talking about. This was the only thing her father had left her. I had no doubt she'd been over it with a fine-tooth comb.

"No," Zara said stiffly.

"Your mother's?"

"No." She brushed off the question in a way that distinctly discouraged follow-up questions, but I had to ask at least one.

"What about August third, nineteen-seventy-five," I said. "Was that the day they got married?"

"No, it was not," Zara replied. "Now, if you could please take that ring and see yourself out, I would greatly appreciate it."

I walked toward the door, then hesitated. "Didn't you wonder?" I asked Zara. "About the inscription?"

Silence. I started to think she had no intention of replying, but just as my hand closed around the doorknob, Zara surprised me. "I did not have to wonder," she said tersely.

I glanced back at her.

Zara shook her head, her grip on her mother's wedding ring

iron-tight. "It's a code, obviously. One of his little games. I'm supposed to decode it. Follow the clue wherever it leads."

"Why didn't you?" If she'd known that there was meaning to this bequest, why hadn't she played?

"Because I don't *want* to know what else my father had to say." Zara pressed her lips together, and something about her expression made her look decades younger. Vulnerable. "I was never enough for him. Toby was his favorite, then Skye. I was last, no matter what I did. That was never going to change. He left his fortune to a total stranger rather than leaving it to me. What else could I possibly need to know?"

Zara didn't seem so formidable now.

"Nan said to tell you something." I cleared my throat. "She said to tell you that 'we all do what we have to do to survive.'"

Zara let out a low, dry laugh. "That sounds like her." She paused. "I was never her favorite, either."

The tree is poison, Toby had written. *Don't you see? It poisoned S and Z and me.*

"Your father left Skye a clue, too." I didn't know why I was telling her this. I shouldn't have been telling her this. Grayson had been very clear in his warning: Zara and Skye couldn't find out that Toby was alive.

"At True North, I assume?" Zara really was Hawthorne. She'd seen the meaning in the will. She just hadn't cared. *No*, I thought. *She cared. She just wasn't going to give him the satisfaction of playing.*

"He left Skye a picture," I said softly. "Of you and her and a guy named Jake Nash."

Zara sucked in a breath. She looked like I'd slapped her. "Now would be a good time for you to leave," she said.

On the way out, I placed her father's wedding ring on an end table. I'd committed the date to memory. I'd gotten what I needed.

There was no reason for me to take this from her, too.

CHAPTER 53

L ate into the night, the five of us dug into the Hawthorne family history, looking for meaning in those dates. *August 3, 1975. September 7, 1948.* Tobias Hawthorne had been born in 1944. Alice had been born in 1948—but in February, not September. The two of them were married in 1974. Zara was born two years later, Skye three years after that, and Toby two years later, in 1981. Tobias Hawthorne had filed his first patent in 1969. He'd founded his first company in 1971.

A little before midnight, I got a phone call from Libby. I answered the phone with a question. "Did you find something?"

We might have hit a wall, but Libby had spent hours in New Castle. She'd had time to ask about Harry. Time to look for him.

"No one at the soup kitchen has seen him for weeks." My sister's tone was hard for me to place. "So we tried the park."

"Libby?" I could hear my own heart beating in the silence that followed. "What did you find?"

"We talked to an older man. Frank. Nash tried to bribe him."

"Didn't work, did it?" I asked. More silence. "Lib?"

"He wasn't going to tell us anything, but then he looked at me for a minute, and he asked me if my name was Avery. Nash told him it was."

I should have been there myself. I should have been the one talking to Frank. "What did he say?"

"He gave me an envelope with your name on it. A message from Harry."

The world came screeching to a halt. *Toby left me a message.* I wanted to stop the thought there, but I couldn't. *My father... left me... a message.*

"Take a picture of the envelope," I told Libby, recovering my voice. "And the letter. I want to read it myself."

"Ave..." Libby's voice got very soft.

"Just do it!" I said urgently. *"Please."*

Less than a minute later, the pictures came through. My first name was written on the envelope in familiar scrawl, part print, part cursive. I scrolled through to the next picture—the message— and my heart sank all the way to my stomach.

The only words that Toby Hawthorne had for me were STOP LOOKING.

><------------------------<

I couldn't sleep. The next day was Monday. I had school, and at this rate, I was going to be up staring at my ceiling all night. Rolling out of bed and walking over to my closet, I withdrew the lone, ratty bag I'd brought from home. I unzipped the pocket on the side and pulled out my mom's postcards—the only thing I had left of her.

I have a secret. I could hear her saying it. I could see her smile, like she was there with me right now.

"Why didn't you just tell me?" I whispered. Why had she

pretended my father was someone else? Why hadn't Toby been a part of my life?

Why didn't he want me looking for him now?

Something snapped inside of me, and before I knew it, I was walking. Out of my room, past Oren, who was positioned outside my door. I barely heard his objections. My pace picked up, and by the time I rounded the corner to Toby's wing, I was running.

The brick wall stared back at me. The Laughlins thought I had no business in Toby's wing. I'd been warned away. I'd walked into my bedroom to find it bloody, and right now, I didn't care if they were the ones who'd done it, or if it was another member of the staff. I didn't care who'd been the stalker in the woods at True North or who'd "decorated" my locker. I didn't care about Ricky Grambs or Skye Hawthorne or the way the skin over my knuckles split as I punched them into that wall.

Toby thought he could tell me to stop looking? He didn't want to be found?

He didn't get to tell me to stop. Nobody did. Oren moved to restrain me, and I fought him. I wanted to fight someone. Oren let me. He wasn't going to allow me to hurt myself, but he wouldn't stop me from lashing out at him. That just made me angrier.

I ducked his grip and barreled toward the bricks.

"Heiress." Suddenly, Jameson was standing between me and the wall. I tried to stop, but couldn't in time, and my fist connected with his chest. He didn't even blink.

I uncurled my fists, staring at him, realizing what had happened and horrified that I had hit him.

"I'm sorry." I had no excuse for losing it like this. So Toby had told me to stop looking? So he didn't want to be found? So what?

What was that to me?

"Tell me what you need." Jameson wasn't flirting. He wasn't being cryptic. He wasn't using me, in any way that I could tell.

I let out a long, effortful breath. "I need to take this damn wall down."

Jameson nodded. He looked past me to Oren. "We're going to need a sledgehammer."

CHAPTER 54

I took that wall down, brick by brick, and when my arms couldn't hold the sledgehammer any longer, Jameson took over for me. With one last swing, he cleared enough that I could step through the rubble.

Jameson ducked in after me.

Oren let us go. He didn't even try to follow. He stayed positioned at the entrance to Toby's wing, on the lookout for anyone who might decide that we didn't belong there.

"You must think I've lost it." I snuck a look at Jameson as I walked across the marble floor of Toby's hall.

"I think," Jameson murmured, "that you finally let go."

I remembered the way his skin had felt under my hands in the hot tub. *That* was letting go. This was me, hanging on to something. I didn't even know what.

"He doesn't want me to find him." Saying the words out loud made it feel real.

"Which suggests," Jameson added, "that he thinks we might be able to."

We.

I stepped into Toby's bedroom. The black lights were still there. Jameson turned them on. The writing was still on the literal walls.

"I've been thinking," Jameson said, like it was a confession, like his mind wasn't always on the move. "The old man didn't leave Xander an impossible task. He left a game, one originally meant for Zara and Skye. And that means that if we follow this through to the end, there will be an end. This is all leading somewhere. I can feel it."

I took a step toward him. Then another. And another.

"You can feel it, too, can't you?" Jameson said as I closed the space between us.

I *could* feel it. The chase was gaining momentum. The hunt was closing in. Eventually, we'd figure out what the dates on the rings meant. We were barreling forward. *Jameson and me.*

I pushed him up against the closest wall. I could see Toby's writing all around him, but I didn't want to think about Toby, who'd told me to stop looking.

I didn't want to think about anything, so I kissed the boy. This time it wasn't rough or frantic. It was gentle and slow and terrifying and *perfect*. And for once in my life, I didn't feel alone.

CHAPTER 55

The next day at school, I didn't wait for Jameson to find me. I found him. "What if the numbers aren't dates?" I said.

That got me a slow, winding, wicked smile. "Heiress, you took the words right out of my mouth."

I half expected to end up back on the roof, but this time Jameson took me to one of the "learning pods" in the STEM Center. Basically, it was a small, square room where the walls, ceiling, and floor were all painted with whiteboard material. There were two white rolling chairs in the center of the room, and nothing else.

Eli started to follow us inside, and Jameson took that as his cue to run a hand down my back and bring his lips to the spot where my neck met my jawline. I arched my neck, and Eli went bright red and stepped out of the room.

Jameson shut the door—and went to work. There were five dry-erase markers attached to the back of each of the rolling chairs. Jameson grabbed one of the markers and began writing on the wall directly in front of the chair. "Eight, three, seven, five," he said.

I rattled off the next four numbers from memory as he continued writing. "Nine, seven, four, eight."

Writing the numbers without the dashes freed up countless possibilities. "A passcode?" I asked Jameson. "A PIN number?"

"Not enough digits in either of them for a phone number or a zip code." Jameson stepped back, sat down in one of the chairs, and pushed off. "An address. A combination."

I flashed back to the moment when he and I had stepped off a helicopter, with a different sequence of numbers. The air between us had felt electric—just like it did now. We'd been flying high— and thirty seconds later, he'd gone cold.

But this time was different, because this time we were on the same page. This time there were no expectations. I was in control. "Coordinates," I said. That had been one of Jameson's suggestions, the last time around.

He turned the chair and, with a push of his heels, came skidding back to me. "Coordinates," he repeated, eyes alight. "Nine-seven-four-eight. Assuming the numbers are already in the correct order, nine has to be the number of degrees. Ninety-seven is too big."

I thought back to my fifth-grade geography class. "Latitude and longitude run from negative ninety to ninety."

"You two don't know the valence of any of the numbers, obviously."

Jameson and I whipped our heads back toward the door of the pod. Xander was standing there. I could see Eli, still red-faced, behind him. Xander stepped into the pod, shut the door, and, with no hesitation whatsoever, leaped forward to flying-tackle Jameson to the ground.

"How many times do I have to tell you?" the youngest Hawthorne demanded. "This is my game. No one is solving this without me." He plucked the marker from Jameson's hand and stood. "That was a friendly tackle," he assured me. "Mostly."

Jameson rolled his eyes. "We don't know the valence of the numbers." He echoed the last thing Xander had said pre-tackle. "And we also don't know which is latitude and which is longitude, so nine degrees could be nine degrees north, south, west, or east."

"Eight-three-seven-five." I grabbed another marker off one of the chairs and underlined the numbers on the board in different combinations. "The degrees could be eight *or* eighty-three."

Jameson smiled. "North, south, east, or west."

"How many total possibilities?" Xander mused.

"Twenty-four," Jameson and I answered at the exact same time.

Xander gave us a look. "Is there something going on here that I should be aware of?" he asked, gesturing between the two of us.

Jameson shared a brief look with me. "Nothing of note." He said *nothing* like it was *something*.

"None of my business!" Xander declared. "But for the record: You lovebirds are incorrect. There are way more than twenty-four possible locations here."

Jameson narrowed his eyes. "I can do the math, Xan."

"And I can humbly inform you, big brother, that there are three different ways of listing coordinates." Xander grinned. "Degrees, minutes, seconds. Degrees, decimal minutes. And decimal degrees."

"With only four digits," Jameson insisted, "we're probably look-ing at decimal degrees."

Xander winked at me. "But *probably* is never good enough."

➤————————◄

"Pacific Ocean," Jameson called out, and I wrote the location next to the designated coordinates. "Indian Ocean. Bay of Bengal."

Xander picked up right where his brother had left off. "Arctic Ocean. Arctic Ocean again!"

Both of them were entering coordinates into a map search. My brain kicked up a gear with each location they called out. *The*

Arctic. That couldn't be where this clue was supposed to point us, could it? And that was assuming that these numbers were coordinates at all.

"Antarctic Ice Shield," Jameson offered. "Times four."

By the time we were finished, the number of actual, non-arctic land locations on our list was much smaller than I'd expected. There were two in Nigeria, one in Liberia, one in Guinea, and one in . . .

"Costa Rica." I said out loud, unsure at first why that location was the one that had jumped out to me, but a moment later, I remembered the last time I'd read the words *Costa Rica*—in the binder.

"You have that look on your face," Jameson told me, his lips quirking upward. "You know something."

I closed my eyes and focused on the memory, not his lips. Skye's bequest had led to True North, one of the Hawthorne family's many vacation homes—mine, now. I tried to remember the pages I'd flipped through the night of the auction. *Patagonia. Santorini. Kauai. Malta. Seychelles . . .*

"Cartago, Costa Rica." I opened my eyes. "Tobias Hawthorne owned a house there." I pulled out my phone and looked up the latitude and longitude of Cartago, then turned my phone's screen toward the boys. "It's a match."

I tried to remember what the Cartago house looked like, but all I could see in my mind's eye was the surrounding vegetation and flowers, lush and bright and larger than life.

"We need to go to Costa Rica." Xander didn't exactly sound put out about that.

"I can't," I said, frustrated. I'd had to fight to go to Colorado. There was no way that Oren and Alisa would sign off on international travel—not when I could only spend two more nights away from Hawthorne House this month.

"Xander's not going anywhere, either."

For a second time, I found myself turning toward the doorway of the pod. Thea stood there.

"Are you just letting *anyone* in?" I called to Eli.

The reply I got was muffled, but I made out the words "not my job."

"Rebecca needs you," Thea told Xander. For the first time since I'd met her, she wasn't wearing any makeup. She looked almost mortal. "She didn't come to school today. It's her mom. I know it is. Rebecca won't answer my calls, so it's going to have to be you." It was clearly killing Thea to ask him, but there she was.

I expected Xander to put up a fight. How many times had he said that this was *his* game? But Xander just stared at Thea for a moment, then turned back to Jameson. "I guess you're going to Cartago."

Jameson glanced at me. I was fully prepared for him to ask me for another plane. Instead, the expression on his face shifted. "Can you call Libby and Nash?"

CHAPTER 56

t makes no sense," I told Max that afternoon. "Jameson never lets up on a puzzle. What's his angle here?"

Nash and Libby had agreed to go to Cartago. I was sitting in my bedroom, staring at the photograph of the Cartago house. A quartet of columns held a tile roof over a large porch, but the house itself was small, less than a thousand square feet.

"Maybe he doesn't have an angle," Max said.

My eyes narrowed. "He's Jameson Hawthorne. He always has an angle."

A sharp knock at the door cut off whatever Max would have said in reply. I went to answer it, annoyed that a part of me couldn't think about Jameson without thinking about the way it felt when his lips brushed lightly against my neck.

I opened the door to find someone holding a tall stack of fluffy white towels. The towels blocked the person's face, and my mind went to the bloodied heart that someone—likely a staff member—had left in my room. I took a step back. My heart rate jumped. Then Eli stepped into view. "She's clear," he told me.

I nodded and stepped back. The person holding the towels

walked past me. *Mellie.* She didn't say a word to us and made her way into my bathroom.

"I will never get used to someone else doing my—" I didn't get to say the word *laundry* before a gut-rattling scream tore through the air. My body responded before my brain did, launching me into the bathroom just in time to see Mellie slamming closed the doors to my bathroom armoire.

"Snake," she wheezed. "There's a snake in your—"

Eli pulled me back into the bedroom. I heard him making a call, and less than two minutes later, my room was flooded with guards.

"What the elf!" Max demanded. "Did she say *snake*?"

"Rattlesnake." Oren took Max and me aside. "Dead—no actual danger."

I met his eyes and said what he wasn't saying. "Just a threat."

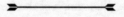

Someone wanted me scared. *Who—and why?* Deep down, some part of me knew the answer. An hour later, I went back to Toby's wing. Max went with me—and so did Oren.

The entire wing had been bricked up again.

I turned back to Oren. "The Laughlins did this." I wasn't sure if I was talking about the wall—or the snake. *They don't want me asking questions about Toby.*

"The threat level has been assessed," Oren told me. "It will continue to be assessed, and we will respond accordingly."

"Avery?"

I turned and saw Grayson making his way down the hall toward us. He always seemed so in control, so certain that the world would bend to his will. If he wanted me safe, I would *be* safe.

"I take it you heard about the snake," I said wryly.

"I did." Grayson arched an eyebrow at Oren. "I trust it's being handled."

Oren did not dignify that comment with a response.

"I also talked to Jameson." Grayson's tone gave away nothing. I saw myself with Jameson at school, in Toby's wing, in the hot tub, and I had to look away from Grayson's piercing silver eyes. "I understand we're in a waiting pattern."

It took me a moment to realize that when he said he'd talked to Jameson, he meant about the numbers—about Cartago. *Not us.*

"I thought perhaps," Grayson said evenly, "you could use a distraction."

"What kind of distraction?" Max asked, her tone just innocent enough to make me think the question wasn't innocent at all.

"A *friendly* one," I told her sternly. That's all Grayson and I were. *Friends.*

He straightened his suit jacket and smiled. "Either of you ladies up for a game?"

CHAPTER 57

The game room at Hawthorne House sent Max into a state of nearly apoplectic joy. The room was lines with shelves, the shelves filled with hundreds—maybe even thousands—of board games from around the world.

We started with Settlers of Catan. Grayson decimated us. We worked our way through four other games, none of which I'd even heard of before. As we were debating our next selection, Jameson strolled into the room.

"How about an old Hawthorne standard?" he suggested wickedly. "Strip bowling."

"What the shelf is strip bowling?" Max demanded, then she looked at me, eyes sparkling.

Don't you dare, I told her silently.

"Never mind!" Max grinned. "Avery and I are in."

Strip bowling was exactly what it sounded like, in that it involved both bowling and, if you were unsuccessful, stripping.

"The goal is to knock over the *least* pins," Jameson explained. "But you have to be careful, because any time your ball ends up in the gutter, you lose an article of clothing."

I could feel heat rising in my cheeks. My entire body felt warm—too warm. This was a horrible idea.

"This is a horrible idea," Grayson said. For a second or two, he and Jameson engaged in a silent standoff.

"Then why are you here?" Jameson volleyed back, waltzing over to pick out a dark green bowling ball with the Hawthorne crest on it. "No one is forcing you to play."

Grayson didn't move, and neither did I.

"So theoretically," Max said, "I want to knock over either zero pins or only one—whichever I can manage without putting the ball in the gutter?"

When Jameson answered, his green eyes locked on to mine. "Theoretically."

>———————◄

It became quickly apparent that excelling at strip bowling required precision and a high tolerance for risk. The first time Jameson cut things too close and his ball landed in the gutter, he took off a shoe.

Then another shoe.

A sock.

Another sock.

His shirt.

I tried not to look at the scar that ran the length of his torso, tried not to picture myself touching his chest. Instead, I focused on taking my turn. I was losing—badly. I'd even bowled a strike once, so determined was I to stay out of the gutter.

This time I cut things a little closer. When I knocked a single pin down, a breath left my chest. Grayson went next and lost his suit jacket. Max made it all the way down to her polka-dotted bra. Then it was Jameson's turn again, and the ball hung to the edge of the lane until the very end—then toppled into the gutter.

I tried—and failed—to look away as Jameson's fingers reached for the waistband of his jeans.

"Help me, Cheez-Its," Max murmured beside me.

Without warning, the door to the room burst inward, and Xander barreled into the bowling alley, then skidded to a halt. He was breathing hard enough to make me wonder how long he'd been running.

"Seriously?" Xander wheezed. "You're playing strip bowling without me? Never mind. Focus! This is me focusing."

"Focusing on what?" I asked.

"I have news," Xander blurted out.

"What kind of news?" Max asked. Xander glanced toward her. He definitely noticed the polka-dotted bra.

"Focus," Max reminded him. "What kind of news?"

"Is Rebecca okay?" Jameson asked, and I remembered Xander's conversation with Thea.

"For some values of okay," Xander said. That sentence made sense to no one except Xander, but he plowed on. "Thea was right. Rebecca's mom is having a rough day. There was vodka involved. She told Rebecca something."

"What kind of something?" Jameson took his turn trying to prompt Xander into spilling. Jameson's pants were still in place, but the top button had been undone.

Okay, now I need to focus.

"Avery, do you remember what Rebecca's mom said at the fundraiser, about all of her babies dying?"

"Nash said there were miscarriages," I said quietly. "Before Rebecca."

"That's what Bex thought she meant, too," Xander said quietly.

"But it wasn't?" I stared at him, having no idea whatsoever where this was going.

"She was talking about Emily," Grayson said, his voice pained.

"Emily," Xander confirmed. "And Toby."

I felt the world slow down around me. "What are you talking about?"

"Toby was a Laughlin." Xander swallowed. "Rebecca didn't know. No one did. Her parents were forty when they had Emily, but twenty-five years earlier—for the math-minded among us, that would be forty-two years ago—when Rebecca's mom was a teenager living in Wayback Cottage..."

"She got pregnant." Jameson stated the obvious.

"And Mr. and Mrs. Laughlin covered it up?" Grayson was intent on getting answers. "Why?"

Xander raised his shoulders up as high as they would go, then let them fall in the world's most elaborate shrug. "Rebecca's mom wouldn't explain—but she did rant to Bex, at length, about the fact that when one of the Hawthorne daughters got pregnant years later, she didn't have to hide her pregnancy. She got to keep *her* baby."

Skye hadn't been forced to put Nash up for adoption. I remembered what Rebecca's mother had said to Libby at the fundraiser. *Never trust a Hawthorne. They take everything.*

"Did Rebecca's mom want to keep her baby?" I asked, horrified. "Did they make her give him away? And why would they force her to hide the pregnancy?"

"I don't know the details," Xander said, "but according to Rebecca, her mother wasn't even told that the Hawthornes were the ones adopting the baby. She thought that our grandmother really was pregnant with a little boy, and that her own baby was adopted by a stranger."

That was horrifying. *That's why they kept Toby's adoption a secret? So she wouldn't know her baby was right there?*

"But as Toby grew up..." Xander shrugged again, the motion understated this time.

"She figured it out?" I imagined giving up a baby and then realizing that a child you'd seen grow up was yours.

I imagined being Toby and discovering this secret.

"Rebecca's been forbidden from seeing any of us." Xander grimaced. "Her mom said that the Hawthorne family takes and takes. She said that we don't play by any rules and don't care who we hurt. She blames our family for Toby's death."

"And Emily's," Grayson added roughly.

"For all of it." Xander sat down, right where he was standing. The room went quiet. Max and Jameson weren't wearing shirts, I was down one shoe, I knew instinctively that our game of strip bowling was over, and none of it mattered, because all I could think was that Rebecca's mom thought Toby was dead.

And so did Mr. and Mrs. Laughlin.

CHAPTER 58

The next day, before school, I went to find Mrs. Laughlin. I located her in the kitchen and asked Eli to give us a moment. The most he would give me was six or seven extra feet.

Mrs. Laughlin was kneading dough. She saw me out of the corner of her eye and kneaded harder. "What can I do for you?" she asked tersely.

I braced myself because I was almost certain this wasn't going to go well. I probably should have just kept my mouth shut, but I'd spent most of the night thinking that if Rebecca's mom was Toby's mom, then the Laughlins hadn't just watched Toby grow up. They hadn't just loved him because he was lovable.

He was their grandson. *And that makes me...*

I pressed my lips together, then decided that the best way to rip a bandage off was quickly. "I need to talk to you about Toby." I kept my voice low.

Wham. Mrs. Laughlin picked the dough up and expertly slammed it back down, then wiped her hands on her apron and whipped her head to look directly at me. "Listen to me, little miss. You may own this House. You may be richer than sin. You could own the sun for all I care, but I will not let you hurt everyone who loved that boy by dredging this up and—"

"He was your grandson." My voice shook. "Your daughter got pregnant. You hid it, and the Hawthornes adopted the baby."

Mrs. Laughlin went pale. "Hush," she ordered, her voice shaking even more than mine had. "You can't walk around here saying things like that."

"Toby was your grandson," I repeated. My throat felt like it was swelling, and my eyes were starting to sting. "And I think he's my father."

Mrs. Laughlin's mouth opened, then twisted, like she'd been on the verge of yelling at me, then run out of air. Both of her hands went to the flour-covered countertop, and she held on to it like what I'd just said was threatening to bring her to her knees.

I took a step toward her. I wanted to reach out, but I didn't press my luck. Instead, I held out the file I had retrieved from Tobias Hawthorne's study. Mrs. Laughlin didn't take it. I wasn't sure she could.

"Here," I said.

"No." She closed her eyes and shook her head. "No, I'm not going to—"

I took a single sheet of paper out of the file. "This is my birth certificate," I said quietly. "Look at the signature."

And bless her, she did. I heard a sharp intake of air, and then finally she looked back at me.

My eyes were stinging worse now, but I kept going. I didn't want to stop, because part of me was terrified about what she might say. "Here are some pictures Tobias Hawthorne had a private detective take of me, shortly before he died." I laid three photographs out on the counter. Two of me playing chess with Harry, one of the two of us in line for a breakfast sandwich. Toby wasn't facing the camera in any of them, but I willed Mrs. Laughlin to look at what she could see—his hair, his body, the way he stood. *Recognize him.*

"That man," I said, nodding to the pictures. "He showed up right after my mother died. I thought he was homeless. Maybe he was. We played chess in the park every week, sometimes every morning." I could hear the raw emotion in my own voice. "He and I had this ongoing bet that if I won, he had to let me buy him breakfast, but if he won, I couldn't even offer. I'm competitive, and I'm good at chess, so I won a lot—but he won more."

Mrs. Laughlin closed her eyes, but they didn't stay closed for long, and when she opened them, she stared right at the photographs "That could be anyone," she said roughly.

I swallowed. "Why do you think Tobias Hawthorne left me his fortune?" I asked quietly.

Mrs. Laughlin's breath grew ragged. She turned to look at me, and when she did, I saw every emotion I felt mirrored in her eyes—and then some.

"Oh, Tobias," she whispered. It was the first time I'd ever heard her call her former employer anything but *Mr. Hawthorne*. "What did you do?"

"We're still trying to figure it out," I said, a ball of emotion rising in my throat. "But—"

I never got the chance to finish that sentence, because the next thing I knew, Mrs. Laughlin was hugging me, holding on to me for dear life.

CHAPTER 59

The downside of modular scheduling was that some days, my classes were scheduled so tightly that I barely even had time for lunch. Today was one of those days. I had exactly one mod—twenty-two minutes—to make it to the refectory, buy food, eat it, and haul myself back to the physics lab, across campus.

While I was waiting in line, I got a text from Libby: a photograph, taken out the window of a plane. The ocean below was a brilliant green-blue. The land in the distance was tree-covered. And coming into view amid those trees was what I recognized as the very top of an architectural marvel. The Basílica de Nuestra Señora de los Ángeles—in Cartago.

I made it to the front of the line and paid. As I sat down to eat, all I could think was that Libby and Nash were landing in Cartago. They would make their way to the house. They would find *something*. And somehow, the puzzle that Tobias Hawthorne had left first for his daughters—and then for Xander—would start to make sense.

"May I sit?"

I looked up to see Rebecca, and for a moment, I just stared at her. She'd cut her long, dark red hair off at the chin. The ends were uneven, but something about the way it flared out around her face made her look almost otherworldly.

"Sure," I said. "Knock yourself out."

Rebecca sat. Without her long hair to hide behind, her eyes looked impossibly large. Her chest rose and fell—a deep breath. "Xander told you," she said.

"He did," I replied, and then my sense of empathy got the better of me, because as much of a mind warp as this revelation had been for me, it might have actually been worse for her. "Don't expect me to start calling you Aunt Rebecca."

That surprised a laugh out of her. "You sounded like her just then," she told me after a moment. "Emily."

That was the exact instant that I realized that if Rebecca was my aunt, then Emily had been, too. I thought about Thea, dressing me up like Emily. I'd never thought we looked anything alike, but when Grayson had seen me coming down the stairs at the charity gala, he'd looked like he'd seen a ghost.

Do I have some Emily in me?

"Was your dad...," I started to ask Rebecca, but I wasn't sure how to phrase my question. "How long have your parents been together?"

"Since high school," Rebecca said.

"So your dad was Toby's father?"

Rebecca shook her head. "I don't know. I'm not even one hundred percent sure my dad knows there *was* a baby." She looked down. "My dad loves my mom, that fairy-tale, all-encompassing, even-our-own-kids-will-never-compare kind of love. He took her name when they got married. He let her make all the decisions about Emily's medical treatment."

I took that to mean that if Rebecca's mother had doted on Emily and ignored Rebecca, her father had backed that decision, too.

"I'm sorry," Rebecca said softly.

"About what?" I asked. As messed up as the Laughlin family secrets were, I wasn't the one who'd grown up in Toby's shadow. This had affected Rebecca's life more than mine.

"I'm sorry about what I did to you," Rebecca clarified. "About what I *didn't* do."

I thought about the night Drake had tried to kill me. After a disastrous make-out session with Jameson, I'd ended up in a room alone with Rebecca. We'd talked. If she'd told me then what she knew about Drake and Skye, there would have been nothing to forgive.

"I've been trying so hard to be okay." Rebecca wasn't even looking at me anymore. "But I'm not. That poem Toby left? The William Blake one? I have a copy on my phone, and I keep reading it over and over, and all I can think is that I wish I had read it sooner, because when I was growing up, I buried all my anger. No matter what Emily wanted or what I had to give up for her—I was supposed to be okay with it. I was supposed to smile. And the one time I let myself get mad, she . . ."

Rebecca couldn't say it, so I said it for her. "Died."

"It messed me up, and I messed up, and I'm so, so sorry, Avery."

"Okay," I said—and to my surprise, I meant it.

"If it's any consolation," Rebecca continued, "I'm angry now, finally—at so many people."

I thought back to her fight with Thea on the plane, and then I thought about the absolutely infuriating message Toby had left me.

"I'm angry, too," I told Rebecca. "And for the record: I like your hair."

CHAPTER 60

When Oren picked Eli and me up after school, Alisa was in the passenger seat—and Landon was in the back, tapping furiously away on her phone.

"Everything is fine," Alisa assured me, which was pretty much the opposite of comforting. "We've got this under control, but—"

"But what?" I glanced over at Landon. "What's she doing here?"

There was a beat of silence. That was all it took for Alisa to craft her reply. "Skye and your father are offering themselves as an interview package to the highest bidder." Alisa expelled an aggrieved breath. "If we want to quash the story, Landon is going to have to make it worth the high bidder's while to bury it."

I'd had enough on my mind these past few days that I'd barely thought about Ricky Grambs. I tried to read between the lines of Alisa's statement. "Are you saying you're going to pay off whoever buys their interview?"

Landon finally looked up from her phone. "Yes and no," she told me before turning her attention to Alisa. "Monica thinks she can make the network pony up, but we're going to have to guarantee them Avery *and* at least one Hawthorne."

"They'll pay for exclusivity from Skye?" Alisa asked. "Complete with an NDA preventing Skye and Grambs from taking their story elsewhere?"

"They'll pay for it. They'll bury it." Landon pinched the bridge of her nose, like she could feel a migraine coming on. "But the latest they'll agree to for a sit-down with Avery is tomorrow night."

"Good lord." Alisa shook her head. "Can she handle it?"

"I'm sitting right here," I pointed out.

"She'll have to." Landon spoke over me. "But we're going to have to crunch."

"*Crunch* what, exactly?" I asked. Everyone in the car ignored the question.

"Avery's interview is nonexclusive," Alisa told Landon, "and they have a deal."

"They'll want an embargo on other interviews for at least a month." Landon's reply was automatic.

"Three weeks," Alisa countered. "And it applies only to Avery, not any of her surrogates."

Since when did I have surrogates? I wasn't running for president here.

"Which Hawthorne am I offering as part of the package?" Landon asked, all business.

My brain was struggling to keep up, but I was pretty sure that what was happening here was that we were giving my first interview to whoever bought Skye's, under the conditions that the interview with Skye and Ricky never aired and whoever bought it contractually prevented the duo from talking to anyone else.

"Why do we even care about *their* interview?" I said.

"We care," Alisa said emphatically. Then she turned back to Landon. "And you can tell Monica that we'll guarantee a sit-down Wednesday evening with Avery and…Grayson."

CHAPTER 61

Grayson, move a little closer to Avery. Tilt your head toward her."

Landon had set us up in the tea room for a mock interview. This was take *seven*. How Alisa had gotten Grayson to agree to this, I had no idea, but there he was, sitting stiffly in the chair next to me. At Landon's instruction, he angled his legs slightly toward mine. Instinctively, I mirrored the movement, and then I was hit with self-consciousness and self-doubt, because Landon hadn't asked *me* to move.

My body had gravitated toward his all on its own.

"Good." Landon nodded at the two of us, then focused on Grayson. "Remember your core message."

"This has been a difficult time for my family," Grayson said, every inch the heir apparent he'd once been. "But some things happen for a reason."

"Good," Landon said again. "Avery?"

I was supposed to respond to what Grayson had said. The more we talked to each other, the easier it would be to sell the fact that I was on good terms with the Hawthorne family.

"Some things happen for a reason," I repeated, but the words came out flat. "I've never believed that," I admitted. I could practically hear Landon groaning internally. "I mean, yeah, things happen for a reason, but most of the time that reason isn't fate or because it was predestined. It's because the world sucks, or someone out there's being an asshole."

A muscle in Grayson's jaw tightened slightly. It was a good enough look for him that it took me a second to realize that he was trying very hard not to laugh.

"Let's try to avoid the word *asshole*, shall we?" Landon said, her British accent pronounced. "Avery, we need for you to project gratitude and awe. It's fine to be overwhelmed, but you need to be overwhelmed in the best possible way."

Gratitude. Awe. I was expected to be some kind of wide-eyed everygirl, and all Grayson had to do was sit there, with those cheekbones and that suit and be a *Hawthorne*.

"Avery's right." Grayson was still in interview mode. He projected confidence, his tone dripping power, like he was an immortal deigning to explain to humans what they should believe, think, and do. "We all make decisions, and those decisions affect other people. They ripple through the world, and the more power you have, the greater the ripple. Fate didn't choose Avery." Grayson's tone brooked no argument. "My grandfather did. We might never know his reasons, but I have no doubt that he had them. He always did."

All I could think was that we *did* know the reasons—or at least, we had theories. But that wasn't something I could say in front of Landon. It wasn't something I could admit on national television.

When you can't tell the truth, I could hear Landon lecturing me, *tell a truth.*

"I wish I knew what those reasons were," I said. *For sure*, I added silently. I shot Grayson a look. "Sometimes, it feels like Hawthornes always just know. Like you're all so sure of everything."

Grayson's eyes locked on to mine. "Not everything."

There was something about the way he looked at me when he said those words that made me realize I might be the one person on the planet with the ability to make Grayson Hawthorne question himself and the decisions he'd made.

Like the decision to step back from me. To be *friends*.

Landon clasped her hands together. "Avery, that's the most natural I've heard you sound. Very relatable! And, Grayson, you're perfection." Like he needed anyone else telling him that. "Just remember, both of you: short answers if they ask about the attempts on Avery's life. Grayson, don't be afraid to seem protective of her. Avery, you know the rest of your 'no' questions."

If they asked if I knew anything about my mother's past: *no*.

If they asked what I had done to work my way into Tobias Hawthorne's will: *nothing*.

"Grayson, whenever possible, talk about your grandfather. And your brothers! The audience will eat that up, and we want them walking away with the idea that your grandfather knew exactly what he was doing when he chose Avery, and no one's worried. And, Avery?"

"Gratitude," I said quickly. "Overwhelmed. Relatable. One day, I'm scrounging to pay the electric bill, and the next, I'm Cinderella. I don't know what I'll do with the money yet—I'm just seventeen. But I'd like to help people."

"And?" Landon prompted.

"Someday I'd like to travel the world." That was something we'd settled on as a talking point, something that made me sound dreamy and wide-eyed and overwhelmed. And it was true.

"Perfect," Landon said. "One more time, from the top."

CHAPTER 62

By the time Landon finally let us go, the sun was starting to set.

"You look like you want to hit something," Grayson observed. He was getting ready to go on his way, and I was getting ready to go on mine—probably to find Max.

"I don't want to hit anything," I said in a tone that did absolutely nothing to sell that statement.

Grayson tilted his head to the side, and his eyes settled directly on mine. "How would you feel about swinging a sword?"

➤━━━━━━━━━━━◄

Grayson took me through the topiary garden to a part of the estate I'd never seen before.

"Is that...," I started to say.

"A hedge maze?" Grayson had a way of smiling: lips closed, slightly uneven. "I'm surprised Jamie's never brought you out here."

The moment he mentioned Jameson, I was hit with the feeling that I shouldn't be out here—not with Grayson. But we were just friends, and whatever Jameson and I were at the moment, it came with no strings attached.

That was the point.

I turned my attention to the maze. The hedges were taller than I was, and dense. *A person could get lost in there.* I stood at the entrance, Grayson beside me.

"Follow me," he said.

I did. The farther into the maze we got, the more I focused on marking our path—not on the way he moved, the shape of his body in front of me.

Right turn. Left turn. Left again. Forward. Right. Left.

Finally, we arrived at what I assumed was the center: a large, square area, surrounded by twinkling lights. Grayson knelt and spread the grass with his fingertips, revealing something metal underneath. In the twilight, I didn't see exactly what he did, but a moment later, I heard a mechanical whirring sound, and the ground started moving.

My first thought was that he'd triggered an entrance to the tunnels, but when I stepped closer, I saw a steel compartment embedded in the ground, six feet long, three feet wide, and not all that deep. Grayson reached into the compartment and removed two long objects wrapped in cloth. He nodded toward the second, and I knelt, unwinding the fabric to reveal a flash of metal.

A sword.

It was nearly three feet long, heavy, with a T-shaped hilt. I ran my fingers over the hilt, then looked up at Grayson, who was unwrapping a second sword.

"Longswords," he said, clipping the word. "Italian. Fifteenth century. They should probably be in a museum somewhere, but..." He gave a little shrug.

This was what it meant to be a Hawthorne. *This should probably be in a museum, but my brothers and I like to hit things with it instead.*

I went to pick up the sword, but Grayson stopped me. "Both

hands," he said. "A longsword is designed to be used with both hands."

I wrapped my hands around the hilt, then managed to stand up.

Grayson placed his own sword down carefully on the cloth it had been wrapped in, then came up behind me. "No," he said softly. "Like this." He moved my right hand up, directly underneath the cross on the *T*. "Quillons," he told me, nodding toward that part of the sword. He nodded toward the end of the hilt. "Pommel. Never put your hand on the pommel. It has its own job to do." He placed my left hand above it, a little below my right. "Grip the sword with the bottom fingers of both hands. Keep the upper ones looser. You move, and the sword moves. Don't fight the movement of the sword. Let it do the work for you."

He stepped back and picked up his own sword. Slowly, he demonstrated.

"Shouldn't I be using some kind of...practice sword?" I asked.

Grayson met my eyes. "Probably."

This was a bad idea. I knew it. He knew it. But I'd spent the last five hours being prepped for an interview I absolutely did not want to give, an interview I only had to give because of Ricky—who *wasn't* my father—and Skye, who had probably hired the stalker at True North.

Sometimes all a girl really needed was a very bad idea.

"Watch your posture. Let the sword lead you, not the other way around."

I corrected, and Grayson gave the slightest of nods. "I'm sorry about all of this," I said.

"You should be sorry. You're getting sloppy again. Already."

I adjusted my stance and my grip. "I'm sorry about the interview," I specified with a roll of my eyes.

Grayson slowly brought his sword to contact mine, the movement so perfectly controlled that I was overcome with the sense that he could cut a hair in half if he wanted to. "It doesn't signify," he assured me. "I'm a Hawthorne. As a general rule, we're press-ready by our seventh birthdays." He stepped back. "Your turn," he told me. *"Control."*

I didn't talk at all until my sword had touched his—a little harder than I'd meant for it to. "I'm *still* sorry that you got dragged into *this* interview."

Grayson lowered his sword and began cuffing his sleeves. "You're sorrier about an interview than you were when I was disinherited."

"That's not true. I *was* sorry—you were just too busy being an asshole to notice."

Grayson gave me his most austere look. "Let's try to avoid using the word *asshole*, shall we?"

His Landon impression was *spot-on*. Grinning, I swung at him again, letting the sword lead me this time, aware of every muscle in my body and every inch of his. I stopped the sword a microsecond before it touched his blade. He stepped forward. Once. Twice.

Longswords weren't meant to be wielded at such close range. And still he came closer, forcing my blade vertical, until there was nothing but inches and two swords separating him from me. I could see him breathing, hear it, *feel* it.

Muscles in my shoulders and arms began to ache—but the rest of me ached more. "What are we doing?" I whispered.

His eyes closed. His body shuddered. He stepped back and lowered the sword. "Nothing."

CHAPTER 63

That night, when I couldn't sleep, I told myself that it was because we still hadn't heard anything from Libby and Nash. Every text I sent went unread and unanswered. That was what kept me up so late that I was guaranteed to wake up the next morning with dark circles under my eyes. *Not Grayson.*

➤━━━━━◄

The next evening, I still hadn't heard from Libby, and Grayson Hawthorne and I were sitting next to each other, under a flood of lights, with Monica Winfield smiling into the camera.

I am so not ready for this.

"Avery, let's start with you. Walk us through what happened the day Tobias Hawthorne's will was read."

That was a softball question. *Gratitude. Awe. Relatability.* I could do this—and I did. Grayson answered his first softball question just as easily.

He even managed to make eye contact with me the first time he said my name.

We got two more softballs apiece before Monica moved on to trickier territory. "Avery, let's talk about your mother."

Keep it short, I could hear Landon telling me. *And sincere.*

"She was wonderful," I said fiercely. "I would give anything for her to be here now."

That was short, and it was sincere—but it also opened me up to a follow-up. "You must have heard some of the...rumors."

That my mom was living under a fake name. That she was a con artist. I couldn't lose my temper. *Spin the question.* That was what I was supposed to do: Start talking about my mother but end up talking about how grateful and awed and gosh darn *normal* I was.

Beside me, Grayson leaned forward. "When the world is watching your every move, when everyone knows your name, when you're famous just by *being*—you stop following rumors pretty quickly. Last I heard, I was supposedly dating a princess, and my brother Jameson had some very questionable tattoos."

Monica's eyes lit up. "Does he?"

Grayson leaned back in his seat. "A Hawthorne never tells."

He was good at this—much better than I was—and just like that, the interviewer was redirected off the topic of my mother. "Your family has been very closemouthed about this entire situation," she told Grayson. "The last the world heard, your aunt Zara was implying there might be a legal solution to your dilemma."

The last public statement Zara had given had more or less accused me of elder abuse.

"You can say a lot of things about my grandfather," Grayson replied smoothly, "but Tobias Hawthorne wasn't known for leaving loopholes."

Something about the way he said that made it clear that the topic was closed. *How does he do that?*

"Avery." Monica zeroed back in on me. "We've talked a bit about your mother. Let's talk about your father."

That was one of my "no" questions. I shrugged. "There's not much to say."

"You're a minor, correct? And your legal guardian is your sister, Libby?"

I could tell where this was going. Just because the network wasn't airing the interview with Ricky and Skye didn't mean that Monica hadn't filed away their statements for future reference. She was going to ask me about custody.

Not if I redirect. "Libby took me in after my mom died. She didn't have to. She was twenty-three. Because our dad was never around, we hadn't spent much time together. We were practically strangers, but she took me in. She is the single most loving person I've ever met in my life."

That was one of the core truths of my existence, and I didn't have to work to sell it.

"I suppose that's one thing Avery and I have in common," Grayson added beside me. He didn't elaborate and forced Monica into asking the follow-up question.

"And what is that?"

"If you're going to come at our siblings," he told her, his smile sharp, his gaze full of warning, "you're going to have to go through us."

This was the Grayson I'd met weeks ago: dripping power and well aware that he could come out on top in any battle. He didn't make threats, because he didn't *have* to.

"Did you feel protective of your brothers after you realized your grandfather had essentially written them out of the will?" Monica asked him. I got the sense that she *wanted* Grayson to say that he resented me. She wanted to poke holes in the message he'd been delivering.

"You could say that." Grayson held her gaze, then broke it to glance deliberately at me.

"I think we're all protective of Avery now. It's not something that

242

my brothers or I expect anyone else to understand, but the simple truth is that we're not normal. My grandfather didn't raise us to be *normal*, and this is what he wanted. This is his legacy." His gaze burned into me. "*She* is."

He sold every single word—enough that I could almost believe that he really thought I was special.

"And you have no reservations about the entire situation?" Monica pressed.

Grayson gave her a wolfish smile. "None."

"No desire to overturn the will?"

"I've already told you: That can't be done."

The trick to answering "no" questions was perfect, bulletproof confidence in your reply. Grayson was a master of the art.

"But if it could?" Monica asked.

"This is what my grandfather wanted," Grayson replied, returning to his core message. "My brothers and I are lucky—luckier than almost anyone else watching this. We've been given every opportunity, and we have a lot of the old man in us. We'll make our own way." He glanced toward me again, but this time it felt more choreographed. "Someday, what I make of myself will give *your* fortune a run for its money."

I grinned. *Take that, Monica.*

"Avery, how does it feel when Grayson says those words: *your fortune?*"

"Unreal." I shook my head. "Before the will was read, back when I knew that I'd been left something but didn't know what, I figured that Tobias Hawthorne had left me a couple thousand dollars. And even that? It would have been life-changing."

"So this?"

"Unreal," I repeated, projecting every ounce of gratitude and awe and bewilderment that I had felt in that moment.

"Do you ever feel like it might all go away?"

Beside me, Grayson shifted slightly, his body angling toward mine. But I didn't need his protection right now. I was on a roll.

"Yes."

"And what if I told you—both of you—that there might be another heir?"

I went still, my face frozen. I couldn't risk even looking at Grayson, but I wondered if he'd sensed something was off the moment before, if that was why he'd shifted. I could see now all the ways the interviewer had been leading up to this. She'd asked Grayson about overturning the will—twice. She'd asked me how I'd feel if it all went away.

"Avery, do you know what the term *pretermitted* means, in the context of inheritance law?"

My brain couldn't catch up fast enough. *Toby. She can't know about Toby. Skye doesn't. Ricky doesn't.* "I . . ."

"It typically refers to an heir who was not yet born at the deceased's time of death, but interpreted a bit more broadly, our experts say that it could refer to any heir who was not 'alive' at the time of death."

She *knew*. I glanced at Grayson. I couldn't help it. His gaze was focused on the interviewer's as he spoke. "I'm sure your experts told you that in the state of Texas, a pretermitted child is entitled only to a share that is equal to the deceased's other children's." Grayson's eyes were sharp—and so was his close-lipped smile. "Since my grandfather left very little to his children, even if he had somehow conceived a child before his death, it would hardly alter the distribution of his assets at all."

In that moment, Grayson didn't seem like he was nineteen years old. He hadn't just spouted off legal precedent—he'd deliberately overlooked the fact that Monica had made it clear she wasn't talking about an unborn child.

"Your family really has been looking for loopholes, haven't they?" Monica said, but she didn't mean it as a question. "Perhaps they should have a sit-down with our experts, because it's not clear, based on precedent, whether a child assumed to be dead would be entitled only to their siblings' share, or to the share left to that child in a prior will."

Grayson stared her down. "I'm afraid I don't follow."

He did. Of course he did. He was just hiding it better than I did, because all I could do was sit there silently and think one name, over and over.

Toby.

"You had an uncle." Monica was still focused on Grayson.

"He died," Grayson said sharply. "Before I was even born."

"Under tragic and suspicious circumstances." Monica swung her head to face me. "Avery." She hit a button on a remote I hadn't even been aware she was holding. A trio of pictures flashed on a large screen behind us.

The same pictures I'd shown Mrs. Laughlin the day before.

"Who is this man?"

I swallowed. "My friend. Harry." *Tell a story.* "We used to play chess in the park."

"Do you have many friends in their forties?"

When you can't tell the truth, tell a truth. Tell a story. "He was the only one who could take my queen. We had a running bet: If I won a game, he had to let me buy him breakfast. I knew he didn't have the money to buy it himself. I was afraid he might not eat otherwise, but he hated charity, so I had to win, fair and square."

I'd done Landon proud—but Monica wasn't deterred. "So it is your statement that this man is not Tobias Hawthorne the Second?"

"How dare you?" Grayson's voice vibrated with intensity. He stood. "Hasn't my family suffered enough? We just lost my grand-father. To dredge up this tragedy—"

"Avery." Monica knew who the weak link here was. "Is this or is this not Tobias Hawthorne's supposedly deceased son? The true heir to the Hawthorne fortune?"

"This interview is over." Grayson turned to block the camera and helped me to my feet. He met my gaze, and even though he didn't say a word, I heard him loud and clear: *We need to get out of here.*

He ushered me to the wings, where Alisa was trying to bust past a security guard. Monica followed us, a cameraman with a hand-held in her wake. "What is your connection to Toby Hawthorne?" she yelled after me.

The world was falling down around me. We hadn't prepared for this. I wasn't ready. But I had an answer to that question. I had a truth, and if they knew this much, then what would the harm be in telling them the rest.

What is your connection to Toby Hawthorne?

"I'm his—"

Before I could get the word *daughter* out, Grayson leaned his head down and crushed his lips to mine. He kissed me to save me from what I'd been about to say. For a small eternity, nothing in the world existed outside of that kiss.

His lips. Mine.

For show.

CHAPTER 64

The kiss ended as the two of us were shuffled off-camera and into an elevator. My heart was thudding. My brain was a mess. My lips felt...my whole body felt...

There were no words.

"What the hell was that?" Alisa waited for the elevator door to close before she exploded.

"That was an ambush," Landon replied, her posh accent doing absolutely nothing to soften the words. "If you keep information from me, I can't keep you from being ambushed. Alisa, you know how I operate. If you won't allow me to do my job, then it is, simply put, no longer my job."

The elevator door opened, and Landon left.

As Max would say: *fax*. My eyes found their way to Grayson's, but he wouldn't even look at me. It was like he *couldn't*.

"I am going to ask one more time," Alisa said, her voice low. "What the hell was that?"

"You'll get your answer," Oren told her. "In the car. We need to move out now. I've sent two of my men to the car and deployed the decoy. We'll go out the back. *Move*."

We made it out of the parking lot before the vultures descended. Alisa let us marinate in silence for a full minute before she spoke again. This time she didn't ask what was going on. "Who knew?" she demanded instead. *"Who knew?"*

I looked down. "I did."

"Obviously." Alisa shifted her gaze to Grayson. "Are you going to lie and tell me you didn't?" Then she glanced to the driver's seat. "Oren?"

My head of security didn't reply.

"This will be easier if we start at the beginning," Grayson said, sounding calmer than he should have. *Like we never kissed at all.* "You will recall that Avery asked you to locate an acquaintance of hers, to whom she was hoping to give economic aid?"

"Harry." Alisa's memory was a sieve—and I knew in my bones that she would *never* forget what had just happened. She probably wouldn't forgive it, either.

"Toby," I corrected. I looked over at Grayson. *You can't do this for me. You can't protect me the way you did back there.* "I didn't know who he was at the time," I continued, "but then I saw a picture of him in Nan's locket."

"You should have told me. Immediately." Alisa was angry, furious enough that she let loose an impressive string of curse words of her own—some in English and some not. "And you *shouldn't* have told anyone else." She shot dagger eyes at Grayson, so it was pretty clear who she was referring to.

"Xander already knew," Grayson said quietly. "My grandfather left him a clue."

That took the wind out of Alisa's sails, but only slightly. "Of course he did." She let out a breath, then took in another, and then repeated the process two or three times. "If you had told me, Avery, I might have been able to get a handle on this. We could have hired a team to—"

"Find him?" I said. "Your team already looked."

"There are teams," Alisa told me, "and there are *teams*. I have a fiduciary duty to the estate—to you. There is no way I could license millions to find *Harry*, but to find *Toby*?"

I dug my phone out and pulled up the picture Libby had sent me of Toby's message. "He doesn't want to be found." I passed the phone into her hands.

"*Stop looking.*" She read the words aloud, completely unimpressed. "Who took this? Where was it taken? Have we verified the handwriting?"

I answered the questions in the order she'd asked them. "Libby. New Castle. The handwriting is definitely Toby's."

Alisa rolled her eyes heavenward. "You sent *Libby* after him?"

I was getting ready to tell her that there was nothing wrong with Libby, when Grayson clarified the situation. "And Nash."

It took Alisa a full four or five seconds to recover from the fact that Nash had known—and that he was with Libby now. "And *you*," she told Grayson heatedly. "You had time to look up the legal precedent, but it didn't occur to you to *talk to a lawyer*?"

Grayson looked down at the cuff link on his right sleeve, considering his response. He must have decided on honesty, because when he lifted his gaze back up to Alisa, all he said was, "We couldn't be certain where your loyalties would lie."

This time Alisa didn't look angry. She looked like she might cry. "How could you say that to me, Gray?" She searched his expression for a response, and I was reminded that she'd grown up with the Hawthorne family. She'd known Grayson and Jameson and Xander their entire lives. "When did I become the enemy here? I have only *ever* done what the old man wanted me to do." She spoke like those words were being physically torn out of her. "Do you have any idea what that's cost me?"

It was clear from the tone of her voice that she wasn't just talking about the will, or me, or anything that had happened in the wake of Tobias Hawthorne's death. She'd called him "the old man," the same way they did, when I'd only ever heard her refer to him as *Mr. Hawthorne* or *Tobias Hawthorne* before. And when she spoke about what her loyalty to the old man had cost her...

She's talking about Nash.

"I am holding this empire together by a thread." Alisa swiped angrily at her face with the back of her hand, and I realized a single tear had escaped. Her expression made it damn clear that it would be the last. "Avery, I will handle this situation. I will put out this fire. I will do what needs to be done, but the next time you keep a secret from me, the next time you lie to me? I will throw you to the wolves *myself*."

I believed her. "There is one more thing." I gulped—there was no way of sugarcoating this. "Well, two more things. One: Toby was adopted, and his biological mother was the Laughlins' then-teenage daughter."

Alisa stared at me for a good three seconds. Then she arched an eyebrow, waiting for the other thing.

"And two," I continued, thinking back to the moment when Grayson had stopped me from saying this on camera—and how. "I have reason to believe that Toby is, in all likelihood, my father."

CHAPTER 65

Well," Max said, flopping down on my bed. "That could have gone better." She'd seen the interview. The whole world had. "Are you sure you're okay?"

Grayson had warned me, from the very beginning, not to pull at this thread. He warned me against telling anyone about Toby, and how many people had I told?

When we'd arrived back at Hawthorne House, I had tried to talk to him, but my mouth had refused to say a single word.

"Grayson didn't *have* to kiss me," I told Max, the words bursting out of my mouth, like I didn't have much bigger things to think about. "He could have cut me off."

"Personally, I find this turn of events *delightful*," Max declared. "But you look like a motherfaxing deer caught in motherfaxing headlights."

I felt like one. "He shouldn't have kissed me."

Max grinned. "Did you kiss him back?"

His lips. Mine. "I don't know!" I bit out.

Max gave me her most innocent look. "Would you like me to pull up the footage?"

I'd kissed him back. Grayson Hawthorne had kissed me, and

I'd kissed him back. I thought about the night before in the hedge maze. The way he'd corrected my form. How close we'd been standing.

"What am I doing?" I asked Max, feeling like I was in a maze now. "Jameson and I are..."

"What?" Max probed.

I shook my head. "I don't know." I knew what Jameson and I were supposed to be: adrenaline and attraction and the thrill of the moment. No strings attached. No messy emotions.

So why did I feel like I'd betrayed him?

"Close your eyes," Max advised me, closing her own. "Picture yourself standing on a cliff overlooking the ocean. The wind is whipping in your hair. The sun is setting. You long, body and soul, for one thing. One person. You hear footsteps behind you. You turn." Max opened her eyes. "Who's there?"

The problem with Max's question was that it assumed I was capable of longing, body and soul, for anything. Anyone. When I pictured myself on that cliffside, I pictured myself alone.

Late into the night, long after Max had retired to her room, I pulled up news searches to see what people were saying about that disastrous interview. Most headlines were calling Toby "the lost heir." Skye was already giving interviews.

Apparently her NDA didn't cover *this*.

In the comments section of nearly every article, there was speculation that I'd slept with Grayson to get him on my side. Some people were claiming that he wasn't the only Hawthorne I'd slept with. It shouldn't have mattered that strangers were calling me a *slut*—or worse—but it did.

The first time I'd ever heard that word, another kid in elementary school had used it to describe my mom. I couldn't ever remember her even dating *anyone*, but I existed, and she'd never been married, and for some people that was enough.

I walked over to my closet and pulled out the bag with the postcards—the ones my mom had given me. *Hawaii. New Zealand. Machu Picchu. Tokyo. Bali.* I flipped through them as a reminder of who I was, who she'd been. This was what we'd daydreamed about—not being swept off our feet.

Not some kind of epic seaside love.

I wasn't sure how long I'd been sitting there when I heard a noise. *Footfalls.* My head whipped up. The last I'd checked, Oren was stationed outside my room. He'd warned me that this news getting out could put me in danger.

A voice spoke, on the other side of the fireplace. "It's me, Heiress."

Jameson. That should have been a relief. Knowing it was him, I should have felt safer. But somehow, as I locked my hand around the candlestick on the mantel, the last thing I felt was safe.

I triggered the passage. "I take it you saw the interview?"

Jameson stepped into my room. "Not your best showing."

I waited for him to say something about that kiss. "Jameson, I didn't—"

He held a finger up to my lips. He never actually touched me, but my lips burned anyway.

"If *yes* is *no*," he said, his eyes on mine, "and *once* is *never*, then how many sides does a triangle have?"

That was a riddle he'd thrown out at me, the first day we'd met. At the time, I'd solved it by converting everything to a number. If you coded *yes*—or the presence of something—as a one, and *no*— or the absence of that thing—as a zero, then the first two parts of the riddle were redundant. *If one equals zero, how many sides does a triangle have?*

253

"Two," I said now, just as I had then, but this time I couldn't help wondering if Jameson was talking about a different kind of triangle—about him and Grayson and me.

"A girl named Elle finds a card on her doorstep. The front of the envelope says *To*, the back says *Elle*. Between them, inside the envelope, she finds two identical letters, then spends the rest of the day underground. Why?"

I wanted to tell him to stop playing games, but I couldn't. He'd thrown out a riddle. I had to solve it. "The front of the card says *To*, the back says *Elle*." I thought as I spoke. "She spends the whole day underground."

There was a gleam in Jameson's eyes, one that reminded me of the time *we* had spent underground. I could practically see him, torch-lit and pacing. And just like that, I saw the method in Jameson's particular brand of madness. "The two letters inside the envelope were *N*," I said softly.

There were probably a thousand adjectives to describe Jameson Hawthorne's smile, but the one that felt truest to me was *devastating*. Jameson Winchester Hawthorne had a devastating smile.

I kept going. "The front of the envelope said 'to'—spelled *t-u*," I continued, resisting the urge to step forward. "The back said 'Elle,' spelled—"

"*E-l*," Jameson finished my sentence. Then *he* took a step forward. "Two *n*'s make *tunnel*, which is why she spent the day underground. You win, Heiress."

We were standing too close now, and a warning siren went off in the back of my head, because if Jameson had seen Grayson kiss me on air, if he was here now, moving toward me—then what were the chances that this wasn't about me?

What were the chances that I was just another prize to be won? Territory to be marked.

"Why are you here?" I asked Jameson, even though I knew the answer, had just *thought* the answer.

"I'm here," he said with another devastating smile, "because I'd be willing to wager five dollars that you aren't checking the messages on your phone."

He was right. "I turned it off," I replied. "I'm thinking of chucking it out that window."

"I'll bet you another five dollars that you can't hit the statue in the courtyard."

"Make it ten," I told him, "and you have a deal."

"Sadly," he replied, "if you did throw your phone out the window, you wouldn't get the message from Libby and Nash."

I stared at him. "Libby and Nash—"

"They found something," Jameson told me. "And they're on their way home."

CHAPTER 66

I woke at dawn the next morning and found Oren standing directly outside my door. "Have you been out here all night?" I asked him.

He gave me a look. "What do you think?"

He'd warned me that if the news about Toby got out, it would be a security liability. I had no idea *how* the news had gotten out, but here we were.

"Right," I said.

"Consider yourself on a six-foot leash," Oren told me. "You're not leaving my side until this dies down. *If* it dies down."

I winced. "How bad is it?"

Oren's reply was matter-of-fact. "I have Carlos and Heinrich posted at the entrance to your wing. They've already had to turn away Zara, Constantine, and both Laughlins, in some cases forcibly. And that's not even touching what Skye tried at the gates, in full view of the paparazzi."

"How many paparazzi?" I asked tentatively.

"Double what we've seen before."

"How is that even possible?" I'd already been front-page news before last night's interview had aired.

"If there's one thing the world loves more than an accidental heiress," Oren replied, "it's a lost heir." He very deliberately did not say, *I told you so*, but I knew he was thinking it.

"I am sorry about this," I said.

"So am I."

"What do *you* have to be sorry for?" I asked flippantly.

Oren's answer wasn't flippant at all. "When I said that I would be within six feet of you at all times, I meant me, personally. I never should have delegated that responsibility, under any circumstance."

"You're human," I said. "You have to sleep." He didn't reply, and I crossed my arms over my chest. "Where's Eli?"

"Eli has been removed from the premises."

"Why?" I demanded, but my brain was already whirring. Oren had apologized to me. He blamed himself for allowing someone else in on my immediate protection detail, and that someone else had been barred from Hawthorne House.

Eli had been the one guarding me when I'd gone to talk to Mrs. Laughlin about Toby.

"He leaked the pictures." I answered my own question. Eli had been on my protection detail for over a week. He'd been in a position to overhear...a lot.

"Eli isn't as good at hiding his digital footprint as my man is at uncovering digital ghosts," Oren told me, his voice like steel. "He leaked the photos. In all likelihood, he's also the one who's responsible for the heart and the snake."

I stared at Oren. "Why?"

"I assigned him to your protection detail at school. He obviously wanted that extended to the estate. I trusted Eli. That trust was clearly misplaced. For whatever reason—possibly a payout from the press—he wanted to be closer to you. I didn't see it. I should have."

I'd never felt unsafe around Eli. He hadn't harmed me, and he could have, if that had been his goal. *For whatever reason*, I replayed Oren's words in my head. *Possibly a payout from the press.*

I thought of Max's ex-boyfriend, who'd tried to access her phone, so he could sell our texts. About my "father" and Skye selling their stories. About the payout that Alisa had arranged, back at the beginning, to have Libby's mother sign an NDA.

It was starting to sink in that for the rest of my life, the people I met, the people I became close to—there would always be a chance that they saw me as a payout.

"This is the second time that my error in judgment has cost you dearly," Oren said stiffly. "If you feel the need to hire new security, I'm sure Alisa could—"

"No!" I said. If Alisa hired someone, that person's loyalty would be to her. Whatever mistakes Oren had made, I believed that his allegiance was to me. He'd do whatever he could to protect me, because Tobias Hawthorne had asked him to.

"Yes?" Oren said curtly. It took me a second to realize that he wasn't talking to me. He was wearing an earpiece and talking to one of his men. *How many of them can we trust? How many of them would sell me out for the right payout?*

"Let them through," Oren ordered, and then he turned back to me. "Your sister and Nash have arrived at the gates."

CHAPTER 67

I waited for Libby and Nash in Tobias Hawthorne's study and requested that security allow Grayson, Jameson, and Xander to come back. I texted the boys to meet me, then waited, alone but for Oren, who stood no more than six feet away. I was jittery and on edge. *Why did it take Libby so long to text me back? What did they find in Cartago?*

"Avery, get behind me." Oren stepped forward, drawing his gun. I had no idea why until I followed his line of vision to the display case on the back wall, the one that housed shelves and shelves of Hawthorne trophies. The wall was moving, rotating toward us.

I moved behind Oren. He took a step forward and called out to the person behind the wall. "Identify yourself. I have a gun."

"So do I." Zara Hawthorne-Calligaris stepped into the room, looking like she was headed to some kind of country club brunch. She was wearing a sweater-set, slacks, and classic, neutral flats.

She was holding a gun.

"Put it down." Oren trained his gun on Zara.

Her own weapon held steady, Zara gave Oren her most unimpressed look. "I think we all know that I'm the least murderous

Hawthorne of my generation," she said, her voice high and clear, "so I will happily lower my weapon once you lower yours, John."

I forgot, most of the time, that Oren had a first name.

"Don't do this," Oren told her. "I don't want to shoot you, Zara, but make no mistake that I will. Put your gun down, and we can talk."

Zara didn't waffle. "You know me, John. Intimately." Her tone never changed, but there was no mistaking what she meant by that. "Do you really believe that I'm capable of harming a child?"

The "child" in question was clearly me, but that barely even registered. My heart was pounding so hard that I felt like it might bruise my rib cage, but I still managed to speak. "Intimately?" I asked Oren.

"Not since my father's death, I assure you," Zara told me. "John has always been quite clear on where his priorities lie. First with my father, and then with you."

Twenty years ago, when Tobias Hawthorne had left Zara his wedding ring, he'd been making a point about her infidelity. Now she was married to a different man, but the text in Tobias Hawthorne's will had remained the same.

She was having another affair. With Oren.

"You shouldn't be here, Zara," Oren said, his gun's aim never wavering.

"Shouldn't I?" she asked. After a moment longer, she lowered the gun, placing it on the desk. "Had your men allowed me entrance in a more traditional fashion, I would not have had to sneak in like a thief, and were I certain you would not have me escorted out, I would have no need of a firearm now. But here are. However, as a show of good will that *none* of you deserve, so long as no one attempts to remove me, my gun will stay right where it is, on that desk."

After a long moment, Oren lowered his own weapon and Zara

turned toward me. "Young lady, you will tell me what that nonsense on the news last night was. *Now.*" Toby was her brother. I could only begin to imagine what her reaction had been to what she had heard.

"Talk," Zara told me. "You owe me that much, at least."

All things considered, I probably did, but before I could say a word, a voice spoke up from the doorway. "Wouldn't you rather hear it from us, Aunt Z?"

All three of us turned to face Jameson. Grayson and Xander stood to his sides. Thus far, Zara had managed to keep her expression schooled into a mix of disdain and calm, but the moment she saw her nephews, that mask wavered.

It was the first time since I'd stepped through the doors of Hawthorne House that it occurred to me that she loved them.

"Please," Zara said quietly. "Boys. Just tell me about Toby."

And so they did, taking turns, working their way through the entire story with brutal efficiency. When Grayson told her that Toby was adopted, she drew in a sharp breath but said nothing. She didn't react again until Xander told her what Rebecca had told him.

"The Laughlins' daughter...," Zara trailed off. "She left for college when I was still in elementary school, and she never came back, not until Emily was born, years later."

I wondered if Zara was imagining, the way I had, how painful this must have been for Rebecca's mother. I wondered if she was questioning, the way I had, what could have led the Laughlins and her own parents to be so cruel.

"It's so easy," Zara murmured, "for all the wrong people to have children."

Silence hit the room like a semitruck.

Zara was the first to overcome it. "Go on," she told the boys. "Out with the rest of it. In this family, there's always a *rest of it.*"

There was only a little more. Zara already knew about the picture that her father had left for Skye at True North. That left only the fact that, along with that picture, he'd left a blank page of paper, and the fact that the numbers inside her parents' wedding rings had pointed us to Cartago, where Libby and Nash had found *something*.

"And what, pray tell, did you find?" Zara asked, and I realized that Libby and Nash had arrived.

Without even meaning to, I took a step toward them. This was it. Everything had been building to this. I felt like I was free-falling at a thousand miles an hour.

"We found my father," Nash said. "And this." He held up a small vial filled with purple powder.

"Your father?" I repeated. *"Jake Nash?"* I thought about the picture of Zara, Skye, and the messy-haired guy.

Nash nodded to Zara. "He asked about you."

Raw vulnerability flashed across Zara's features.

"I reckon you loved him," Nash said quietly.

Zara shook her head. "You don't understand."

"You loved him," Nash repeated. "Skye went after him, and I was the result." I saw a muscle in Nash's throat tighten. "Even then," he said quietly, "you didn't hate me."

Zara shook her head. "How could I? It was easy enough to stay away when you were a baby. I got married. I was starting a life of my own. But then you were a little boy. A wonderful little boy, and the newness of it all had worn off for Skye, and you were so lonely because she was never there."

"But you were," Nash replied. "For a time. Memory's a bit hazy, but before Toby died, you used to take care of me."

"I found Jake," Zara said quietly. "For you."

Slowly, the gears in my brain started turning. At the time that Tobias Hawthorne had first rewritten his will—right after Toby had "died"—Zara had been having an affair. Tobias Hawthorne had been aware of it.

"You and Nash's father?" I said.

"I brought Jake pictures of his son," Zara replied crisply. "I was working on convincing him to go against my father, to be a part of Nash's life, but then he disappeared for parts unknown. Cartago, apparently, at what I can only assume was my father's behest."

"He's been the caretaker at the Cartago property ever since," Nash confirmed. "The old man gave him strict instructions that if you ever came to call, he was to give you this." Nash nodded again to the vial in his hands. "Took a bit for Libby and me to persuade him to give it to us."

I looked at the powder in the vial. This was what we needed to decode Skye's message. *This is it.* Twenty years ago, Tobias Hawthorne had woven a puzzle to set his daughters on the trail of the truth. That trail had led to a picture from before their relationship had splintered—and to Jake Nash, over whom they'd apparently fought.

"I have the note from True North," Xander said. "I think we all know what we're supposed to do with that powder."

"You Hawthornes and your invisible ink," I said, shaking my head. "Will we need anything except the powder?"

"A makeup brush," Zara answered immediately. Then the boys chimed in, all four of them in unison: "And a heat source."

CHAPTER 68

The blank page was unfolded and laid out. The powder was poured onto the page; the brush dusted it over the surface of the letter. And it *was* a letter. That much became clear the moment the heat source—a nearby lamp bulb—was applied.

Words appeared on the page in tiny, even scrawl—Tobias Hawthorne's. All I saw before Zara snatched the letter up was the salutation: *Dearest Zara, Dearest Skye.* Zara stalked to the corner of the room. As she read, her chest rose and fell with heavy breaths. At some point, tears overflowed and began carving paths down her face. Finally, she let the letter go. It dropped from her hand, floating gently toward the ground.

The boys were all frozen in place, like they'd never seen their aunt shed a single tear before now. Slowly, I walked forward. Zara didn't tell me to stop, so I stooped to pick up the letter, and I read.

Dearest Zara, Dearest Skye,

If you are reading this, then I am dead. I cannot express how sorry I am to leave you in this way—or how necessary I believe what I have done for you truly is. Yes, <u>for</u> you, not to you.

If you are reading this, my daughters, then you have set aside your differences long enough to follow the trail I left you. If this has happened, then everything I have done has served at least one purpose. And perhaps, my dears, you are now ready for the other.

As you might have gathered, depending on how closely you examined the charities to which I left my fortune, your brother did not perish on Hawthorne Island. Of that I am certain. He was, as far as I have been able to piece together, pulled from the ocean, severely burned, by a local fisherman. It has taken me years to piece together even this much. I have written and rewritten this letter to you countless times as my investigation into your brother's disappearance has evolved.

I have never found him. I came close once but found something else instead. I can only conclude that Toby does not want to be found. Whatever happened on the island, he has been running from it for half his life.

Or perhaps, he has been running from me.

I have made mistakes with all of you. Zara, I asked too much of you at times and gave you too little of my approval at others; Skye, of you I never asked enough. I treated both of you differently because you were female.

I hurt Toby worst of all.

I won't make the same mistakes with the next generation. I will push them, all in equal measure. They'll learn to put each other first. I will do for them everything I should have done for you, including this: Not one of you will see my fortune. There are things I have done that I am not proud of, legacies that you should not have to bear.

Know that I love you, both of you. Find your brother. Perhaps, once I am gone, he will finally stop running. Below,

you will find a list of locations to which I have traced his
whereabouts these past twelve years. In a safe-deposit box at
Montgomery National Bank, number 21666, you will find a
police report about the incident on Hawthorne Island, as well
as extensive files put together by my investigators over the years.

You'll find the key to the safe-deposit box in my toolbox.
There is a false bottom. Be brave, my dears. Be strong. Be true.

Yours sincerely,
Father

I looked up from the letter, and the boys came to me—Grayson, Jameson, and Xander. Nash, Libby, and Oren stayed where they stood. Zara sank to her knees behind me.

As the boys read the letter, I processed its contents. We had confirmation now that Tobias Hawthorne had known that his son was alive, that he had been searching for him, and that, just as Sheffield Grayson had claimed, the old man had buried a police report about what had happened on the island. There might be more details in the safe-deposit box, once we found the key.

"The toolbox," I said suddenly. I turned toward Oren. "Tobias Hawthorne left you his toolbox."

That had been a part of the updated will. Had the old man realized that Oren was sleeping with Zara? Was that why he'd made him a part of this? Tobias Hawthorne had written the phrase *these past twelve years* in the letter, suggesting that it hadn't been updated recently. *Eight years. He wrote this eight years ago.*

When Tobias Hawthorne had updated his will the year before, leaving me everything, he'd laid a new trail to follow. A new game. A new attempt at mending family bonds that had been torn asunder.

But he'd included the same words to Zara and Skye—the same clues.

Had he continued to add information to the safe-deposit box over the last eight years?

"What do you think he meant," Grayson said slowly, "about legacies we shouldn't have to bear?"

"I care less about that," Jameson replied, "than about the list at the bottom. What do you make of it, Heiress?"

Coming to stand between Jameson and Grayson should have been awkward. It should have been unbearable—but in this moment, it wasn't.

Slowly, I looked back down at the letter, at the list. There were dozens of locations listed, scattered all over the world, like Toby had never stayed in one place for long. But one by one, certain locations jumped out at me. *Waialua, Oahu. Waitomo, New Zealand. Cuzco, Peru. Tokyo, Japan. Bali, Indonesia.*

I literally stopped breathing.

"Heiress?" Jameson said.

Grayson stepped toward me. "Avery?"

Oahu was one of the islands of Hawaii. Cuzco, Peru, was the nearest city to Machu Picchu. My eyes roved back over the list. *Hawaii. New Zealand. Machu Picchu. Tokyo. Bali.* I stared at the page.

"Hawaii," I said out loud, my voice shaking. "New Zealand. Machu Picchu. Tokyo. Bali."

"For a guy on the run," Xander commented, "he sure made his way around."

I shook my head. Xander didn't see what I was seeing. He couldn't. "Hawaii, New Zealand, Machu Picchu, Tokyo, Bali—I know this list."

There were more. At least five or six that I recognized. Five or six places that I had imagined going. Places that I had held in my hand.

"My mother's postcards," I whispered, and took off running. Oren bolted after me, and the others weren't far behind.

I made it to my room in a matter of seconds, to my closet in less than that, and soon I was holding the postcards in my hand. There was nothing written on the back, no postage. I'd never questioned where my mother had gotten them.

Or from whom.

I looked up at Jameson and Grayson, Xander and Nash.

"You Hawthornes," I whispered hoarsely, "and your invisible ink."

CHAPTER 69

A black light revealed writing on the postcards, the same way it had on Toby's walls. *The same handwriting.* Toby had written these words. The answers we were looking for—there was a chance that they were all *here*, but it took everything in me just to read the salutation, the same on every postcard.

"Dear Hannah," I read, *"the same backward as forward."*

Hannah. I thought about the tabloid's accusations that my mom was living under a fake identity. I'd spent my whole life thinking she was Sarah.

The words on the postcards blurred in front of me. *Tears. In my eyes.* My thoughts were detached, like this was all happening to someone else. The room around me was still filled with the buzzing electricity of the moment, of what I'd just discovered, but all I could think was that my mom's name was *Hannah*.

I have a secret.... How many times had we played? How many chances had she had to tell me?

"Well," Xander piped up, "what do they say?"

Everyone else was standing. I was on the floor. Everyone was waiting. *I can't do this.* I couldn't look at Xander—or Jameson or Grayson.

"I'd like to be alone," I said, my voice rough against my throat. I realized now how Zara must have felt reading her father's letter. *"Please."*

There was a beat of silence and then: "Everyone out." The realization that it was Jameson who had spoken those words, Jameson who was willingly stepping back from the puzzle—for me—rocked me to my core.

What was his angle here?

Within moments, the Hawthornes were gone. Oren was a respectful six feet away. And Libby knelt beside me.

I stole a glance at her, and she squeezed my hand. "Did I ever tell you about my ninth birthday?" Libby asked.

Through a fog, I managed to shake my head.

"You were about two then. My mom hated Sarah, but sometimes she'd let her babysit. Mom always said it didn't count as charity if *that bitch* did it, because if it weren't for Sarah and for you, maybe Ricky would have come back to us. She said your mom owed her, and your mom acted like she did so she could spend time with me. So I could spend time with you."

I didn't remember anything like that. Libby and I had barely seen each other growing up—but at two, I wouldn't have remembered much.

"My mom dumped me at your place for almost a week. And it was the best week of my life, Ave. Your mom baked me cupcakes on my birthday, and she had all these cheap Mardi Gras beads, and we must have been wearing about ten apiece. She got these clip-on hair streaks in a rainbow of neon colors, and we wore them in our hair. She taught you to sing 'Happy Birthday.' My mom didn't even call, but Sarah tucked me in every night, into *her* bed, and she slept on the couch, and you would crawl into bed with me, and your mom would kiss us both. Every night."

The tears in my eyes were falling now.

"And when my mom came back and she saw how happy I was—she never let me come over to your place again." Libby's breath went ragged, but she managed to smile. "My point is that you know who your mom was, Avery. We both do. And she was *wonderful.*"

I closed my eyes. I willed myself to stop crying, because Libby was right. My mom was *wonderful.* And if she'd lied to me or kept too many secrets—maybe she'd had to.

Taking a deep breath, I turned back to the postcards. There were no dates, so it was impossible to tell the order in which they'd been written; no postmarks, so they hadn't ever been mailed. I spread the postcards out on the floor and started with the one on the far left, aiming the black light at it. Slowly, I read it.

I drank up every word.

There were things in that first postcard that I didn't understand—references whose meaning was lost with my mom. But near the end, there was something that caught my eye. *I hope you read the letter I left you that night. I hope that some part of you understood. I hope you go far, far away and never look back, but if you ever need anything, I hope you do exactly what I told you to do in that letter. Go to Jackson. You know what I left there. You know what it's worth.*

"Jackson," I said, my voice coming out wispy. What had Toby left for my mother in Jackson? *Mississippi?* Had that even been on Tobias Hawthorne's list?

Setting the first postcard aside, I kept reading and realized that Toby had never meant to send these messages. He was writing to her, but for himself. The postcards made it clear that he was staying away from her on purpose. The only other thing that was clear was that they were in love. Epic, incomplete-without-the-other, once-in-a-lifetime love.

The kind of love that I'd never believed in.

The next postcard read:

Dear Hannah, the same backward as forward,

Do you remember that time on the beach? When I didn't know if I would ever walk again, and you cursed at me until I did? It sounded like you'd never cursed before in your life, but oh, how you meant it. And when I took that step and swore right back at you, do you remember what you said?

"That's one step," you spat. "What now?"

You were backlit, and the sun was sinking into the horizon, and for the first time in weeks, it felt like my heart had finally remembered how to beat.

What now?

It was hard to read Toby's words without feeling a wealth of emotion. My whole life, my mom had never been involved with anyone but Ricky. I'd never seen anyone adore her the way she deserved to be adored. It took me longer to focus on the implications of the words. Toby had been injured—badly enough that he wasn't sure if he would walk again, and my mother had *cursed* at him?

I thought about what the old man had said in his letter to Zara and Skye, about a fisherman pulling Toby from the water. How badly had he been injured? And where had my mother come in?

My mind spinning, I read on. Another postcard and then another, and I realized that, yes, my mom had been there, in Rockaway Watch, in the wake of the fire.

Dear Hannah, the same backward as forward,

Last night, I dreamed of drowning, and I woke up with your name on my lips. You were so quiet in those early days. Do you remember that? When you couldn't stand to look at me.

Wouldn't speak to me. You hated me. I felt it, and I was awful
to you. I didn't know who I was or what I'd done. I remembered
nothing of my life or the island. But still, I was horrid.
Withdrawal was a beast, but I was worse. And you were there,
and I know now that I didn't deserve a damn thing from you.
But you changed my bandages. You held me down. You touched
me, more gently than I could ever deserve.

Knowing what I know now, I don't know how you did it.
I should have drowned. I should have burned. My lips should
never have touched yours, but for the rest of my life, Hannah,
O Hannah—I will feel every kiss. Feel your touch when I was
halfway dead and wholly rotten and you loved me despite myself.

"He lost his memory." I looked up at Libby. "Toby. Jameson and
I thought that he might have had amnesia—there was a hint to that
in Tobias Hawthorne's old will. But this letter confirms it. When he
met my mom, he was hurt and in withdrawal—probably from some
kind of drug—and he didn't know who he was."

Or what he'd done. I thought about the fire. About Hawthorne
Island and the three people who hadn't survived it. Had my mom
been from Rockaway Watch? Or another nearby town?

More postcards, more messages. One after the other, without
answers.

Dear Hannah, the same backward as forward,

Ever since the island, I'm terrified of water, but I keep
forcing myself onto ships. I know that you would tell me that I
don't need to, but I do. Fear is good for me. I remember all too
well what it was like when I had none.

If I had met you then, would your touch have broken
through to me? Would you have hated me until you loved me?

*If we'd met in a different time, under different circumstances,
would I still dream of you every night—and wonder if you
dream of me?*

*I should let you go. When everything came crashing back,
when I realized what you'd been hiding from me, I promised
that I would. Promised myself. Promised you.*

Promised Kaylie.

The name stopped me dead in my tracks. *Kaylie Rooney.* The
local who'd died on Hawthorne Island. The girl on whom Tobias
Hawthorne had pinned much of the blame in the press. I scoured
the rest of the postcards, all of them, looking for something that
would tell me what exactly to make of Toby's words, and finally—
finally—I found it, near the end of a message that started off with
a much dreamier tone.

*I know that I will never see you again, Hannah. That I
don't deserve to. I know that you will never read a word I write,
and because you will never read this, I know that I can say what
you forbade me to say long ago.*

I'm sorry.

*I'm sorry, Hannah, O Hannah. I'm sorry for leaving in the
dead of night. I'm sorry for letting you love me even a fraction
as much as I will, to the day I die, love you. I'm sorry for what I
did. For the fire.*

And I will never stop being sorry about your sister.

CHAPTER 70

Sister. That word echoed in my mind over and over again. *Sister. Sister. Sister.* "Toby told my mom—told *Hannah*—that he was sorry about her sister." Thoughts crashed into one another in my brain, like a ten-car pileup, the cacophony deafening. "And in another postcard, he mentioned Kaylie. Kaylie Rooney—she's the girl who died in the fire on Hawthorne Island. Sometime after that, my mom helped nurse Toby back to life. He didn't remember what had happened, but he said that she hated him. She must have known."

"Known what?" Libby asked, reminding me that I wasn't just talking to myself.

I thought about the fire, the buried police report, Sheffield Grayson saying that Toby had purchased accelerant. "That Toby was responsible for her sister's death."

The next thing I knew, I had my laptop out, and I was doing yet another internet search on Kaylie Rooney. At first I didn't find anything I hadn't already seen, but then I started adding search terms. I tried *sister* and got nothing. I tried *family*, and I found the one and only interview with a member of the Rooney family. It wasn't much of an interview. All the reporter had gotten out of Kaylie's

275

mother was, and I quote, *My Kaylie was a good girl, and those rich bastards killed her.* But there was also a picture. A photograph of... *my grandmother?* I tried to wrap my mind around that possibility. Then I heard the door open behind me.

Max poked her head into the room. "I come in peace." She squeezed by the door and strolled past Oren. "For the record, I'm armed only with sarcasm." Max ended her stroll right next to me and hopped up on the desk. "What are we doing?"

"Looking at a picture of my grandmother." Saying the words made them feel just a little bit more real. "My mom's mom. Maybe."

Max stared at the picture. "Not maybe," she said. "She even *looks* like your mom."

The woman in the picture was scowling. I'd never seen my mom scowl. She had her hair pulled into a tight bun, and my mom always wore hers loose. Twenty years ago, this woman had looked decades older than my mom had when she died.

But still, Max was right. Their features were the same.

"How has no one made this connection?" Max asked incredulously. "With all the rumors about your mom, and people trying to find a connection between you and the Hawthornes, no one thought to look at the family of a girl they pretty much murdered? And what about your mom's relatives and the people who knew her growing up? Someone must have recognized her, once you made the news. Why hasn't anyone tipped off the press?"

I thought about Eli, selling me out for a payday. What kind of town was Rockaway Watch that no one would have done the same?

"I don't know," I told Max. "But I do know that whatever Tobias Hawthorne left in that safe-deposit box—that police report, his investigators' files—I want to see it all. I *need* to see it. Now."

CHAPTER 71

Oren retrieved the key from his toolbox, but he didn't give it to me. He gave it to Zara, then told me to get ready for school.

"Have you lost your mind?" I asked him. "I'm not going to school."

"It's the safest place for you right now," Oren said. "Alisa will agree with me."

"Alisa's doing damage control from the interview," I retorted. "I'm sure the last thing she wants is me out in public. No one would question why I might want to stay home."

"Country Day isn't public," Oren told me, and a few seconds later, he had Alisa on speakerphone, and she was echoing what he had said: I was to put on my private school uniform, put on my best face, and pretend that nothing had happened.

If we treated this like a crisis, it would be seen as a crisis.

Since I'd promised to keep Alisa in the loop, I told her everything, and she still didn't change her mind. "Act normal," she told me.

I hadn't been *normal* in weeks. But less than an hour later, I was dressed in a pleated skirt, a white dress shirt, and a burgundy blazer, with my hair tousled just so and my makeup minimal, except for the eyes. Preppy with an edge, for all the world to see—or at least all the denizens of Heights Country Day School.

I felt like I had on my very first day. No one looked directly at me, but the way they were not-looking at me felt far more conspicuous. Jameson and Xander slipped out of the car after me, and each of them took one of my sides. At least this time, it was me *and* the Hawthornes against the world.

I made it through the day bit by bit, and by lunch, I was done. Done with the stares. Done pretending everything was normal. Done trying to put on a happy face. I was hiding—or making an attempt at it—in the archive when Jameson found me. "You look like someone who needs a distraction," he told me.

A few feet away, Oren crossed his arms over his chest. "No."

Jameson shot my bodyguard his most innocent look.

"I know you," Oren replied. "I know your *distractions*. You're not taking her skydiving. Or parasailing off the coast. No racetracks. No motorcycles. No ax throwing—"

"Ax throwing?" I looked at Jameson, intrigued.

He turned back to Oren. "What are your feelings on roofs?"

Ten minutes later, Jameson and I were back on top of the Art Center. He rolled out the turf and teed up a ball.

"Keep away from the edge," Oren told me, and then he turned deliberately away from us both.

I waited for Jameson to ask me about the postcards. I waited for him to flirt with me, to touch me, to Jameson Hawthorne the answer out of me. But all he did was hand me a club.

I lined up the shot. Part of me wanted him to come stand behind me, wanted his arms to wrap around mine. *Jameson on the roof. Grayson in the maze.* My mind was a mess. I was a mess.

I dropped the club.

"My mother was Kaylie Rooney's sister," I said. And so it began. It was hard to put into words everything I'd learned, but I managed. The more I said, the easier it was to see Jameson thinking.

The more he thought, the closer to me he came.

"What do you think Toby left in Jackson that's worth so much?" he asked. "And where in Jackson?" Jameson studied me like my face held the answers. "How long did Toby's amnesia last? Why stay 'dead' once his memory returned?"

"Guilt." I almost choked on the word, though I couldn't have explained why. "Toby loathed himself almost as much as he loved my mom."

That was the first time I'd said that last bit out loud. *Toby Hawthorne loved my mother. She loved him.* It had been an epic, seaside kind of love. Literally. Just knowing that made me feel like I'd been lying to myself every time I'd pretended that I didn't have feelings, that things didn't have to be messy.

That I could have what I wanted without ever really longing for anything, body and soul.

"Heiress?" There was a question in Jameson's deep green eyes. I wasn't sure what he was asking, what he wanted from me.

What I wanted from him.

"Knock, knock!" Xander stuck his head out the door to the roof. "I just happened to have my ear pressed to this door. I might have overheard some things, and I have a suggestion!"

Jameson looked like he might actually throttle his brother. I glanced at Oren, who was still pointedly ignoring all three of us. I could practically hear him thinking, *Not my job.*

"Call her!" Xander tossed something at me. It wasn't until I'd caught it that I realized it was his phone—and a number had already been plugged in.

"Call who?" Jameson asked, his eyes narrowing.

"Your grandmother," Xander told me. "Like I said, I inadvertently overheard some things while my ear was casually pressed to this steel door. Kaylie Rooney's mother is your grandmother, Avery. That's a piece of the puzzle we've never had before, and *that*"—he nodded to the phone—"is her phone number."

"You don't have to call," Jameson told me, which made about as much sense as the fact that he'd willingly stepped back from the postcards.

"Yes." I swallowed. "I do." My heart jumped into my throat just thinking about it, but I hit the Call button. The line rang and rang and rang, with no one picking up and no voicemail. I couldn't bring myself to hang up, so I just let it ring, and then finally someone answered. All I got out was a hello and my name before the person who'd answered cut me off.

"I know who you are." At first I thought the gravelly voice belonged to a man, but as the words kept coming, I realized that the speaker was a woman. "If my worthless daughter had taught you the first damn thing about this family, you wouldn't dare have dialed my number."

I wasn't sure what I'd been expecting. My mom had always told me that she didn't have a family. But still, each word her mother— my *grandmother*—spoke cut into me.

"If that little bitch hadn't run, I would have put a bullet in her myself. You think I want a dime of your blood money, girl? You think you're family? You hang up that phone. You forget my name. And if you're *lucky*, I'll make sure this family—this whole town— forgets yours."

The sound on the other end of the line cut out. I stood there, the phone still pressed to my ear, frozen.

"You okay there, buddy?" Xander asked.

I couldn't reply. I couldn't say anything. *You think I want a dime of your blood money, girl? You think you're family?*

I wasn't even sure if I was breathing.

If that little bitch hadn't run—

Jameson came up beside me. He put his hands on my shoulders. For a second, I thought he might force my eyes to his, but he didn't. He walked me over to the edge of the roof. The very edge, close enough that Oren called out, but in response, all Jameson did was spread my arms to each side, until his and mine were both held out in a *T*. "Close your eyes," he whispered. "Breathe."

If that little bitch hadn't run—

I closed my eyes. I breathed. I felt him breathing. The wind picked up. And I told them everything.

CHAPTER 72

By the time the SUV passed the gates of Hawthorne House that afternoon, I was still shaken. To my surprise, Zara met Jameson, Xander, and me in the foyer. For the first time since I'd met Tobias Hawthorne's firstborn, she looked less than perfect. Her eyes were puffy. Stray hairs were stuck to her forehead. She was holding a folder. It was only an inch or so thick, but even that was enough to stop me in my tracks.

"That's what was in the safe-deposit box?" Xander asked.

"Do you want an overview?" Zara replied crisply. "Or would you prefer to read it for yourself?"

"Both," Jameson said. First, we'd take the big picture, and then we'd comb through the actual materials, looking for subtle hints, clues, anything Zara might have missed.

Where's Grayson? The question came into my mind unbidden. Some part of me had expected him to be here, waiting. Even though he'd barely spoken to me since the interview. Even though he'd barely been able to look at me.

"Overview?" I asked Zara, forcing myself to focus.

Zara gave a slight dip of her chin—assent. "Toby had been in and out of rehab for a year or two at the time of his disappearance. He was obviously angry, though at the time I didn't know why. From what my father was able to piece together, Toby met two other boys at rehab. They all went on a road trip together that summer. It very much appears that the boys partied—and slept—their way across the country. One young woman in particular, a waitress at a bar where the boys stopped, was quite informative when my father's investigator tracked her down. She told the investigator exactly what Toby had been snorting, and exactly what he had said the morning after they had intercourse."

"What did he say?" Xander asked.

Zara's tone never wavered. "He told her that he was going to burn it all down."

I stared at Zara for a moment, then shifted my gaze to Jameson. He'd been there when Sheffield Grayson had claimed that Toby was responsible for the fire. Even after reading the postcards and seeing the kind of guilt Toby carried, some part of me had still thought the fire was an accident, that Toby and his friends were drunk or high, and things got out of control.

"Did Toby happen to specify *what* he was going to burn down?" Jameson asked.

"No." Zara kept her reply curt. "But right before they got to Rockaway Watch, he purchased a great deal of accelerant."

He set the fire. He killed them all. "Was that in the police report?" I managed to ask. "What Toby said about burning it all down—did the police know?"

"No," Zara replied. "The woman Toby said that to—she had no idea who he was. Even when our private investigators tracked her down, she remained entirely in the dark. The police never found her. They never had motive. But they knew about the accelerant.

From what the arson investigators were able to tell, the house on Hawthorne Island had been thoroughly soaked. The gas had been turned on."

I felt my hand pressing to my mouth. A sound escaped around my fingers, somewhere between a horrified gasp and a mewl.

"Toby wasn't an idiot." Jameson's expression was sharp. "Unless this was some kind of suicide pact, he would have had a contingency plan to make sure that he and his friends weren't caught in the flames."

Zara closed her eyes tightly. "That's the thing," she whispered. "The house was soaked in accelerant. The gas was turned on—but no one ever lit a match. There was a lightning storm that night. Toby might well have been planning to burn down the house from a safe distance. The others might have helped him. But none of them actually set the fire."

"Lightning," Xander said, horrified. "If the gas was already on, if they'd soaked the floorboards in accelerant..."

I could see it in my mind. Had the house exploded? Had they still been inside, or had the fire spread quickly across the island?

"For months, my father believed that Toby truly had died. He convinced the police to bury the report. It wasn't arson, not technically. At best, it was *attempted* arson."

And they'd never gotten to finish the attempt.

"Why didn't the police just blame it on the lightning?" I asked. I'd read the articles in the press. They hadn't mentioned the weather. The picture they'd painted was one in which a teenage party had gotten out of hand. Three upstanding boys had died— and one not-so-upstanding girl from the wrong side of the tracks.

"The house went up like a fireball," Zara replied evenly. "They could see it from the mainland. It was obvious it wasn't just a lightning strike. And the girl who was there with them, Kaylie Rooney, she'd just gotten out of juvenile detention for *arson*. It was easier to deflect blame toward her than to try to pin it on nature."

"If she was a juvenile," Xander said slowly, "the record would have been sealed."

"The old man unsealed it." Jameson didn't phrase that as a question. "Anything to protect the family name."

I could understand why my mother's mother had called Tobias Hawthorne's fortune blood money. Had he left it to me in part out of guilt?

"I wouldn't feel too sorry for Kaylie Rooney," Zara said coldly. "What happened to her—what happened to all of them—it was a tragedy, of course, but she was far from innocent. From what the investigator was able to piece together, the Rooney family runs just about every drug that comes through Rockaway Watch. They have a reputation for being merciless, and Kaylie was almost certainly already elbow-deep in the family business."

If my worthless daughter had taught you the first damn thing about this family, you wouldn't dare have dialed my number. The conversation I'd had that afternoon came back to me.

If that little bitch hadn't run, I would have put a bullet in her myself.

If what Zara was saying about my mother's family was true, that statement probably wasn't metaphorical.

"What about the fisherman who pulled Toby from the water?" I asked, trying to concentrate on the facts of the case and not think too long or hard about where my mom had come from. "Did the file elaborate on that at all?"

"The storm was severe that night," Zara replied. "Initially, my father believed there were no boats out, but eventually the investigator talked to someone who swore that there was one boat on the water during the storm. Its owner was practically a shut-in. He

285

lives in a shack near an old abandoned lighthouse in Rockaway Watch. The locals steer clear of him. Based on the investigator's discussions with townsfolk, most seem to think he's not quite well in the head. Hence, taking his boat out that night, in the midst of a man-killing storm."

"He finds Toby," I said, thinking out loud. "Pulls him from the water. Brings him home. And no one's the wiser."

"My father believed that Toby had lost his memory, though whether this was the result of an injury or psychological trauma is unclear. Somehow this man, this Jackson Currie, managed to nurse him back to health."

Not just the man, I thought. *My mom was there, too.* She'd helped nurse him back to life.

I was so busy thinking about my mom and reassembling that part of the story in my head that I missed the rest of what Zara had said. The *name* she'd said.

"Jackson," Jameson breathed. "Heiress, the fisherman's name was *Jackson.*"

I froze, just for an instant. *I hope you go far, far away,* Toby had written, *but if you ever need anything, I hope you do exactly what I told you to do in that letter. Go to Jackson. You know what I left there. You know what it's worth.*

Not Jackson, Mississippi.

Jackson Currie. The fisherman who'd pulled Toby from the water.

"What I don't understand," Zara said, "is why Toby was so intent on running once he got his memory back—assuming he got it back. He had to have known that our security could protect him from any threat. The Rooneys may run Rockaway Watch, but it's a small town. They're small people with a small reach, and the legal situation had already been taken care of. Toby could have come home, but he fought it."

He didn't come home, because he didn't think he deserved to. Having read the postcards, I understood Toby. Wasn't that how I would have felt if I'd done what he'd done?

A ringing sound jarred me from that thought. My phone. I looked down. Grayson was calling.

I flashed back to the moment he'd kissed me. I'd kissed him back. Since then we hadn't even managed to look at each other. We hadn't really talked. So why was he calling now?

Where is he? "Hello?" I answered.

"Avery." Grayson lingered on my name, just for a moment.

"Where are you?" I asked. There was a pause at the other end of the line, and then he sent me an invite to switch over to a video chat. I accepted it, and the next thing I saw was his face. Gray eyes, sharp cheekbones, sharper jawline. In the sunlight, his light blond hair looked platinum.

"After some convincing, Max told me about what was written on your postcards," Grayson said. "About your mother. Do you remember when I told you that I was in this? That I would help you?" He turned his phone, and I saw ruins. Charred ruins. Burned trees. "That's what I'm doing."

"You went to Hawthorne Island without us?" Xander was absolutely indignant.

He did this for me. I wasn't sure how I was supposed to feel about that when, if he'd waited a few hours, we could have gone together. This didn't feel like a larger-than-life gesture. It felt like Grayson running away.

Keeping his promise as far away from me as he could.

"Hawthorne Island," Grayson confirmed in response to Xander's accusation. "And Rockaway Watch. I wouldn't call the locals friendly, but I'm optimistic that I'll find our missing piece, whatever that might be."

He was optimistic that *he* would find the answer. Had he even considered dealing me in?

"Rockaway Watch," Xander said slowly.

The town's name echoed in my mind. *Rockaway Watch. My mother's family.* Suddenly, I had much bigger concerns than what Grayson's behavior did or did not mean—and what it did or did not make me feel.

"Grayson." My voice sounded urgent, even to my own ears. "You don't understand. My mother changed her name and left that place because her family is dangerous. I don't know what they know about Toby. I don't know if that's the reason they hated her so much—but they blame the Hawthornes for their daughter's death. You have to get out of there."

Beside me, Oren cursed. Grayson turned the phone back around and those gray eyes locked on mine. "Avery, have I ever given you reason to believe that I'm particularly averse to danger?"

Grayson Hawthorne was arrogant enough to consider himself bulletproof—and honorable enough to see a promise through to its end.

"You have to get out of there," I said again, but the next thing I knew, Jameson was sticking his head over my shoulder, yelling to his brother.

"You're looking for a man named Jackson Currie. He's a recluse, living near an abandoned lighthouse. Talk to him. See what he knows."

Grayson smiled, and that smile cut into me, every bit as much as his kiss. "Got it."

CHAPTER 73

I t was another hour before we heard from Grayson again, and Oren spent a good chunk of that time calling in favors on the West Coast. I wasn't the only one concerned about the safety of a Hawthorne anywhere near the town of Rockaway Watch.

When my phone did ring again, Grayson was less than happy about the security detail that had descended on him.

"Did you find him?" Jameson squeezed in beside me to talk to his brother. "Jackson Currie?"

"He has a very colorful vocabulary," Grayson reported. "And the land near his shack is booby-trapped."

"Father and his investigator ran into similar issues," Zara said behind us. "They never got a word out of the man. Grayson, you should come home. This is a fool's errand. There are other leads that we could follow."

In any other circumstances, I would have asked what those leads were, but all I could think was that Toby had told my mom to go to Jackson if she needed anything. That seemed to suggest that if my mom had shown up, he would have opened the door.

"Can you get close enough to put me on the phone with him?" I asked.

"Assuming no one tries to restrain me..." Grayson glanced pointedly back over his shoulder at what I could only assume was his security detail and then turned back to look straight into the camera—straight at me. "I can try."

———✦———

Jackson Currie's shack really *was* a shack. I would have laid money that he'd built it himself. It wasn't large. There were no windows.

Grayson knocked on what appeared to be a metal door. *Then again, maybe* shack *is the wrong word*, I thought. What Jackson Currie had built was closer to a bunker.

Grayson knocked again, and all he got for his effort was a large rock chucked at him from somewhere up above.

"I don't like this," Oren said stonily.

Neither did I, but we were so close—not just to Toby but to answers. *I have a secret....*

I knew so much now that I hadn't before. Maybe I knew everything. but I couldn't help feeling like this was my chance—maybe my last chance—to know for sure, to know my mom in a way that I'd never known her before.

To understand what she and Toby had.

"See if he'll talk to me," I told Grayson. "Tell him..." My voice caught. "Tell him that Hannah's daughter is on the phone. Hannah Rooney." That was the first time I had said the name my mom had been born with. The name she'd never told me.

The image on the phone screen went blurry for a moment. Grayson must have lowered the phone. I heard him in the background, yelling something.

Talk to me, I willed Jackson Currie from a distance. *Tell me anything and everything you know. About Toby. About my mom. About whatever it is that Toby left with you.*

"I told him." Grayson's face came back into focus. "No reply. I think we—"

I never got to hear the rest of what Grayson thought, because a moment later, I heard the distinct sound of metal on metal. *Dead bolts*, I realized, *being thrown open.*

Grayson turned the camera in time for me to see the metal door creak open. All I saw at first was Jackson Currie's enormous beard—but then I saw his narrowed eyes.

"Where is she?" he grunted.

"Here," I said, my voice verging on a yell. "I'm here. I'm Hannah's daughter."

"No." He spat. "Don't trust phones." And just like that, he slammed the door.

"What does he mean, he doesn't trust phones?" Jameson demanded. "What's not to trust?"

My thoughts were elsewhere. We knew now that Jackson Currie would talk to me. He wouldn't talk to Grayson. He hadn't talked to Tobias Hawthorne's investigators. He was paranoid and pretty much a shut-in. He didn't trust phones.

But he would talk to me—in person.

"I'll call you back," I told Grayson, and then I placed another phone call—to Alisa. "I'm allowed to spend three nights per month away from Hawthorne House. So far, I've only spent one."

CHAPTER 74

Alisa didn't like the idea of my visiting Hawthorne Island. Oren liked it even less. But there was no stopping me now.

"Fine." Oren gave me a look. "I will arrange security for you." His eyes narrowed. "And *only* you."

Beside me, Xander jumped to his feet. "I object!"

"Overruled." Oren's reply was immediate. "We will be flying into a high-threat situation. I want at least an eight-person security team on the ground. We can't afford a single distraction. Avery is the package—the only package—or I will duct-tape all three of you to chairs and call it a day."

All three of us. My eyes found their way to Jameson's. I waited for him to argue with Oren. Jameson Winchester Hawthorne had never sat out a race in his life. He wasn't capable of it. So why wasn't he attempting to negotiate with Oren now?

Jameson noticed something about the way I was looking at him. "What?"

"You're not going to complain about this?" I stared at him.

"Why would I, Heiress?"

Because you play to win. Because Grayson's already there. Because this was our game—yours and mine—before it was anyone else's. I tried to stop myself there. *Because your brother kissed me. Because when you and I kiss, you feel it, the same way I do.*

I wasn't about to say a single word of that out loud. "Fine." I kept my eyes on Jameson's a moment longer, then turned to Oren. "I'll go alone."

—————◆—————

It took a little under four hours to fly from Texas to the Oregon coast. Including travel time to and from the airport on each side, that was closer to five. I was standing on Jackson Currie's doorstep—such as it was—by dusk.

"Are you ready?" Grayson asked beside me, his voice low.

I nodded.

"Your men will have to stay back," Grayson told Oren. "They can set up a perimeter, but I'd bet a very large amount of money that Currie will not open the door if Avery shows up with her own army."

Oren nodded to his men and made some kind of hand signal, and they spread out. If this went as planned, my mother's family would never even know I was here. But if they figured it out, small-time criminals didn't hold a candle to the power of the Hawthornes.

My power, now. I tried to really believe that as I reached forward and knocked on Jackson Currie's door. My first knock was hesitant, but then I banged with my fist.

"I'm here!" I said. "For real this time." No response. "My name's Avery. I'm Hannah's daughter." If I had come all this way and he still wouldn't open the door, I didn't know what I would do. "Toby wrote my mother postcards." I kept yelling. "He said that if she ever needed anything, she should come here. I know you saved Toby's life after the fire. I know my mom helped you. I know that they were in love. I don't know if her family found out, or what happened exactly—"

The door opened. "That family always finds out," Jackson Currie grunted. Over the phone, I hadn't realized just how big he was. He had to have been at least six foot six, and he was built like one of Oren's men.

"Is that why my mom changed her name?" I asked him. "Is that why she ran?"

The fisherman stared at me for a moment, his expression hard as rocks. "You don't look much like Hannah," he grunted. For one terrifying moment, I thought he might slam the door in my face. "Except for the eyes."

With that, he let the door swing the rest of the way inward, and Oren, Grayson, and I followed him inside.

"Just the girl," Jackson Currie growled without ever turning around.

I knew Oren was going to argue. "Please," I told him. "Oren, *please*."

"I'll stay in the doorway." Oren's voice was like steel. "She stays in my sight at all times. You don't come closer than three feet to her."

I expected Jackson Currie to balk at all of that, but instead he nodded. "I like him," he told me, then he issued another order. "The boy stays outside, too."

The boy. As in Grayson. He didn't like stepping back from me, but he did it. I turned for just a moment to watch him go.

"That the way it is?" Currie asked me, like he'd seen something in that moment that I hadn't meant to show.

I turned back to him. "Please, just tell me about my mother."

"Not much to tell," he said. "She used to come check on me now and then. Always nagging at me to go to the hospital over every little scrape. She was in school to be a nurse. Wasn't half-bad at stitches."

She was in nursing school? That felt like such a mundane thing to be learning about my mother.

"She helped you nurse Toby after you pulled him from the water?" I said.

He nodded. "She did. Can't say she particularly enjoyed it, but she was always going on about some oath."

The Hippocratic oath. I dug through my memory and remembered the gist of it. "First do no harm."

"It was the damnedest thing for a Rooney to say," Currie grunted. "But Hannah always was the damnedest Rooney."

The muscles in my throat tightened. "She helped you treat Toby even though she knew who he was. Even though she blamed him for her sister's death."

"You telling this story, or am I?"

I went silent, and after a second or two, my silence was rewarded. "She loved her sister, ya know. Always said Kaylie wasn't like the rest of 'em. Hannah was going to get her out."

My mom couldn't have been more than three or four years older than me when all of this had gone down. Kaylie would have been her younger sister. I wanted to cry. At this point, I wasn't even sure what else to ask, but I pushed on. "How long did Toby stay here after the accident?"

"Three months, give or take. He mostly healed up in that time."

"And they fell in love."

There was a long silence. "Hannah always was the damnedest Rooney."

In other circumstances, it might have been harder for me to understand, but if Toby had been suffering from amnesia, he wouldn't have known what had happened on the island. He wouldn't have known about Kaylie—or who she was to my mother.

And my mom had a big heart. She might have hated him at first, but he was a Hawthorne, and I knew all too well that Hawthorne boys had a way about them.

"What happened after three months?" I asked.

"Kid's memory came back." Jackson shook his head. "They had a big fight that night. He came damn near close to killing himself, but she wouldn't let him. He wanted to turn himself in, but she wouldn't let him do that, either."

"Why not?" I asked. No matter how in love with him she'd been, Toby was responsible for three deaths. He'd planned to set a fire that night, even if he'd never lit a match.

"How long you think the person who killed Kaylie Rooney would last in any jail hereabouts?" Jackson asked me. "Hannah wanted to run away, just the two of them, but the boy said no. He couldn't do that to her."

"Do what to her?" I asked. My mom had ended up running anyway. She'd changed her name. And three years later, there was me.

"Hell if I could make sense of either of 'em," Jackson Currie muttered. "Here." He tossed something at my feet. Behind me, Oren twitched, but he didn't object when I moved forward to pick up the object on the ground. It was wrapped in linen. Unrolling it, I found two things: a letter and a small metal disk, the size of a quarter.

I read the letter. It didn't take me long to realize that it was the one Toby had mentioned in the postcards.

Dear Hannah, the same backward as forward,
    Please don't hate me—or if you do, hate me for the right reasons. Hate me for being angry and selfish and stupid. Hate

me for getting high and deciding that burning the dock wasn't enough—we had to burn the house to really hit my father where it hurt. Hate me for letting the others play the game with me—for treating it like a game. Hate me for being the one who survived.

But don't hate me for leaving.

You can tell me over and over again that I never would have struck the match. You can believe that. On good days, maybe I will, too. But three people are still dead because of me. I can't stay here. I can't stay with you. I don't deserve to. I won't go home, either. I won't let my father pretend this away.

Sooner or later, he'll figure this out. He always does. He'll come for me, Hannah. He'll try to make it all better. And if I let him find me, if I let him wag his silver tongue in my ear, I might start to believe him. I might be tempted to let him wash away my sins, the way that only billions can, so you and I can live happily ever after. But you deserve better than that. Your sister deserved better. And I deserve to fade away.

I won't kill myself. You extracted that promise, and I will keep it. I won't turn myself in. But we can't be together. I can't do that to you. I know you—I know that loving me must hurt you. And I won't hurt you again.

Leave Rockaway Watch, Hannah. Without Kaylie, there's nothing holding you here. Change your name. Start anew. You love fairy tales, I know, but I can't be your happily-ever-after. We can't stay here in our little castle forever. You have to find a new castle. You have to move on. You have to live, for me.

If you ever need anything, go to Jackson. You know what the circle is worth. You know why. You know everything. You might be the only person on this planet who knows the real me.

Hate me, if you can, for all the reasons I deserve it. But don't hate me for leaving while you sleep. I knew you wouldn't let me go, and I cannot bear to say good-bye.

Harry

I looked up from the letter, my ears ringing. "He signed it Harry."

Jackson tilted his head to the side. "That's what I called him 'fore I knew his name. It's what Hannah called him, too."

Something gave inside me. I closed my eyes and let my head fall, just for a moment. I had no idea what had happened between Toby leaving this shack twenty years ago and my mother's death. If he was my father, he had to have found her at some point. They had to have been together again, if only once.

"He found me after she died," I whispered. "He told me his name was Harry."

"She's dead?" Jackson Currie stared at me. "Little Hannah?"

I nodded. "Natural causes." Given the context, that seemed important to clarify. Jackson turned suddenly. A second later, he was rummaging around in the cabinets. He thrust another object at me, coming close enough for our fingertips to brush this time.

"I was supposed to give this to Harry," he grunted. "If he ever came back. Hannah sent them here, year after year. But if she's gone—only seems right to give them to you."

I looked down at the thing he'd just handed me. I was holding another bundle of postcards.

CHAPTER 75

It was one thing to read Toby's love letters to my mother. It was another entirely to read hers to him. She sounded like herself, so much that I could hear her voice with every single word I read.

She loved him. The muscles in my chest tightened. *It hurt to love him, and she loved him anyway.* I breathed—in and out. *He left her, and she loved him anyway.* That string of thoughts cycled through my head on repeat as we drove back to the airstrip where the jets awaited. What my mom and Toby had—it was tragic and messy and all-consuming, and if the postcards made one thing clear, it was that she would have done it all again.

"Are you okay?" Grayson asked beside me, like it was just the two of us in this SUV, like we weren't surrounded by Oren's men. There were two other SUVs, one in front of us and one at our rear. There were four armed men, including Oren, in this car alone.

"No," I told Grayson. "Not really." My entire life, I'd grown up knowing that I was enough for my mom. She hadn't dated. She hadn't wanted or needed a damn thing from Ricky. Her life was full of love. *She* was full of love—but romance? That wasn't something she'd needed. It wasn't something she'd wanted. It wasn't even something she was open to—and now I knew why.

Because she'd never stopped loving Toby.

Close your eyes, I could hear Max telling me. *Picture yourself standing on a cliff overlooking the ocean. The wind is whipping in your hair. The sun is setting. You long, body and soul, for one thing. One person. You hear footsteps behind you. You turn.*

Who's there?

And my answer had been: *no one.*

But after reading even just a couple of my mom's postcards? It was getting harder to ignore Grayson's presence beside me, harder not to think about Jameson. My eyes stung, even though there was zero reason for me to be crying.

I stared through my tears at the postcards my mom had written to Toby and forced myself to keep reading. Soon, the focus of my mom's writing shifted from what they'd had to a different kind of love story. From that point on, every single postcard was about me.

Avery took her first steps today.

Avery's first word is "uh-oh!"

Today, Avery invented a game that combines Candy Land, Chutes and Ladders, and checkers.

On and on it went, up until the postcards stopped. Up until she died.

My hand shook, holding the last postcard, and Grayson's hand made its way to mine.

"She wrote these," I said, my voice catching in my throat, "to Toby about me." It couldn't have been clearer reading them: He really was my father. I'd been working off that assumption for so long that it shouldn't have come as a shock.

Beside me, Grayson's phone buzzed. "It's Jameson," he said.

My heart skipped a beat, then made up for it. "Answer it," I told Grayson, pulling my hand back from his.

Grayson did as I'd asked. "We're on our way back to the plane," he told Jameson.

He'll want to know what I found. I knew that, knew Jameson. I held up the small metal disk that Jackson Currie had given me. "This is what Toby left with Jackson." Grayson stared at it, then switched Jameson over to a video chat, so he could see it, too.

"What do you think this is?" I asked. The disk was gold and maybe an inch in diameter. It looked like some kind of a coin, but not any I'd seen before, its surface engraved with nine concentric circles on one side and smooth on the other.

"It doesn't look like it's worth much," Jameson commented. "But in this family, that means nothing." The sound of his voice did something to me—something it shouldn't have done. Something it wouldn't have done before I'd read my mother's postcards.

Close your eyes, I could hear Max telling me. *Who's there?*

"We're incoming," Oren announced curtly—to whom, I wasn't sure. "Sweep the plane."

When we arrived at the airstrip, he opened my door, and I got three escorts to the plane. Behind me, Grayson had switched the phone off video, but he was still on the line with Jameson.

My mind was full with images of them both—and with the words my mother had written to Toby.

The night air was cold and getting colder. As I walked toward the jet, a brutal wind picked up, then gave way to sudden and utter stillness. I heard a single, high-pitched beep, and the world exploded. Into fire. Into nothing.

CHAPTER 76

Everything hurt. I couldn't hear. I couldn't see. When blurred images finally began to form, all I saw was fire. Fire and Grayson, standing a hundred feet away from me.

I waited for him to come running.

I waited.

I waited.

He didn't.

And then, there was nothing.

➤————◄

The world around me was dark, and then there was a voice. "Let's play a game."

I couldn't tell if I was standing up or lying down. I couldn't feel my body.

"I have a secret."

If I had eyes, I opened them. Or maybe they were already open? Either way, I did *something*, and the world was flooded with light.

"I'm tired of playing," I told my mom.

"I know, baby."

"I'm so tired," I said.

"I know. But I have a secret, Avery, and you have to play—just one more time, just for me. Okay, baby? You can't let go."

I heard a long and distant beep. Lightning tore through my body. "Clear!" a voice yelled.

"Come on, Avery," my mom whispered. *"I have a secret...."*

Another round of lightning tore through me. "Clear!"

I wanted to stop breathing. I wanted to go where the lightning and the fire and the pain couldn't touch me.

"You have to fight," my mom said. "You have to hang on."

"You're not real," I whispered. *"You're dead.* So either this is a dream, and you're not even here, or I'm..."

Dead, too.

CHAPTER 77

I dreamed that I was running through the halls of Hawthorne House. I hit a staircase, and at the bottom, I saw a dead girl. At first, I thought it was Emily Laughlin, but then I got closer—and I realized it was me.

I was standing at the edge of the ocean. Every time a wave crested and came toward me, I thought that it would swallow me whole. I was ready for it to swallow me whole.

But each time, as the darkness beckoned, I heard a voice: Jameson Winchester Hawthorne.

"You son of a bitch." The words cut through the darkness in a way that nothing else had since I'd been here. The voice was Jameson's again, but louder this time, sharper, like the edge of a knife. "She was dying, and you just stood there! And don't tell me it was shock."

I tried to open my eyes. I tried—but I couldn't.

"You would know, Jamie, about standing there and watching someone die."

"*Emily.* It always comes back to Emily with you."

I wanted to tell them that I could hear them, but I couldn't move my mouth. Everything was dark. Everything hurt.

"You know what I think, Gray? I think the whole martyr act was a lie you told yourself. I don't think you stepped back from Avery for my sake. I think you needed an excuse to draw a line so you could stay safe on the other side."

"You don't know what you're talking about."

"You can't let go. You couldn't when Emily was alive, no matter what she did, and you can't now."

"Are you done?" Grayson was yelling now.

"Avery was dying, and you couldn't run toward her."

"What do you want from me, Jamie?"

"You think I didn't fight the same fight? I halfway convinced myself that as long as Avery was just a riddle or a puzzle, as long as I was just playing, I'd be *fine*. Well, joke's on me, because somewhere along the way, I stopped playing."

I can hear you. I can hear every word. I'm right here—

"What do you want from me?"

"Look at her, Gray. Look at her, damn it! *Est unus ex nobis. Nos defendat eius.*"

She is one of us. We protect her. Whatever Grayson said in response was lost to the sound of a crashing wave.

———————

I sat at a chessboard. Across from me was a man I hadn't seen since I was six years old.

Tobias Hawthorne picked up his queen, then set it back down. Instead, he laid three new pieces on the board. A corkscrew. A funnel. A chain.

I stared at them. "I don't know what to do with these."

Silently, he laid a fourth object on the board: a metal disk.

"I don't know what to do with that, either."

"Don't look at me, young lady," Tobias Hawthorne replied. "This is *your* subconscious. All of this—it's a game of your making, not mine."

"What if I don't want to play anymore?" I asked.

He leaned back, picking up his queen once more. "Then stop."

CHAPTER 78

The first thing I was aware of was pressure on my chest. It felt like a cinder block was holding me down. I struggled against the weight of it, and like a switch had been flipped, every nerve in my body began to scream. My eyes flew open.

The first thing I saw was the machine, then the tubes. So many tubes, connected to my body.

I'm in the hospital, I thought, but then the rest of the world came into focus around me, and I realized that this wasn't a hospital room. It was *my* room. At Hawthorne House.

Seconds passed like molasses. It took everything I had not to claw the tubes out of my body. Memory settled in around me. Jameson's voice—and Grayson's. Lightning and fire and—

There was a bomb.

A nearby monitor began sounding some kind of alarm, and the next thing I knew, a woman in a white doctor's coat rushed into the room. When I recognized her, I thought I was dreaming again.

"Dr. Liu?"

"Welcome back, Avery." Max's mother fixed me with a no-nonsense look. "I need you to lie back and breathe."

I was poked and prodded and dosed with pain medication. By the time Dr. Liu let Libby and Max into my room, I was feeling downright loopy.

"I gave her some morphine," I heard Dr. Liu tell Libby. "If she wants to sleep, let her."

Max approached my bed, as tentative as I'd ever seen her.

"Your mom is here," I said.

"Correct," Max replied, taking a seat next to the bed.

"At Hawthorne House."

"Very good," Max said. "Now, tell me what year it is, who's president, and which Hawthorne brother you're going to let fax your brains out first."

"Maxine!" Dr. Liu sounded like *she* was the one with a splitting headache.

"Sorry, Mama," Max said. She turned back to me. "I called her when Alisa brought you back here. Lawyer Lady more or less stole your fine comatose self from the hospital in Oregon, and everyone was pretty faxing mad. We weren't about to let her staff you up with doctors of her choosing. We needed someone we could trust. I might have been disowned, but I'm not stupid. I called. The great Dr. Liu came."

"You were not disowned," Max's mom said sternly.

"I distinctly remember disowning," Max countered. "Agree to disagree."

If you'd told me a few hours ago that Max and her mom would be in the same room, and it wouldn't be painful or awkward or painfully awkward, I wouldn't have believed you.

A few hours ago. My brain latched on to that thought, and I realized the obvious: If there had been time for Alisa to steal me from a hospital, and time for Max to call her mom...

"How long was I out?" I asked.

Max didn't answer, not right away. She looked back at her mom, who nodded. Max opened her mouth, but Libby beat her to speaking. "Seven days."

"A full week?"

Libby's hair was dyed again—not one color, but dozens. I thought about what she'd said about her ninth birthday. About the cupcakes my mom had baked for her, and the rainbow colors she'd clipped into her hair, and I wondered how much of her life Libby had spent trying to get that one perfect moment back.

"They told me you might not wake up." Libby's voice was shaking now.

"I'm okay," I said, but then I realized that I had no idea if that was true. I stole a look at Dr. Liu.

"Your body's been healing nicely," she told me. "The coma was medically induced. We tried to wake you up two days ago, but there was some unexpected swelling in your brain. That's all under control now."

I looked past her toward the doorway. "Do the others know?" I asked. "That I'm awake?" *Do the boys?*

Dr. Liu walked over to my bedside. "Let's take this one step at a time."

CHAPTER 79

Eventually, they let Oren in to see me.

"The bomb was planted inside the plane's engine—forensics suggests it had been there for days and was triggered remotely." Oren had partially healed wounds running down the side of his jaw and across the backs of his hands. "Whoever triggered the explosion must have mistimed things. If you'd been two steps closer, you would have died." His voice got tighter. "Two of my men didn't make it."

Devastating guilt drilled through me, a needle-thin icicle straight to the heart. I felt heavy and numb. "I'm sorry."

Oren didn't tell me not to be. He didn't say that if I hadn't pushed to go to Rockaway Watch, those men would still be alive.

"Wait…" I stared at him. "You said that the bomb was planted days before it exploded? Then the Rooneys"—the reason we'd brought so much security with us—"they weren't the ones who…"

"No," Oren confirmed.

Someone planted that bomb. "It must have been planted sometime after True North." I tried to be logical about this, tried to view it from a distance without thinking about the fire, the lightning, the *pain*. "That man at True North, the professional..." My voice caught in my throat. "Who was he working for?"

Before Oren could answer, I heard the familiar sound of heels on the wood floor. Alisa appeared in the doorway. She stepped across the threshold, and when her eyes landed on me, she reached out to a nearby armoire, her fingers gripping the edge with knuckle-whitening ferocity. "Thank God," she muttered. She closed her eyes, battling for calm, then opened them again. "I appreciate you telling your men to stand down."

That was directed at Oren, not me.

"You have five minutes," he said coldly.

Hurt flashed across Alisa's features, and I remembered what Max had said. Alisa had moved me back here without permission. With my life on the line, she'd acted to save my inheritance.

"Don't look at me like that," Alisa said—to me this time. "It worked, didn't it?"

I was here. I was alive. And I was still a billionaire.

"It cost me dearly." Alisa held my gaze. "It cost me this family. But *it worked*."

I didn't know what to say to that. "What's the status of the police investigation about the bombing?" I asked. "Do they have any idea who..."

"The police made an arrest yesterday." Alisa's tone was brisker now, no-nonsense. Familiar. "The job was a professional one, obviously, but the police traced it back to Skye Hawthorne and..." She had the decency to hesitate, just for a moment. "Ricky Grambs."

That answer shouldn't have been surprising. It shouldn't have mattered to me, but for a split second, I saw myself at four years old. I saw Ricky lifting me up and putting me on his shoulders.

I swallowed. "His name is on my birth certificate. If I die, he and Libby are my heirs." It was the same song in a different key, courtesy of Skye Hawthorne.

"There's something else you should know," Alisa told me quietly. "We got back the DNA test you ordered."

Of course she had. I'd been out for a week. "I know," I said. "Ricky's not my father."

Alisa walked to stand beside my bed. "That's the thing, Avery. He is."

CHAPTER 80

I stared at my birth certificate. At the signature. This made no sense. None. Every single clue had pointed in the same direction. Toby had sought me out after my mother's death. He'd signed my birth certificate. He and my mom had been in love. Tobias Hawthorne had left me his fortune.

I have a secret, my mother had told me, *about the day you were born.*

How was it even remotely possible that Toby wasn't my father?

"Upside, downside, inside, outside, left side, right side." Jameson Hawthorne stood in the doorway. When I saw him, something clicked. It was the feeling of a wave crashing over me—at last. "What's missing?" Jameson asked. He walked toward me, and I tracked every step. He repeated his riddle. "Upside, downside, inside, outside, left side, right side. What's missing?"

He stopped next to my bed, right next to it. "Beside," I whispered.

He stared at me—at my eyes, at the lines of my face, like he was drinking it in. "I have to say, Heiress, I'm not a big fan of comas." Jameson sounded just the same, wry and darkly tempting, but the expression on his face was one I'd never seen before.

He wasn't joking.

I flashed back to something like a dream. *Well, joke's on me, because somewhere along the way, I stopped playing.* Jameson Hawthorne and I had an understanding. No emotions. No mess. This wasn't supposed to be an epic kind of love.

"I came to see you," Jameson told me. "Every day. The least you could have done was wake up while I was here, tragically backlit, unspeakably handsome, and waiting."

Picture yourself standing on a cliff overlooking the ocean. The wind is whipping in your hair. The sun is setting. You long, body and soul, for one thing. One person. You hear footsteps behind you. You turn.

Who's there?

"Every day?" I asked, my voice foreign in my throat. I remembered standing at the edge of the ocean. I remembered a voice. *Jameson Winchester Hawthorne.*

"Every single day, Heiress." Jameson closed his eyes, just for an instant. "But if I'm not the one you want to see..."

"Of course I want to see you." That was true. I could say it. "But you don't have to—" *Tell me I'm special. Tell me I matter.*

"Yes," Jameson cut in, "I do." He sank down beside my bed, bringing his eyes level with mine. "You aren't a prize to be won."

I wasn't hearing this. He wasn't saying this. He *couldn't* be.

"You're not a puzzle or a riddle or a clue." Jameson had laser focus. On me. All on me. "You aren't a mystery to me, Avery, because deep down, we're the same. You might not see that." He gave me a long, searing look. "You might not believe it—yet." He held up his hands, his fingers curled into a loose fist. "But there's no one besides the two of us who would have gone back in the wake of that bomb to look for *this*."

He uncurled his fingers, and I saw a small metal disk in his palm.

Every muscle in my body tightened. Everything in me wanted to reach out to him. "How did you—"

Jameson shrugged, and that shrug, like his smile, was *devastating*. "How could I not?" He stared at me a moment longer, then pressed the disk into my hand. I felt his fingertips on my palm. He left them there for a moment, then trailed them along the inside of my wrist.

I sucked in a breath and looked from Jameson's face to the disk. Concentric circles ringed the metal on one side. The other was smooth.

He was still trailing his fingers down my arm.

"Have you figured out what it is?" I asked, every nerve in my body alive.

"No." Jameson smiled, that crooked, devastating Jameson Hawthorne smile. "I was waiting for you."

Jameson wasn't patient. He didn't *wait*. He lived with his foot on the gas. "You want to figure it out." I stared at him, feeling his stare on me. "Together."

"You don't have to say anything." Jameson stood. I could still feel the ghost of his touch on the inside of my arm. I could see the vein in my wrist and *feel* my heart pumping. "You don't have to kiss me now. You don't have to love me now, Heiress. But when you're ready..." He brought his hand to the side of my face. I leaned into it. His breath went ragged, and then he pulled his hand back and nodded to the disk in my hand. "When you're ready, *if* you're ever ready, if it's going to be me—just flip that disk. Heads, I kiss you." His voice broke slightly. "Tails, you kiss me. And either way, *it means something*."

I stared at the disk in my hand. It was the size of a coin. Every clue we'd followed, every trail that had been left, led to this.

I swallowed and looked back up at Jameson. "Toby wasn't my father," I said, and then I corrected the tense. "He *isn't* my father."

Toby Hawthorne was out there somewhere. He still didn't want to be found.

Beside me, Jameson cocked his head, eyes sparking. "Well then, Heiress. Game on."

CHAPTER 81

I made it through that day. That night. The next day. The next night. And on it went. On the morning that I was cleared to go back to school, I heard a sound on the other side of my fireplace.

Jameson. I made my way to the mantel and closed my hand around the candlestick. With a breath, I pulled it forward.

Jameson wasn't the one standing on the other side.

"Thea?" I said. I was confused. I had no idea what she was doing at Hawthorne House or why she'd come through the passage. My gaze darted toward my door. Oren was in the hall. Even now, with Skye and Ricky in prison, he was staying close.

"Don't say anything," Thea implored me, her voice low. "I need you to come with me. It's Grayson."

"Grayson?" I repeated. He'd been like a ghost in the House since I'd woken up. He either didn't want to see me or couldn't face me. I'd watched him swimming laps every night.

"He's in trouble, Avery." Thea looked like she'd been crying, and that scared me, because Thea Calligaris wasn't a person who cried. She didn't *do* vulnerable.

She didn't do scared.

"What's going on? *Thea.*"

She disappeared back into the passageway. I followed her, and an instant later, hands gripped me from behind. Someone slammed a damp cloth down over my mouth and nose. I couldn't breathe. I couldn't scream.

The smell of the cloth was sickly sweet. Everything started going dark around me, and the last thing I heard was Thea.

"I had to, Avery. They have Rebecca."

CHAPTER 82

I woke up tied to an antique chair. The room around me was packed tight with boxes and knickknacks. The entire place smelled like it had been soaked in gasoline.

Two people stood across from me: Mellie, who looked like she might throw up any second. And Sheffield Grayson.

"Where am I?" I asked, and then the memory of what had happened in the passageway came flooding back. "Where's Thea? And Rebecca?"

"I assure you, your friends are fine." Sheffield Grayson was wearing a suit. He had me tied to a chair in what appeared to be some kind of storage unit, and he was *wearing a suit.*

He has Grayson's eyes.

"I am sorry about all of this," Grayson's father said, flicking a speck off the cuff of his shirt. "The chloroform. The restraints." He paused. "The bomb."

"The bomb?" I repeated. The police had arrested Ricky and Skye weeks ago. They had motive, and there was evidence—there had to be, for an arrest. "I don't understand."

"I know you don't." Grayson's father closed his eyes. "I am not a

319

bad man, Ms. Grambs. I take no joy in...this." He didn't specify what *this* was.

"You kidnapped me," I said hoarsely. "I'm tied to a chair." He didn't reply. "You tried to kill me."

"Injure you. If I'd meant for you to die, my man would have timed the explosion differently, wouldn't he?"

I thought of Oren telling me that if I'd been a few steps closer to the plane when the bomb had detonated, I would have died.

"Why?" I said lowly.

"Why what? The bomb or—" Sheffield Grayson gestured to the bindings on my wrists. "The rest?"

"All of it." My voice shook. *Why kidnap me? Why bring me here? What is he planning to do to me next?*

"Blame your father." Sheffield Grayson broke eye contact then, and for reasons I couldn't quite pinpoint, that sent a chill down my spine. "Your real father. If Tobias Hawthorne the Second weren't such a coward, I wouldn't have had to go to such lengths to lure him out."

My captor's voice was calm, commanding. Like he was the rational one here.

The muscles in my chest tightened, threatening to wring the air from my lungs, but I forced myself to breathe, to stay focused. *Stay alive.* "Toby," I said. "You're after Toby."

"The bomb should have worked." Sheffield began cuffing the sleeves on his dress shirt, a furious motion—and a familiar one. "You were rushed to the hospital. It made worldwide news. I was ready. The trap was set. All that was left to do was wait for that bastard to come to your bedside, the way any self-respecting father would. And then your lawyer had the audacity to have you *moved*."

To Hawthorne House, with all its security.

"So here we are," Sheffield Grayson said, "as unfortunate as that may be."

I tried to read between the lines of what he was saying. It had been clear from Grayson's meeting with his father that the man blamed Toby for Colin's death. My captor must have realized, somehow, that Toby was alive. He'd convinced himself that I was Toby's daughter.

And this entire place smelled like gasoline.

"I'm sorry." Mellie's voice shook. "It wasn't supposed to be like this."

My head pounded. My body was screaming at me to flee, but I couldn't. I had no idea why Mellie would have helped this man kidnap me—or what exactly he planned to do to me now.

"Toby won't come for me," I said. Emotion welled up in my throat, and I bit it back. "He isn't my father." That hurt—more than it should have. "I'm nothing to him."

"I have reason to believe he's in town. He stuck his head out of whatever hole he's hiding in long enough for me to verify that much. You are his daughter. He will come for you."

It was like he wasn't hearing me. "I'm not his daughter." I'd wanted to be. I'd believed that I was.

But I wasn't.

Sheffield Grayson's achingly familiar eyes settled on mine. "I have a DNA test that says otherwise."

I stared at him. What he'd just said made no sense. *Alisa* had done a DNA test. Ricky Grambs *was* my father. That meant, obviously, that Toby wasn't. "I don't understand." I really didn't.

I couldn't.

"Mellie here was quite obliging about providing a sample of your DNA. I'd acquired a sample of Toby's from the Hawthorne

Island investigation years ago." Sheffield Grayson straightened. "The match was definitive. You have his blood." Sheffield gave me a chilling smile. "And you really should pay your help more."

For the first time, I looked at Mellie, really looked at her. She wouldn't meet my eyes. Was she the one who'd knocked me out in the passageway?

Why? Like Eli, had she sold me out for money?

"You can go now, dear," Sheffield Grayson told her. Mellie shuffled toward the door.

She's leaving me here. Panic began slithering up my spine.

"You think he's just going to let you go?" I called after her. "You think he's the kind of man who leaves loose ends?" I didn't know Sheffield Grayson. I didn't even know Mellie, really, but everything in me was saying that I couldn't let her leave me here with him alone. "What do you think Nash would say if he knew what you're doing?"

She hesitated, then kept walking. I was getting frantic—and she was getting farther away. The sound of her footsteps grew fainter.

"And now," Sheffield Grayson told me, in the same calm, commanding voice, "we wait."

CHAPTER 83

Toby wasn't coming. Sooner or later, my captor would realize that. And when he did... well, he couldn't just let me go.

"What makes you think Toby's close by?" I tried not to sound scared. I tried not to *be* scared. Pissed was better—much. "How is he even supposed to know that you took me? Or where to come?"

He's not my father. He's not coming.

"I left clues," Sheffield said, inspecting one of his cuff links. "A little game for your father to play. I understand Hawthornes are prone to such things."

"What kind of clues?"

No answer.

"How did you send clues to him if you don't where he is?"

No response.

This was useless. Toby had told me to stop looking for him. He'd been in hiding for decades. I wasn't his daughter.

He wasn't coming.

That was the only thought my brain was capable of producing. It rang in my mind over and over again, until I heard footsteps. They were too heavy to be Mellie's.

"Ah." Sheffield Grayson inclined his head. He walked toward

me, assessing me, then reached a hand out to my face and put two fingers under my chin. He angled it backward. "It's important that you know, Avery: This isn't personal."

I jerked back, but it was useless. I was still bound. I wasn't going anywhere. And the footsteps were getting closer.

Someone was coming for me. It probably just wasn't the person he expected.

"What if you're wrong?" I said, rushing the words. "What if the person who found your *clues* wasn't Toby? What are you going to do if that's Jameson? Xander? *Grayson?*"

The sound of his son's name—his *own* name—gave Sheffield Grayson only the briefest moment of pause. He closed his eyes again for a moment, then opened them, resolute and steeled against whatever unwanted thoughts my questions had raised.

"These were my nephew's things." Sheffield gestured to the items in the storage unit. His voice tightened. "I never could bear to part with them."

The footsteps were almost here. Sheffield Grayson turned toward the entrance to the front of the storage unit. He withdrew a gun from his suit jacket. Finally, the footsteps stopped as a man stepped into view. He'd shaved since the last time I'd seen him, but he was still wearing layers of worn and dirty clothes.

"Harry." That was the wrong name, and I knew it, but I couldn't keep the word from bursting past my lips. *He's here. He came.* Tears welled in my eyes, carving trails down my cheeks as the man I'd known as Harry looked past Sheffield Grayson, past the gun, toward me.

"Horrible girl." Toby's voice was tender. He'd called me a lot of things when we played chess—that was one of them. *Especially when I won.* "Let her go," he told my captor.

Sheffield Grayson smiled, his gun held steady. "Ironic, isn't it? My son carries the last name Hawthorne, and your daughter doesn't. And now…" He walked slowly out of the storage unit toward Toby. "I'm the one holding the match."

I didn't see a match, but he had a gun. This place had been doused in accelerant. If he fired that gun—

"Get in there," Sheffield ordered.

Toby did as he was told. "Avery isn't my daughter." His voice was even.

I'm not. Am I? "He said he has a DNA test," I told Toby, stalling for time, trying to think of a way—any way—out of this, before the whole place went up in flames.

A few feet away from me, Tobias Hawthorne the Second took his eyes off Sheffield Grayson—and the gun—just for a moment. "Queen to rook five," he told me. That was a chess move—one I'd used on him in our last game, as misdirection.

Misdirection. My brain managed to latch on to that. *He's going to distract Sheffield.* I tested the security of the bindings that held me to the chair. They were just as tight as they'd been a minute before, but a surge of adrenaline hit me, and I thought about the fact that mothers had been known to lift cars off their toddlers in crises. This chair was an antique. With enough pressure, could I break the chair's arms?

"I told you." Toby turned his attention back to the man with the gun. "Avery is not my daughter. I don't know what kind of DNA test you think you got, but when Hannah got pregnant, I hadn't seen her for years."

I tried to focus on the chair, not his words, and worked the restraints back to the thinnest part of the wood.

"You came for the girl." Sheffield Grayson sounded different now. Harder. "You're here." He lowered his voice. "You're here, and my nephew is not." That was clearly an accusation—and the man with the gun was judge, jury, and executioner.

"He hated you," Toby shot back.

"He was going to be great," Sheffield said intently. "I was going to make him great."

Toby didn't bat an eye. "The fire was Colin's idea, you know. I kept saying that I wanted to burn everything down, and he dared me to put my money where my mouth was."

"You're a liar."

I jerked my arms upward. Again. And again. I threw the weight of my body into it, and the right arm on the chair gave. The noise it made was loud enough that I expected Sheffield Grayson to whip his gaze toward me, but he was 100 percent focused on Toby.

"Colin dared me to do it," Toby said again. "But it wasn't his fault I took the dare. I was angry. And high. And the house on Hawthorne Island meant something to my father. I was going to make sure that everyone was clear of it. We were supposed to watch it burn *from a distance*."

The second arm on the chair gave, and Toby raised his voice. "We didn't count on the lightning."

Sheffield Grayson stalked toward him. "My nephew is dead. He burned, because of you."

This entire place had been soaked in accelerant. Deep down, I knew why. *He burned, because of you.*

"I am what I am," Toby said. "If you want to kill me, I won't fight it. But let Avery go."

Sheffield Grayson's eyes—*Grayson's eyes*—shifted toward me. "I am truly sorry," he told me. "But I can't leave any witnesses behind. Unlike some people, I don't fancy the idea of disappearing for decades. My family deserves better than that."

"What about Mellie?" I asked, stalling for time. "Or the man you had plant the bomb?"

"You don't need to worry about that." Sheffield aimed the gun at Toby. He was still calm, still in control.

He's going to kill us both. I was going to die here with Toby Hawthorne. My mother's Toby. *No.* I stood, ready to fight, aware that there was no use in fighting—but what else was I supposed to do?

I launched myself forward. Instantly, a gun fired. The sound of it was deafening.

I expected an explosion. I expected to burn. Instead, as I watched, Sheffield Grayson crumpled to the ground. An instant later, Mellie stepped into view, her eyes wide and unseeing, holding a gun.

CHAPTER 84

killed him." Mellie sounded dazed. "I...He was holding a gun.
And he was going to...And I..."

"Easy," Toby murmured. He stepped forward and removed the
gun from her hand. Mellie let him.

What just happened here? Trying not to look at the body on the
ground—at *Grayson's father*—I made my way out of the unit. "I
don't understand." That was probably the biggest understatement
of my life. "You sold me out, Mellie. You left. Why would you—"

"It wasn't supposed to be like this." Mellie shook her head, and
for a few seconds, it seemed like she couldn't stop shaking it. "And
we didn't sell you out. This was never about the money."

We? I thought dizzily.

"Who's we?" Toby asked.

In answer, Mellie swallowed and reached a finger up to her eye.
I wasn't sure what she was doing at first, but then she removed a
contact lens. I walked toward her, and she blinked up at me. The
contact she'd removed was colored. Her left eye was still brown, but
her right eye was a vibrant blue, with an amber circle around the
center. *Just like Eli's.*

"My brother and I agreed that I should be the one to wear contacts," Mellie said, her voice still a little shaky.

"Eli's your brother." My mind raced. "He engineered a threat against me so he could stay close, then he leaked information about Toby to the press. And then you—"

"It wasn't supposed to be like this," Mellie repeated. "We were just trying to flush Toby out of hiding. We just wanted to talk. When Mr. Grayson offered his assistance—"

"You kidnapped me for him."

"No!" Mellie's response was instantaneous. "I mean...*kind of*." She shook her head again. "After Grayson and Jameson went to see him in Arizona, Sheffield Grayson sent a man to follow them to True North. To watch them." I thought about the professional in the woods. Oren had pulled me out of the tub—and sent one of his men after the interloper. "Eli caught the guy," Mellie continued. "He tackled him, and then...they talked."

"About me?" I paused. "About Toby?"

Mellie didn't answer either question. "We didn't know who the man was working for," she said instead. "Not at first. But we all wanted the same thing."

Toby. "So Eli leaked those pictures," I said, my throat constricting. "And then a few days later, someone blew up my plane."

"That wasn't us! Eli and I never wanted to hurt you. We never wanted to hurt anyone!" Mellie's eyes drifted toward Toby's. "We just needed to talk."

"Why?" I demanded, but Mellie didn't answer me. Now that she'd looked over at Toby, she couldn't stop staring at him.

"Do I know you?" he asked her, his brow furrowing.

Mellie looked down. "You knew my mother."

The world shifted under my feet—suddenly, abruptly. *Sheffield*

Grayson said he had a DNA test linking me to Toby. I sucked in a breath. *But Toby's not my father. It wasn't my DNA.*

"This is my mom." Mellie pulled out her phone and showed Toby a picture. "I don't expect you to remember her. Pretty sure she was just another wild night for you that summer."

The summer he "died," I thought. Across from me, Toby looked at the photo, and I remembered Zara saying that Tobias Hawthorne's investigators had talked to at least one of the women that Toby had slept with that summer. *Mellie's mother?*

Across from me, I could see Toby working his way through it, too.

"Sheffield Grayson said you gave him a DNA sample to test," I said, staring at Mellie. "He was certain I was Toby's daughter." I glanced toward Toby, and the muscles in my stomach twisted. "But I'm not. Am I?"

"Not by blood." Toby held my gaze a moment longer, then turned back to Mellie. "You're right. I don't remember your mother."

"I was five," Mellie told him. "Eli was six. Our parents were in a bad place, and suddenly, Mom was pregnant. She didn't know your name. She didn't know the kind of money you came from."

"But you figured it out?" I said. I couldn't stop staring at Mellie. Alisa had told me once that she was one of the ones that Nash had "saved" from unfortunate circumstances. I had no idea what those circumstances were, but it couldn't be coincidence that both she and her brother had ended up in the Hawthornes' employ.

How long had they been planning this?

"You said your mother was pregnant," Toby said quietly. "Did she have the child?"

The child, I thought, my stomach sinking. *His child.* The DNA that Mellie had given Sheffield Grayson, the DNA that had come up as a match for Toby's—it wasn't mine.

"My sister," Mellie replied. "Her name is Evelyn. She goes by Eve."

I saw something—just a hint of emotion—in Toby's eyes. "A palindrome."

"She chose it herself," Mellie replied quietly, "when she was three years old, for that reason. She's nineteen now." Mellie turned to me. "And everything *you* have should be hers."

For the first time, I heard surety burning in Mellie's tone, and I understood that while she hadn't meant for me to be hurt, it was a risk she'd been willing to take, because Toby Hawthorne did have a daughter.

It just wasn't me.

Did the old man know? Did Mellie ever try to tell him?

"What do you want from me?" Toby asked.

"I want Eve taken care of," Mellie said fiercely. "She's a Hawthorne."

My gaze cut to Toby's. "And a Laughlin," I said quietly. I wasn't Mrs. Laughlin's great-granddaughter. I wasn't Rebecca's niece, Emily's niece. Eve was.

She was the one who belonged here.

I swallowed. "Bring her to Hawthorne House." The words chafed against my throat, but I wasn't going to give in to that hurt. "There's plenty of room."

"No." Toby's voice was blade-sharp.

Mellie scrolled furiously through her phone and shoved another picture in his face. "Look at her," she demanded. "She's your *daughter*, and you have no idea what her life has been like."

Toby looked at the photo. Without meaning to, I stepped forward. I looked, too, and the second I saw Mellie's sister's face, I stopped breathing.

Eve was a dead ringer for Emily Laughlin. Strawberry-blonde

hair, like sunlight through amber. Emerald eyes, too big for her face. Heart-shaped lips, a scattering of freckles.

"My daughter isn't coming to Hawthorne House," Toby told Mellie. "If you bring me to her, I will see that she's taken care of. Discreetly."

"What's that supposed to mean?" I asked, finally recovering my voice. Toby was talking about leaving. Like he was just going to walk away. After everything I'd been through, everything that Jameson, Xander, Grayson, and I had done to look for him.

"Do you promise?" Mellie stared at Toby like I wasn't even in the room.

"I promise." Toby's eyes traveled to mine. "But first," he continued softly, "Avery and I need to have a conversation alone."

CHAPTER 85

Y ou're going to keep her a secret?" I demanded, once we were out of Mellie's earshot. "Eve?"

Toby took my elbow and guided me to the exit. "There's a car outside," he told me. "Key's in the ignition. Take it and drive north."

I stared at him. "That's it?" I said. "That's all you have to say to me?" Eve's face—Emily's—was still fresh in my mind.

Toby reached out and brushed the hair off of my forehead. "In my heart," he said quietly, "you were always mine."

I swallowed. "But biologically, I'm not."

"Biology isn't everything."

I knew in that moment that I'd gotten this much right: Toby *had* sought me out after my mother died. He had been watching me. He had wanted to make sure that I was okay.

"My mom and I had this game," I told him, trying my best not to cry. "We had lots of games, actually—but this one, her favorite, it was about secrets."

He stared off into the distance for a moment. "I made her promise never to tell you—about me, about my family. But if it was just a game, if you guessed..." He looked back at me, and his own eyes were shining. "Damn it, Hannah."

"How the hell was I supposed to guess?" The words burst out of my mouth. I was furious suddenly—at her, at him. "She said that she had a secret about the day I was born."

Toby said nothing.

"You signed my birth certificate." I wanted answers. He owed me that at least.

He reached out to lay a hand against my cheek. "There was a storm that night," he said quietly. "Worst one I'd ever seen— Hawthorne Island included. I shouldn't have been there in the first place. I'd managed to stay away from Hannah for three long years. But something brought me back. I just wanted to *see* her again, even if I couldn't let her see me.

"She was pregnant. Forecasts were calling for a hurricane. And she was alone. I was going to stay away. She was never supposed to know that I was there, but then the power went out—and she went into labor."

With me. I couldn't say that out loud, couldn't say anything, couldn't even tell him that my mother had been capable of making decisions for *herself.*

"The ambulance didn't make it in time," Toby said, his voice growing hoarse. "She needed *someone.*"

"You." I managed one word this time—just one.

"I brought you into this world, Avery Kylie Grambs."

There it was. My mother's secret. Toby was there the night I was born. He'd delivered me. I wondered what my mom had felt, seeing him again after years. I wondered if he'd called her *Hannah, O Hannah,* and if she'd tried to make him stay.

"Avery Kylie Grambs." I repeated the last words Toby had said to me. There was something about the way he'd said my full name. "It's an anagram." I swallowed again, and for some reason, whatever force had been holding back my tears gave way. "But you knew that."

Toby didn't deny it. "Your mom had a middle name all picked out. Kylie—like Kaylie but minus a letter."

That hit me hard. I'd never known that I was named after my mother's sister. I'd never known about Kaylie at all.

"Hannah was set on giving you Ricky's last name," Toby continued. "But she didn't like the first name he'd picked out."

Natasha. "Ricky wasn't there." I blinked back tears and stared at Toby. "You were."

"*Something* Kylie Grambs." Toby smiled and gave a little shrug. "I couldn't resist."

He was a Hawthorne. He loved puzzles and riddles and codes. "You chose my name." I didn't phrase it as a question. "You suggested Avery."

"A Very Risky Gamble." Toby looked down. "What I took that night. What Hannah took when she nursed me back to life, knowing what her family would do to her if they found out."

A Very Risky Gamble—the reason Tobias Hawthorne had left me his fortune. Had he recognized his son's fingerprints all over that name? Had he suspected, from the moment he heard it, that I was a link to Toby?

"When the ambulance got there, I disappeared," Toby continued. "I snuck into the hospital one last time to see you both."

"You signed the birth certificate," I said.

"With your father's name, not mine. It was the least he owed her."

"And then you left." I stared at him, trying not to hate him for that.

"I had to."

335

Something like fury rose up inside me. "No, you didn't." My mom had loved him. She'd spent her entire life loving him, and I'd never even known.

"You have to understand. My father's resources were unlimited. He never stopped looking for me. I had to stay on the move if I wanted to stay dead."

I thought about Tobias Hawthorne, eating at a hole-in-the-wall diner in New Castle, Connecticut. Had it taken him six years to track Toby there?

Had he thought his son would come back?

Had he realized who my mother was?

Had he thought, even for a moment, that I was Toby's?

"What are you going to do now?" I asked, my voice like sand-paper in my throat. "The world knows you're alive. Your father is dead. As far as we know, Sheffield Grayson was the only person who realized the old man had buried the police report about Hawthorne Island. He's the only one who knew—"

"I know what you're thinking, Avery." Toby's eyes hardened. "But I can't come back. I promised myself a long time ago that I would never forget what I did, that I would never move on. Hannah wouldn't let me turn myself in, but exile is what I deserved."

"What about what other people deserve?" I asked vehemently. "Did my mother deserve to die without you there? Did she deserve to spend my entire life in love with a ghost?"

"Hannah deserved the world."

"So why didn't you give it to her?" I asked. "Why was punishing yourself more important than what *she* wanted?"

Why was it more important than what I wanted now?

"I don't expect you to understand," Toby told me gently—more gently than he'd ever spoken to me as Harry.

"I do understand," I said. "You're not staying gone because you have to. You're making a choice, and it's selfish." I thought about Mr. and Mrs. Laughlin, about Rebecca's mother. "What gives you the right to deceive the people who love you? To make that kind of decision for everyone else?"

He didn't answer.

"You have a daughter now," I told him, my voice low.

He looked at me, his expression never wavering. "I have two."

In the span of a heartbeat, fury gave way to devastation. Tobias Hawthorne the Second wasn't my father. He hadn't raised me. I didn't carry a single drop of his blood.

But he'd just called me his daughter.

"I want you to go outside, princess. Get in the car and drive north."

"I can't do that," I said. "Sheffield Grayson is dead! There's a body. The police are going to want to know what happened. And as screwed up as what Mellie did is, she doesn't deserve to go down for murder. If we tell the police what really happened—"

"I know men like Sheffield Grayson." Toby's expression shifted, until it was utterly impossible to read. "He's covered his tracks. No one knows where he is or who he was after. There will be nothing to tie him to this warehouse—nothing to even suggest he was in the state."

"So?" I said.

Toby looked past me, just for a moment. "I know more than I wish I did about what it takes to make something—or some*one*—disappear."

"What about his family?" I asked. *Grayson's family.* "I can't let you—"

"You're not *letting* me do anything." Toby reached out to touch my face. "Horrible girl," he whispered. "Don't you know by now? No one *lets* a Hawthorne do anything."

That was the truth.

"This is wrong," I said again. He couldn't just make that body disappear.

"I have to, Avery." Toby was implacable. "For Eve. The spotlight, the media circus, the rumors, the stalkers, the threats—I can't save you from that, Avery Kylie Grambs. I would if I could, but it's too late. The old man did what he did. He pulled you onto the board. But if I stay in shadows, if I make this disappear, if *I* disappear—then we can save Eve."

It had never been clearer: To Toby, the Hawthorne name, the money—it was a curse. *The tree is poison, don't you see? It poisoned S and Z and me.*

"It's not all bad," I said. "Kidnapping and murder attempts aside, I'm doing fine."

That was a ridiculous statement, but Toby didn't even laugh. "And you will stay fine, as long as I stay dead." He sounded so certain of that. "Go. Get in the car. Drive. If anyone asks you what happened, claim amnesia. I'll take care of the rest."

This was really it. He was really going to walk away from me. He was going to disappear again. "I know about the adoption," I said, desperate to keep him here—to make him stay. "I know your biological mother was the Laughlins' daughter and that she was coerced into the adoption. I know that you blame your parents for keeping secrets, for ruining the three of you. But your sisters—they need you."

Skye was sitting in a jail cell, but she wasn't guilty—this time, at least. Zara was more human than she wanted to admit. And Rebecca? Her mother was still mourning Toby.

"I read the postcards you wrote to my mom," I continued. "I talked to Jackson Currie. I know everything—and I'm telling you: You don't have to stay away anymore."

"You sound just like her." Toby's expression softened. "I never could win an argument with Hannah." He closed his eyes. "Some people are smart. Some people are good." He opened his eyes and put a hand on each of my shoulders. "And some people are both."

I knew, with a strange kind of prescience, that this moment would never leave me. "You're not staying, are you?" I asked. "No matter what I say."

"I can't." Toby pulled me in. I'd never been much of a hugger, but for a moment, I let myself be held.

When Toby finally let me go, I reached into my pocket and pulled out the small metal disk, the one he'd told my mother was valuable. "What is this?"

It was the last question I had for him. The last chance I had of making him stay.

Toby moved like lightning. One second, I held the disk in my hand, and the next, he had it. "Something I'll be taking with me," he said.

"What aren't you telling me?" I asked.

He shook his head. "*Horrible girl*," he whispered, his voice tender.

I thought of my mother, of every word she'd written to him about me, of the way he'd come for me tonight.

You have a daughter, I'd told him.

I have two.

"Am I ever going to see you again?" I asked, my throat closing in on the words.

He leaned forward, pressed a kiss to my forehead, and stepped back. "It would be a very risky gamble."

I opened my mouth to reply, but the door to the warehouse flew inward. Men poured inside. Oren's men.

My head of security stepped between me and Toby Hawthorne and then leveled a deadly look at Tobias Hawthorne's only son. "I think it's time we had a little talk."

CHAPTER 86

I wasn't able to overhear whatever words were exchanged between Oren and Toby. I was shuttled into the SUV, and when Oren took his place in the driver's seat a few minutes later, I noted that he'd left several of his men inside.

I thought about Sheffield Grayson, dead on the floor. About Toby's plan for that body. "Is disposing of corpses part of your job description?" I asked Oren.

He met my eyes in the rearview mirror. "You want a real answer to that?"

I looked out the window. The world blurred as the SUV picked up speed. "Skye and Ricky didn't plant that bomb," I said. I tried to focus on the facts, not the flood of emotions I was barely holding back. "They were framed."

"*This time*," Oren said. "Skye has already tried to have you killed once. Both of them are threats. I suggest we let them cool their heels in prison at least until your emancipation goes through."

Once I was legally an adult, once I could write my own will, Ricky and Skye would stand to gain nothing by my death.

"Rebecca." I lunged forward in my seat suddenly, remembering. "Thea helped Mellie abduct me because someone had Rebecca."

"It's been handled," Oren told me. "They're fine. So are you. The rest of the family is none the wiser." From his tone, you would have thought this was just business as usual. The kidnapping. The body. The cover-up.

"Was it like this for the old man?" I asked. "Or am I just lucky?"

I thought about Toby, sparing Eve from my fate, like inheriting this fortune was less blessing than curse.

"Mr. Hawthorne had a list." Oren took his time with his reply. "It was a different kind of list from yours. He had enemies. Some of them had resources, but by and large, we knew what to expect. Mr. Hawthorne had a way of seeing things coming."

I was starting to think that if I was going to survive being the Hawthorne heiress, I was going to have to start doing the same. I would have to learn to think like the old man.

Twelve birds, one stone.

Back at Hawthorne House, Oren made it clear that he intended to escort me all the way to my room. When we hit the grand staircase, I cleared my throat.

"We'll need to disable the passageway," I told him. "Permanently."

I paused on the staircase, in front of Tobias Hawthorne's portrait. Not for the first time, I stared at the old man. Had he known who Mellie and Eli were? Had he known about Eve? I was certain he would have run a DNA test on me at some point. He knew I wasn't Toby's daughter—not by blood.

But he'd still used me to lure Toby out—the same way Sheffield Grayson had, the same way Mellie and Eli had. *You're not a player,* Nash had told me a small eternity ago. *You're the glass ballerina—or the knife.*

Maybe I was both. Maybe I was a dozen different things, chosen for a dozen different reasons—none of them having a damn thing to do with who I was or what made me special.

I met the portrait's eyes and thought about my dream—about playing chess with the old man. *You didn't choose me. You used me. You're still using me.* But as of this moment?

I was done being used.

CHAPTER 87

An hour later, I went in search of a Hawthorne. "I have something to tell you."

Xander was in his "lab," a hidden room where he built machines that did simple things in complicated ways. "Something to tell me? Is it possible you have me confused with one of my brothers?" he asked. "Because people don't tell me things."

He was tinkering with some kind of miniature catapult mechanism, part of a complicated chain reaction born from the brain of Xander Hawthorne.

"This was your game," I said. "The old man left it to you."

"Or so it appeared." Xander settled a metal ball on the catapult. "At first."

I gave him a look. "What do you mean?"

"Jameson has laser focus. Grayson always finishes what he starts. Even Nash, he might take the scenic route, but he's wired to go from point A to point B." Xander finished tinkering and finally turned to face me. "But me? I'm not wired that way. I start at point A, and somewhere along the way, I end up at the intersection of one hundred and twenty-seven and purple." He shrugged. "It's one of my many charms. My brain likes diversions. I follow the paths that I find. The old man knew that." Xander shrugged. "Did he expect me to start the ball rolling this time? Yes. But where I'd end up?" Xander stepped back from his work and took in the entirety of the Rube Goldberg machine he'd built. "The old man knew damn well that it wasn't going to be point B."

I needed to tell someone what had happened. I'd chosen him because I felt like I owed it to him—like the universe, or maybe his grandfather, owed it to him. And now Xander was seeming an awful lot like someone who didn't want closure.

Someone who didn't need it.

"So where did you end up?" I asked.

Xander leaned forward and triggered the catapult. The metal ball sailed into a funnel, spiraled down a series of ramps, and hit a lever, dumping a bucket of water, releasing a balloon...

Eventually, the entire machine parted, revealing the wall behind it. That wall was covered with pictures—photographs of men with brown skin. The placards beneath the photographs informed me that every one of them had the last name Alexander.

I thought about the game we'd spent the past weeks playing. *Sheffield Grayson. Jake Nash.* Was this the detour that the old man had expected Xander to take?

"Do you want to know what I found?" I asked Xander.

"Sure," he said gamely. "But before I forget: two things." He held up his middle and index fingers. "First, this is Thea's phone number." He handed me a scrap of paper with the number scrawled across it. "I'm supposed to call her and let her know you're alive."

I frowned. "So why give me her number?" I asked.

"Because," Xander replied, "when it comes to Thea, forewarned is forearmed."

I narrowed my eyes. "What's the second thing?" I asked suspiciously.

Xander pressed a button, and the wall slid to reveal a second workshop. "Voilà!"

My eyes widened as I took in the contents of that workshop. "Is that ..."

"Life-sized re-creations of the three most lovable droids in the *Star Wars* universe." Xander grinned. "For Max."

CHAPTER 88

You beautiful beaches." Max was beyond pleased with
Xander's offering—enough so that it took her a moment
to shoot me a reproving look. "I feel obliged to warn you, you're looking a little pale, and the great Dr. Liu is not going to be pleased."

I took that to mean that my doctor would have been really dis-
pleased to know what I'd actually been up to in the last twelve
hours. "Thank you." I waited until Max looked at me before I continued. "For bringing your mom here."

I knew enough about my best friend to know that it hadn't been
an easy call to make.

"Yeah, well…" Max shrugged. "Thank you. For getting blown up."

*For giving you a reason to call—and giving her a reason to pick
up.* "Do you think you'll be headed home soon?"

I didn't want Max to leave, but at the same time, my best friend
had her own life to live, and I couldn't help thinking that she'd be
safer doing that far away from Hawthorne House. Away from me,
from the Hawthorne family, from everything I'd inherited along
with Tobias Hawthorne's billions.

Poison tree and all.

When Thea called, I almost didn't pick up. That was why Xander had given me her number. And yet...

"Hello?" I said darkly.

There was a moment of hesitation, and then: "I did some digging and found out who vandalized your locker. It was a freshman. You want the name?"

Silly me. I'd been expecting an apology. "No." I was tempted to leave it there, but I couldn't. "Is Rebecca okay?"

"She's shaken, but fine." Thea's voice was soft, but she spoiled the effect by scoffing audibly. "Fine enough to yell at me for putting you in danger."

"Yeah, well..." I shrugged, even though Thea couldn't see me. "Rebecca's one to talk." That I could joke about this was a true testament to how far Rebecca and I had come.

"I had a choice." Thea's voice shook. She was diabolical and complicated and about a thousand other things, but she wasn't evil. She'd been worried about me. "I had to choose her. Can you understand that, Avery?" Thea didn't wait for my answer. "For me, it's always going to be Rebecca. She doesn't believe that, but no matter how long it takes, I'm going to keep choosing her."

I had never understood what it felt like for one person to be your everything, to look at that person and *know*. I'd never believed myself capable of that. I hadn't wanted to be capable of it.

When Thea and I hung up the phone, I went to see Grayson.

CHAPTER 89

I told Grayson what had happened to his father. I didn't tell him about Eve. The entire time, his face was like stone. "You look like you want to hit something," I told him.

He shook his head.

I made him look at me. "How about swinging a sword?"

Grayson corrected my stance. "Let the blade do the work for you," he reminded me, and in that moment, I was reminded of more.

Of the first day I'd met him. How arrogant he'd been, how sure of himself and his place in the world. I thought about the first time I'd caught him really looking at me, and the way he'd told me that I had an expressive face. I thought about bargains struck and promises made and stolen moments and words spoken in Latin.

But mostly I thought about the ways that the two of us were alike. "I had a dream," I told him. "When I was in the coma. You and Jameson were fighting. About me."

"Avery..." Grayson lowered his sword.

"In my *dream*," I continued, "Jameson was angry that you didn't run toward me. That I was lying there at death's door, and you couldn't move. But, Grayson?" I waited for him to look at me, with silver eyes and the weight of the world on his shoulders. "I'm not angry. I've spent my entire life not running toward anyone. I know what's it like to just stand there—to not be able to do anything else. I know what it's like to lose someone."

I thought about my mom, then Emily.

"I am an expert at not wanting to want things." I held my sword up for a moment longer, then lowered it, the way he'd lowered his. "But I'm starting to realize that the person I need to be, the person I'm becoming—she's not that girl anymore."

I'd been given the world. It was time to stop living scared, time to take the reins.

It was time to take risks.

CHAPTER 90

Ms. Grambs, you understand that if you are emancipated, you will be considered a legal adult. You will be responsible for yourself. You will be held to adult standards. You are literally signing away the rest of your childhood."

In the past six weeks, I'd been shot at, blown up, kidnapped, and paraded around as the living, breathing embodiment of Cinderella stories. To the world, I was a scandal, a mystery, a curiosity, a fantasy.

To Tobias Hawthorne, I'd been a tool.

"I understand," I told the judge. And just like that, it was done.

"Congratulations," Alisa said as we stepped out of the courthouse. Oren's men cleared a path through the paparazzi, and I made my way to the SUV. "You're an adult." Alisa sounded pretty darn satisfied with herself. "You can write your own will."

I leaned back in my seat and thought about how carefully my lawyer had been managing my public image, how much she wanted the world to believe that the firm was calling the shots.

I smiled. "I can do a lot more than that."

Three hours later, I found Jameson on the roof. He was holding a familiar knife in his hands. He faked like he was going to toss it to me, and my heart sped up.

His eyes met mine, and it sped up more.

"I have a lot to tell you." The wind caught my hair, whipping it around my face. "I met Toby, face-to-face. He has a daughter, but it's not me. She looks just like Emily Laughlin."

Jameson's green eyes looked fathomless. "I'm intrigued, Heiress."

I reached into my pocket and pulled out a coin. This felt more dangerous than riding on the back of a motorcycle or speeding down a racetrack or getting shot at in the Black Wood. This wasn't just a rush.

This was a risk—one the old Avery never would have been capable of taking.

My eyes on Jameson's, I uncurled my fingers, revealing the coin in my palm. "Toby took the disk," I said. "We might never know what it was."

Jameson's lips ticked up at the edges. "This is Hawthorne House, Heiress. There will always be another mystery. Just when you think you've found the last hidden passage, the last tunnel, the last secret built into the walls—there will always be one more."

There was an energy in his voice when he spoke about the House. "That's why you love it." I locked my eyes on his. "The House."

He leaned forward. "That's why I love the House."

I held up the coin. "It's not the disk," I said. "But sometimes you have to improvise." My heart was racing. I was vibrating with the same energy I'd heard in his tone.

And like Jameson, I loved it.

"Heads, you kiss me," I said. "Tails, I kiss you. And this time..." My voice cracked. "It means something."

Jameson shot me one of those devastating, crooked Jameson Winchester Hawthorne grins. "What are you saying, Heiress?"

I tossed the coin into the air, and as it turned, I thought about everything that had happened. All of it.

I'd found Toby.

I knew my mother's secret.

I understood, more than ever, why my name had caught the attention of a billionaire who'd only met me once. Maybe that was all there was to it. Or maybe I was one stone meant for twelve birds, most of them still undiscovered.

Like Jameson had said, this was Hawthorne House. There would always be another mystery. Like me, Jameson would always be driven to solve them.

The coin landed. "Tails," I said. "I kiss you." I wrapped my arms around his neck. I pressed my lips to his. And this time, the joke was on me—because I wasn't playing.

This wasn't nothing.

This was the beginning—and I was ready to be bold.

ACKNOWLEDGMENTS

This book was written and revised in the spring and summer of 2020, largely while I was locked down at home with my husband and small children; *The Inheritance Games* came out in September 2020, mid-pandemic. Due to the tireless work and incredible support of my amazing publishing team, the book somehow managed to find its audience during this tumultuous time. More than any other book or series I have written, this one owes an incredible debt of gratitude toward the people without whom it simply could not have happened.

First, I would like to thank my incredible team at Little, Brown Books for Young Readers. What you have done for the Inheritance Games series and for me as an author astounds and humbles me. I have no idea how I got so lucky as to work with a group of people whose enthusiasm, work ethic, generosity, and just all-around brilliance are so far off the charts that the chart isn't even visible anymore. What all of you have done for these books—in unprecedented and incredibly challenging times, no less!—is more amazing than I could possibly say. I get tears in my eyes just thinking of all that this team has put into getting *The Inheritance Games* and *The Hawthorne Legacy* into the hands of readers.

Thank you to my incredible editor, Lisa Yoskowitz, whose brilliant editorial mind is only matched by the kindness and grace she extends to those she works with. Getting to work together again has been a dream come true.

Thank you to Megan Tingley and Jackie Engel; I cannot begin to express what an absolute joy it has been to be published by LBYR under your leadership.

Huge thanks to cover designer Karina Granda and artist Katt Phatt; the covers you have given *The Inheritance Games* and *The Hawthorne Legacy* are nothing short of perfection. I smile literally every time I see them!

To my incredible marketing and publicity teams, thank you, thank you, thank you for helping *The Inheritance Games* and *The Hawthorne Legacy* find so many readers. Thank you to Emilie Polster, who has been an incredible champion for these books from day one, and to Bill Grace, Savannah Kennelly, Christie Michel, Victoria Stapleton, Amber Mercado, and Cheryl Lew, for your tremendous work on *The Hawthorne Legacy*, as well as to Katharine McAnarney and Tanya Farrell, for your help with book one! Huge thanks also go out to the wonderful LBYR sales team: Shawn Foster, Danielle Cantarella, Celeste Risko, Anna Herling, Katie Tucker, Claire Gamble, Naomi Kennedy, and Karen Torres.

I am also incredibly grateful to the production team, who went out of their way to configure our schedule so that I could go on maternity leave with a new baby mid-process. Thank you, Marisa Finkelstein, Barbara Bakowski, Virginia Lawther, and Olivia Davis. Thank you also to Lisa Cahn, Janelle DeLuise, and Hannah Koerner, for helping bring this series to life in audio and overseas.

In addition to my publishing team in the United States, I would also like to thank my wonderful UK publishing team, including Anthea Townsend, Phoebe Williams, Ruth Knowles, Sara Jafari,

Jane Griffiths, Kat McKenna, Rowan Ellis, and everyone else at Penguin Random House UK!

Thank you also to Josh Berman, who is developing *The Inheritance Games* for television. Josh, you were one of the first people to read *The Inheritance Games*, and your belief in this project means the world. To the rest of the team hard at work on this project, including Grainne Godfree, Jeffrey Frost, Jennifer Robinson, Alec Durkheimer, and Sam Lion—thank you!

This is my twenty-second book, and I have been incredibly lucky to have had Curtis Brown as my agency home since I was pretty much a kid myself! Thank you, Elizabeth Harding, for fighting for me for all these years. Holly Frederick, thank you not only for finding these books a wonderful Hollywood home but also for your insightful feedback on the early stages of book one. Thank you, Sarah Perillo, for your incredible work advocating for this series all over the globe. And thank you to the rest of my Curtis Brown team, including Nicole Eisenbraun, Sarah Gerton, Michaela Glover, Madeline Tavis, and Jazmia Young.

Writing is a solitary profession; this year, that solitude was taken up a notch. I am grateful for all the writing friends who made this process less lonely along the way. Thank you to Ally Carter, Rachel Vincent, Emily Lockhart, Sarah Mlynowski, and all of BOB for the tremendous amounts of writerly support, and to the fellow authors who have been incredibly supportive of this series, including Katharine McGee, Karen McManus, Kat Ellis, Dahlia Adler, and so many more.

As is probably obvious by this point, the writing and publishing of a book is a true team effort. For this book, written in one of the hardest and most chaotic periods of my life, I am also hugely indebted to my team at home. Thank you to Avery Eshelman and Ruth Davis, for helping take care of my kids while I wrote, and thank you to my family, for EVERYTHING. Anthony, I could not ask for a better partner. Thank you for all you do; I could not do this without you. To my mom and dad, thank you for always being just a phone call away and for all you have done to help us through this difficult time. And to my children, thank you for the snuggles and fun, but also for understanding that sometimes Mommy has to write!

Finally, thank YOU, dear reader! After all these years and twenty-two books, I am still in awe that the stories I write are read by people like you.

Kim Haynes Photography

JENNIFER LYNN BARNES

is the *New York Times* bestselling author of over twenty novels for young adults, including *The Inheritance Games* and the Naturals series. She is also a Fulbright Scholar with advanced degrees in psychology, psychiatry, and cognitive science. She received a PhD from Yale University in 2012 and is currently a professor of psychology and professional writing at the University of Oklahoma. She invites you to follow her on Twitter @jenlynnbarnes and to visit her online at jenniferlynnbarnes.com.